What's her Secret?

HER SECRET PAST

VICTORIA BLISSE

Her Secret Past
ISBN # 978-1-78430-082-1
©Copyright Victoria Blisse 2014
Cover Art by Posh Gosh ©Copyright May 2014
Interior text design by Claire Siemaszkiewicz
Totally Bound Publishing

Published in 2014 by Totally Bound Publishing, Newland House, The Point, Weaver Road, Lincoln, LN6 3QN, United Kingdom.

HER SECRET
PAST

Dedication

To my husband, the man of infinite patience and love.
Thank you for all the support you give me through
procrastination, writer's block and word binges that
keep me typing when I should be tidying.

Chapter One

Katrina Quinn

"Ms Quinn, how long has it been going on?"

The microphone pressed insistently under my nose was nothing new, but the question puzzled me. It didn't make sense. I didn't answer or inquire further. That's the first lesson of Celebrity 101 — *Do not engage with a journo unless you're in a predetermined interview.*

As far as I was concerned it was just another work day — I hadn't expected the media hordes to greet me outside my Hollywood mansion that morning. The warm sun, the chirping birds, the gentle introduction to another day was completely disturbed by the clamor of camera flashes, hot bodies and microphones. I was completely confused by the mass of yelling at first. I was still waking up. Matt, my blond Adonis of a bodyguard, did his best to push back the eager media but it was a losing battle. I was hurried back into the house while he called for back-up.

Victoria Blisse

"What the hell was that?" he growled after pushing the door shut and locking it.

My stomach sucked and bubbled with nerves. How did I explain it to Matt?

A few days earlier, Brian Paxton had come over to my place for a meal after confessing that he was missing his home comforts.

"God, you're a wonder, Kat, taking care of an old man like me."

"Oh hush, you're not old," I'd exclaimed, picking up his plate and carrying it over to the sink. There hadn't been a scrap left on it, just a smear of sauce from the homemade lasagna I'd made.

"Do you want dessert?"

"Does the president live at the White House? Hell yeah, I want dessert. Fuck Cameron. I don't care if I look bloated tomorrow—this is the best food I've eaten in months." Brian had tapped his stomach, which was still as flat and toned as it had been back in the days when I'd lusted over him from afar.

I'd served up the pavlova, and the conversation had stayed light. The sweet treat had been enjoyed and Brian had even had seconds of dessert. The problem had started after we'd opened that second bottle of wine.

"I'm stuffed," he'd sighed, throwing himself down onto my red leather sofa. "I wish I didn't have to go back to the hotel."

"Well, I've got rooms. You could stay here if you want." I'd shrugged and dropped myself down on the seat beside him.

"Really?"

"Yeah of course. No problem." I'd radiated laissez-faire but inside I had been a tumult of sexual chemistry. Brian had been beside me, exuding

8

sexiness, smelling of wood, salt and manliness. It had been all I could do not to grab hold of him and snog his face off. But he was married. I'd had to hold myself in check.

I should have thought, should have sent him away and I really shouldn't have drunk that last glass of wine. We'd sat there in the living room chatting quite innocuously. I had flicked on the TV and hopped through the channels. It had all gone downhill when I'd seen a particular film listing and giggled.

"What's so funny?" Brian had asked.

"I used to watch this film over and over again when I was younger 'cause I fancied the arse off you," My answer had spurted out before I'd thought about it properly.

"Oh, is that right?" He'd crooked his eyebrow at me.

"Yeah, and I used to imagine I was the Mina to your Mike and that we'd kiss and cuddle and, well, you know. You fueled many an orgasm, I can tell you."

"Dear God, tell me you were of legal age." He wiped his brow dramatically.

I nodded, cheeks bursting with heat.

"That is fucking hot. I bet you wouldn't touch me with a barge pole these days, though, would you?"

"I'd fuck you right here and right now if I could," I had answered bluntly.

"You're only saying that to save my ego." Brian had run his fingers through his hair, quickly, his hand quivering.

"No way, I've been trying to keep my hands off you all the time we've been filming. You're the hottest man I've ever met."

Bar one. But that one wasn't in my house or even in my life anymore.

He hadn't spoken—we'd just looked at each other. My eyes had been wide, I was hyper-aware of the thumping of my heart and the deep, languid brown of his eyes. And the real man had been there, it wasn't a poster—I hadn't been fantasizing, he was really there.

Had he moved toward me or had I moved toward him? I didn't know, but what mattered was that our lips had clashed together and the sea of excitement that swamped me every time I saw him on screen had swelled and the waves had swept me away. I hadn't fought that, like I did in filming, I had just let it flow and allowed the tumult of lust to toss me about. I had been lost in a dream come true.

I should have stopped at the kiss. We had both been a bit drunk, both lonely and both hyped up after a week of crying scenes and heartbreak. It was just a kiss, we could have stopped, and although it might have proven a little awkward at future filming, we'd probably have laughed about it and carried on as before. But I hadn't stopped kissing him and at some point he had gone from kissing me, to holding me, then I'd wrapped my arms around his shoulders—and the holding had turned to caressing and clothing had come off.

It had been a whirlwind of body heat and lust. My brain had switched off and my body had been in control. I'd run my fingers across planes I'd etched in my fantasies, that I'd played in my head so many times while I masturbated. The heat of his body, the soft caress of his flesh on mine far exceeded my dreams. It hadn't been a long, drawn out seduction. I had been wet from him before we'd even started kissing.

Brian had concentrated on me and my pleasure, stroked my breasts, pulled my nipples, dragged his hands down over my hips and sought out my pussy. He'd fingered me as we'd kissed, his breath had danced with mine and I'd come explosively over his fingers.

He'd stood and dragged me with him, pushed me over the back of my sofa and fucked me with ferocity. He'd gripped my hair and pulled my head back. I had been able to see out of the huge window into the garden bathed with softening sunlight. The pool, to the left, bright blue, contrasting with the white marble surrounding it and leading out into the expanse of green lawn edged with trees and bushes created to shelter me from the gaze of the public.

My body had vibrated with ecstasy — rolling orgasms had made me scream and croon his name, my cunt had tightened around him and he'd come inside me. Well, luckily he'd not been that drunk. He'd slipped on a condom before entering me. Thank God he'd come prepared because I had been so lost in the excitement I hadn't been able to separate the reality from my dreams and had forgotten about the protection I kept in the coffee table drawer.

He had stayed the night. We hadn't fucked again but we'd snuggled in bed together. It had been comforting, and even when I'd woken in his arms in the morning I hadn't panicked. It felt so good to be with him. It had been Brian who had done the panicking.

"This can't happen again, it can't. Fuck, Katrina, it shouldn't have happened at all." He'd scrambled the sheets between his hands, letting out his irritation in the folds of my bed linen.

"I know, I know. I won't tell anyone, I won't expect anything more. Brian, it was just a tipsy shag."

"For you, yes. You're single. I have a wife and kids and I love them to bits and I should be able to hold my desires in. Fuck." He'd pressed his face into one hand and massaged his brow.

At first I had felt guilty and a bit sorry for him, then I'd realized he was calling me loose and incapable of controlling myself, and I'd become offended. What right did he have to judge me like that? My affront had escalated to anger in a matter of moments.

"I'll call you a cab. Get your clothes."

I'd stalked from the room stark naked. I hadn't been able to bear being with him anymore. He'd made me feel dirty. I had told him when the cab would arrive, showered then dressed in clothes from my second best wardrobe in the spare room. I'd wanted him to leave without saying anything, but he'd found me before he left.

"I'm going now."

"Yes, fine. Bye," I'd snapped.

"See you Monday. You won't tell anyone, will you?" The guilt in his gaze had changed his handsome face, twisted it into something far uglier.

"No, I won't, okay? I get it. It shouldn't have happened. I won't tell a soul."

"Good. Thanks. I'm sorry. Shit, Katrina. I'm so sorry."

If he was, he was only sorry for himself.

"Whatever." I'd shrugged. "Your cab is waiting."

How the paps had gotten the photos I had no clue but that was what the shit storm outside was about. Usually my security was spot on. I spent a lot of my hard-earned wages employing a small army of security guards to patrol the walls and grounds of my million dollar mansion and they'd not let me down before. So how had some photo-taking perv gotten hold of such clear and damning photos?

The phone rang, bringing me back from my ponderings, it was the director of *Cupful*. "What the fuck do you think you're doing?" Cameron yelled.

"What do you mean?" My stomach plunged, my chest tightened—I started to suspect what had upset him so much.

"You and Brian are all over the fucking papers, Katrina. All over them. He's gone ape-shit and left in a huff. I've had to cancel filming today. I might have to cancel it indefinitely—all because you can't keep it in your pants."

"Hey, wait a minute, I wasn't the only person involved with all this, you know—"

"But you knew he was married, Kat. That's just unforgiveable. Anyway, you've got the day off. I'll get someone to ring you tomorrow and let you know what's going on."

Cameron clicked the phone off before I could respond with affirmation or express my regret.

I didn't know what to do with myself. I imagined other people might have rung their mum or a girlfriend. I had neither. My parents had died years ago and I didn't make friends easily. Loneliness wasn't a problem of mine, though. I was forever around people, I threw myself into every film I made and the people on set became my friends and family for the time I was with them.

I felt like I'd kicked my family in the nuts. My mobile kept ringing and I just ignored it. The only person I contemplated talking to was my gran but she wasn't fantastic at phone conversation. At eighty-eight she was doing well for her advancing years but her hearing was not as good as it'd been, and she was too proud to wear a hearing aid, which made non-face-to-face communication almost impossible with her.

A new stab of guilt ripped through me. I'd not written to her in a while. It was the way we kept in touch. I couldn't go back to England to visit her and she wasn't good on the phone. We both wrote fabulous letters, though.

Hey, Gran,

How are you? Has Bernard shown his hand yet or is he still pussy-footing around? Remember to make him buy you dinner and chocolates before you put out, all right?

Things are good this side of the pond – my latest film is almost in the can and I've got the next queued up already. I'm still single, Gran, but I'm really not looking for love. I think it's overrated and I don't have a charming Bernard to sweep me off my feet with indigestion pills and muscle rub. Who said romance is dead, huh?

Send my love to that hot male nurse you sent me the picture of, and remember to keep on growing old disgracefully.

Looking forward to your next missive,

Your loving granddaughter x

I felt better for reaching out to Gran. For the first time in years I felt like leaping on a plane and paying her a visit. I'd not seen her since I'd come over to America. Even when she'd moved into the home after a fall I hadn't visited, as much as I had wanted to. She was meant to be in the home for a short period of respite but she liked the company so much she stayed. I was just happy to know that she was content where she was. She understood why I had to stay away but often asked me to visit anyway. I wished I could but I'd distanced myself from Thornleydale and I couldn't risk being caught there in case someone discovered my secret. She even kept Copse Cottage instead of selling it just in case I ever decided I wanted to go home. Mostly though, I didn't think she could bear parting with all those memories. Having her home sitting there waiting for her or me was her safety blanket.

As far as the public knew I was born in Leeds, orphaned at an early age and brought up by loving adoptive parents who had died while I was still young. It was a tragic tale that gave me opportunity to practice my acting skills. I couldn't afford anyone finding out who I really was and where I'd started out life. No, I'd wiped the slate clean.

But I missed Gran. She was the one connection to my old life I couldn't bear to give up.

The phone ominously blasting out the first bars of *The Phantom of the Opera* jolted me from my melancholy daydreams. It was the tone I'd associated with my director.

"Hey, Cameron, look I'm really sorry—"

"Yeah, save it. I'm having to rewrite the fucking movie because of you. Brian has quit."

"Oh, shit. We've just got a few more scenes to shoot, though, right? Can't you use his double?" I thought I was being helpful.

"Good idea," he exclaimed snidely, "I hadn't thought of that. I've got to get my head around this problem. If I could I'd fire you, you know that? You've ruined the integrity of my dream."

"I know, I'm sorry. It wasn't meant to happen." My heart wrapped around itself to appease the guilt lodged there. "And I don't know how the papers got those photos, my security is usually so good."

"Whatever, Kat. I'm pissed but I want you in at seven a.m. tomorrow. We're going to have to finish this up quick so I have more time to edit and fill in the holes you've blown through my storyline."

"I'll be there at seven." I knew it was no use me apologizing and begging anymore. Cameron was angry at me and rightly so. He was well within his rights to fire me then and there. I'd work as hard as was needed to make things right for him.

"Good." He put down the phone.

I shook my head. Life had been so good and I'd ruined it because I hadn't been able to keep my libido on a leash.

Chapter Two

Ryan Taylor

"Bloody spoiled bitch," Eve muttered into her cornflakes. "Not got enough with her mansion and her millions, she's got to steal some other woman's man."

"What?" I looked up from my second slice of toast to work out what my girlfriend was ranting about again.

"That bloody Katrina Quinn. She's been caught shagging that Brian Whatshisface she was filming with. It's a damn disgrace."

"Oh, I wouldn't believe all you read in the papers."

Especially not the pile of tabloid trash Eve read every morning with her breakfast. The tabloid I always got up at six thirty to walk to the other end of the village to pick up. She used to read it at seven every morning but since her job at the biscuit factory had fallen through six months ago it was later and later before she got up—sometimes not until the afternoon.

"You would say that, you fancy the arse off her."

"And it's a fact—they make up most of the stories these days," I protested, picked up my plate then carried it to the sink.

"Whatever," Eve snapped, shaking her head so that her piled high bright blonde locks shook.

"Right, I've got to go. Mrs Ebberson needs some firewood chopping, it's coming into the winter months now."

"I don't like you doing it," she sighed. "Can't you just stay home today, babe? You know, and we'll have some fun?" Eve lowered the left corner of the paper and winked suggestively, pouting her lips and flashing her big blues at me.

Not so long ago I'd have dropped anything to answer that seductive call but not now.

"I wish I could, babe, but I need the money. We've got a million bills due this week." I shrugged. "And I'll be careful. I'm good with the ax. I only nearly chopped my foot off once."

"It's not that." Eve flipped up the paper to block the view between us again, before shaking it vigorously with irritation. "I don't like you working for women."

"Mrs Ebberson is seventy, Eve. I don't have a thing for grannies!"

"How do I know? You could be off getting up to all sorts with these women who employ you. Every time you tell me you've got a new job it's a woman's name I hear. What else am I meant to think?"

"Look, sweetheart, I work for a lot of women because there are loads of older ladies in the village who need some help. Some because they're widows, some because their husband works all day. There's not many men in this world who'll admit to needing help from a bloke to get something done."

"Yeah, whatever. I think you're shagging about 'cause you're sure not shagging me." She slammed the paper down and violently pushed the chair back, her bright pink dressing gown flapping against her thighs.

"That's because I've been tired, babe," I crooned. It was true. Since I'd had to support both of us, I'd been taking on any odd job to keep the cash flowing, which meant I didn't have the energy to get anything else flowing.

"Or because you're dicking about with another woman." She crossed her arms by her waist, pushing up her breasts to bubble over the cleavage of her pink nightie.

"You're the only one for me, Eve. Always have been. Don't be angry."

"Yeah, well" — she shrugged — "I don't feel like you love me anymore."

"I do." I strode over and planted a kiss on her scrunched up lips. "But I have to go make some money today, all right? Once I've dealt with all Mrs Ebberson's firewood I'll have some spare time. We'll do something special then, okay?"

"Suppose so." She shrugged again.

My Eve had perfected stroppy at an early age. Her arms were still wrapped around herself.

"I'll see you later then."

I'd never been very good at dealing with confrontation. Which was ironic really, considering I'd been the boyfriend to the most 'in your face' woman in the whole of West Riding for the past twelve years. I just used to do whatever Eve wanted me to do to avoid the slanging matches. But one of us had to be responsible.

I was just an odd job man. I'd never gotten any qualifications. I'd worked with my dad for years, so at least I'd gotten my electric and gas accreditations. That was something. I was going to start my own firm filled with electricians, gas safety people and other tradesmen and women. People based in rural areas like me. A network of guys who could get out to anyone, anywhere. It was my grand plan. It was a good one, I knew it could work.

When Dad had passed away, he'd left me nothing. I'd always been told I'd get half of his estate, my sister would get the other. It would have been a tidy sum. My dad had been minted. But no. Dad had taken against Eve and written me out of his will completely.

"Son," he'd told me as he'd lain in his bed, chest heaving to pull in breath. "I love you, I do, but I'm not going to let my money go to keeping that recalcitrant, harridan bitch Eve."

Even on his deathbed Dad had liked to use his excessive vocabulary.

"But I love her, Dad," I'd replied, gripping his bony hand in mine. It was horrid to see my vibrant father wasted away and clinging to life by a thread. His soul had left him piece by piece—the shell left behind wrinkled, old and unfamiliar.

"You think you do, son. But I know different. If you want your share, you've got to lose the leech."

He'd broken into a fit of coughing and the nurse in the room had hurried me away. Those were the last words he had ever said to me. I didn't dump Eve, though, I kept with her. I'd always been bloody-minded. We'd gotten by well enough in those days. She'd had her packing job with the other girls she'd gone to school with. It hadn't brought in a lot but had paid for the television and the phone since she used them the most. I'd continued with Dad's company for a bit—my older sister, Helen, kept it on. But after three years she'd closed it down and left me jobless without thinking twice about it.

That's how I'd ended up as Thornleydale's odd job man. I knew enough people and I could turn my hand to most things. People who lived in villages tended to stick together, too. I was sure that several jobs I'd done over the years had been made up just so I had been able to feel useful and make some money. Again, we'd ticked over all right until Eve had lost her job at the factory. Everything had gone downhill in the six months since, including my mood.

It was a short walk over to Mrs Ebberson's so I didn't take the van. It would save on my petrol costs. The sun was shining but there was no warmth to its beams. Winter was coming, and out in the wilds on the edge of the moors they set in early. Frost coated the grass and the gravel, patches of ice glistened under the light. A few lonely birds chirruped in the trees, hidden behind the last thin veils of autumnal leaves, hanging on the branches in shades of red and gold waiting to fall and add to the patchwork beneath my feet.

Mrs Ebberson lived by the village green. It was more of a glassy, frosted sheet of prickly ice as I crunched across it, past the shop and post office to the cute, chocolate box cottage. Mrs Ebberson kept me busy. In the summer I tended to her extensive gardens, both front and back. I mowed the lawn weekly, weeded, trimmed bushes and more. She was a good lady and I liked to keep her sweet because I relied on her regular money to pay my bills.

I knocked on the door with the polished brass knocker and waited. She was bad on her pins and used one of those trolley frames to move about. I looked down at the floor, my steel toecap boots dusty and worn. I could probably have done with a new pair but I just hoped they'd be sturdy enough to protect me if the ax went astray.

I'd never been one for sharp clothes, fashion and all that. But even I felt scruffy in my ancient work overalls, torn at the knee and the elbow, splattered with paint of several hues and more of a washed out gray than the blue they were originally. The old T-shirt and sweater underneath keep me warm but wouldn't be fit for anything else.

The door before me rattled open, and a few moments later I saw the top of a little gray head.

"Oh." Mrs Ebberson looked up and smiled. "Ryan, it's you. You're early."

"I know, I just couldn't keep away from your lovely smile, Mrs Ebberson." I grinned.

"You charmer, you," she chuckled. "Anyway, come in, come in."

The elderly lady led me down the wood clad corridor, through into her chintz covered kitchen and to the back door.

"The key's hung there, love, be a dear and open up for me."

Mrs Ebberson had arthritis and found fine motor skills a challenge. She had a carer who came in three times a day otherwise she'd be helpless. Especially in her house, which didn't have central heating. Just the wood-fired boiler, hence why my firewood chopping was so important.

Once I got the door open she directed me to the pile of wood and retold me where to find the ax. I could have found both blindfolded but I humored her.

"I'll make us a brew in a bit, once I've worked up a sweat." I smiled.

"That'd be lovely, dear. I'll see you later."

I pulled the door closed and headed across the lawn to the outhouse. I'd collected together the logs and firewood over the summer months. Mrs Ebberson's backed onto the copse and there was plenty of downed wood to keep her fueled up for the winter.

I loved working for her but it also stirred up some uncomfortable memories. I never knew my own grandparents. I was too small when they had died but there was a gran in my past whom I remembered with fondness. Mary Davey. She was my best friend Janet's grandma with a heart of gold.

Me and Janet had been inseparable when we were little. Constant companions, I'd often led her into trouble. It had gone downhill in secondary and we'd completely lost contact when we left college. I'd no idea where she'd gone.

I pulled forward a large branch and started stripping off the smaller twigs. I broke them into six inch lengths for tinder. Even after so many years my stomach rolled when I remembered the shit I'd given Janie in school.

* * * *

Wakefield, 1994

"Her, I want you to pull her hair and run away." Eve was two years older than me. I loved her blonde-haired, blue-eyed good looks and was totally flattered when a third year pupil had taken notice of me, a squirty year one. To get in her group, though, I had to do something to prove my worth.

"Janet?" My voice was high-pitched with shock so I said it again in a lower register.

"Yes, her. I'm picking something easy for you to start with."

I think it was just a sad and unfortunate coincidence that Eve's eye had fallen on Janet as she'd walked up to me at the end of the day.

"But she's my best friend," I continued, conflicted. Janet and I spent so much time together, at her gran's house, mostly. We were inseparable. I'd stuck up for her on many occasions and the idea of picking on her was completely alien to me.

"If you want to be my boyfriend you'll do what I tell you, okay?"

I nodded. I really wanted to be her boyfriend, to be someone. Not just the thick boy with a rich dad. And it was only tugging my mate's hair. It wasn't like it was anything truly cruel.

So I tugged Janet's ponytail and ran away laughing.

I thought that would be it. But no, Eve had taken a real dislike to Janet. It was probably because she was so sweet and innocent and not in Eve's group of sycophants.

"Oh my God, Janet's wetting herself!" I exclaimed as she walked past me down the antiseptic-blue, gum-splattered school corridor. The lads around me turned to look and laughed. Skinny Steve's face went as red as his big ears, Keano dug his big, hard elbow in my ribs, nearly cracking one.

"She's a knicker-wetting baby," he bellowed.

Janet ran past, her ponytail bobbing, the PE bag slung over her shoulder jiggling. That didn't help matters as I'd just poured a bottle full of water into the top of it. More of it splattered down her back and legs, intensifying the laughter that echoed down the corridor.

I felt awful but that wasn't the worst thing I'd done. I'd told all the lads she was frigid, that she had syphilis, fleas, nits... Basically anything I'd been able to think of that would prevent them from talking to her. Why? Because Eve had told me to.

I watched Janet on sports day. She looked fabulous in her little maroon gym skirt with the white-collared T-shirt tucked in at the waist. Her full figure was on display and I appreciated it. She'd been nominated to run the fifteen hundred meters. I knew she was hating it, her face was tight, but she would never back down from a responsibility. She was running for her form and even if she came in last she'd have done what she had to.

Some older girls were laughing and pointing at her. Of course Eve was amongst them. Janet pointedly ignored them, her chin lifting, her jaw tightening. I was proud of her, striding on and ignoring the taunts. My heart dropped when I locked my gaze with Eve's. She nodded at me, the chosen symbol for my next act of dedication to her.

I pretended to get cramp in my leg just as Janet rounded the track before me. I extended and felt her foot slam into my calf. It hurt me a little but as she fell forward, flashing her maroon gym knickers to the assembled school, I was sure it hurt her more.

Of course I got into trouble but I knew I deserved it. I'd betrayed my best friend for a little social mobility.

* * * *

Thornleydale 1998

It was years of cruelty later when I snapped and very nearly changed the course my life was taking.

"What the hell did you think you were doing?" Eve screamed. "How the fuck are you going to get anywhere in life if you don't take your exams seriously?"

"God, Eve, you're just pissed off because I went out without you. I needed to let off steam—these tests are fucking me right off and I was sick of revising."

"Well if you're serious about wanting to be with me you've got to get serious about your fucking future. I've not got a qualification to my name and I'm staying here in the back of fucking beyond for you. Just you, Ryan."

"Nice," I snarled, "Just pile some more pressure onto me, why not? Clearly I've not got enough on my plate right now."

I stormed out, jumped into Dad's Jag and drove out of Thornleydale without a further thought or plan. On my way to Wakefield I passed a familiar figure sat by the side of the road.

"Hey, Janie, what are you doing all the way out here?"

Janet always hated being called Janie, so of course I called her it all the more. I think she grew to like it in the end. She responded half-heartedly and a mad thought flitted through my mind and I spoke it before I could convince myself that it wasn't right.

"I'm running away, Janie. I'm pissed off. Want to come with me?"

How cool could life be with my old best mate Janie? I knew I'd given her shit for the last seven or so years but when push came to shove I still saw her as *my* Janie.

She agreed in the end and we sat in the car in silence, contemplating the adventure ahead of us. Until we got hungry and pulled in at The Golden Fry for some chips. We ate 'em in a lay-by, conversation flowing. I found out she was running away too.

"My dad left us, my mum's not been the same since and I'm the butt of everyone's joke at school. I can't take all that anymore."

My heart ceased, and I dropped my next chip back into the paper bag. I felt awful.

"Oh, Janie, it's been really tough for you, hasn't it?"

I reached out and touched her cheek. I wanted to make it all better, take back all the snide things I'd said and done.

"I still think you're the best girl in the world," I smiled.

"And you're not bad, for a boy." Her eyes lit up again and her smile warmed me deep inside. I had ended our first big argument when we were little with those words. Janie had still been a bit mad at me so she hadn't been so complimentary. But we'd laughed it off and I'd managed to finish most arguments since with those exact words.

It was weird, though, I wasn't just seeing her as my best mate. Something to do with rampant teenage hormones, I'm sure, because I kissed her. What would have happened if the police officer hadn't knocked on the window at that moment I don't know, but the connection between me and Janie was potent. I had an overwhelming desire pull her tighter and hold her forever. But I couldn't. I had to go home.

* * * *

I'd ended up working for Dad. She'd ended up at a posh university. That's where we had lost touch and I just didn't know where she was. I had looked for her, even asked her gran a time or two, but Mary wouldn't tell me anything.

"She's happy, Ryan, that's all you need to know. She's really happy now."

Mary had been a great lady but she'd never really approved of me hanging around with her Janet. Janet was too good for me in her gran's eyes. And I was pretty certain she was right.

After my mental trip down memory lane I wiped the sweat off my brow and carried some of the chopped wood into the shed. I took up another armful then carried it into the house.

"I've brought some wood in, Mrs Ebberson," I called, moving it to the wood-powered boiler before feeding it in. I left a few logs in the nook beside the boiler as it had gaps that needed filling in.

"I'll put the kettle on," I called.

I sat in the quaint cottage front room on the golden brown sofa and sipped at my tea while Mrs Ebberson talked about the good old days when her husband had been alive and they both used to chop their own wood for the winter.

"What would I do without you, Ryan, lad? I'd be lost, I tell ye."

"Oh, you're just flattering me so I'll chop you more wood. I know the games of you attractive young girls."

Mrs Ebberson cackled and rested her wrinkly, cellophane-thin hand on my knee. I'd not felt the real warmth of a touch in a long time, so I coughed to cover the rising sadness that brought tears pricking at the corners of my eyes then hurried back out into the yard to chop more wood.

Chapter Three

Katrina Quinn

I had a cavalcade of bodyguards the next morning and still it was a challenge pushing my way through the boiling sea of questions, microphones and flashing bulbs. I got into the limo then onto the film set in relative peace—Matt knew when to leave me alone and I wasn't in the mood to chat.

The car drove slowly up to the studio—bodies pushed against the windows, cameras flashed desperately—but I knew my tinted glass would protect me from them. I pasted on a smile anyway, just in case. You never knew in this business, and I didn't want pictures of me looking miserable hitting the papers and magazines for the journos to make up appropriate—at least in their minds—headlines.

The greeting on set was icy. The makeup and wardrobe ladies nattered on as usual, but that was what they did. Fellow actors completely blanked me—Cameron wouldn't even look at me and I had to go all method actor and absorb myself in the role. I completely became Zarika, female assassin to the king. The last person I wanted to be was Katrina Quinn because everyone was ignoring her.

I gave my all to the scenes, even learnt a whole new one in my lunch hour. I had to do everything I could to make Cameron see I was sorry for what I'd done. He didn't soften. When I caught a glimpse of the newspapers in the canteen I saw why.

Apparently I'd been conducting an illicit affair with Brian throughout the whole of the filming process. Shots from the movie of Brian and me holding hands, staring lovingly into each other's faces, were declared to be evidence of the beginnings of a love affair. Cameron had apparently turned a blind eye—he was tarred with the same brush as me.

I was the wicked temptress. Brian, apparently, had given an exclusive interview to one of the seedier tabloids decrying me as an evil seductress. He was heart-broken and hoping his wife would take him back. I steamed about it for the rest of the day and was relieved when it was time to go home.

"Shit day at work?" Matt asked when I threw myself back against the comforting leather of the limo's back seat.

"You could say that, yes."

"A ham and pineapple pizza with extra cheese will be delivered at eight."

"Oh, Matt, you're a Godsend." I sighed, tears pooling. It was just the kind of food I didn't eat. I avoided processed, fat-laden, over-sweet foodstuffs at all cost but when I needed comfort, then pizza was the go to food. A rare treat to give me an emotional pickup. It would mean a day of nothing but fruit and veg smoothies the next day but it'd be worth it.

"Hey, boss, just doing what I can to keep my job." He leaned forward from his seat facing me and covered my hand with his, briefly. A reassuring gesture.

"Thanks," I whispered, coughed and looked out of the window, a single tear tracing down my cheek.

Matt was big, tough and gay. The perfect bodyguard. He made me feel completely safe. I knew he'd do everything he could to protect me and he was so thoughtful, too. I wanted him as my PA but he wouldn't hear of it. Things like calling for pizza when I was depressed were just part of his friendly service. I tried not to dwell on the fact that my best friend in all the world was my bodyguard and we weren't that close. No one understood me like Matt, though.

Except maybe Ryan Taylor, but I'd not seen him in many, many years and that friendship had turned sour way back in high school. It frustrated me that even after so many years he was the first person I thought of when I needed to be looked after. When he'd been such a bastard to me for so long.

There were a few less paps at the mansion thankfully, and I got into the safety of my home with little battle. I went straight upstairs, showered, threw on my PJs and unwound with cheesy pizza and an equally cheesy film. *Never Been Kissed* had always been a favorite of mine and was just the kind of mindless movie-watching I needed after such a long and intense day.

Just as I was eyeing up the last piece of pizza and wondering if I could find space in my very full stomach for a bit more comfort, my mobile rang. I looked down and saw the word *Gran*.

"Hey, Gran. It's so good to hear from you…"

"Hello, is this Ms Quinn?"

"Yes, speaking. But who is this? Where's my gran?"

"Are you seated, Ms Quinn?"

"I am." I knew what the softly spoken British man was going to say next but I couldn't believe it.

"I'm Conrad McAlister from McAlister and Sons Solicitors. I'm afraid to inform you that your grandmother passed away last night peacefully in her sleep."

"Oh." The tears that had bubbled below the surface all day spilt over and spattered my cheeks.

"I'm taking care of her will and the arrangements for her funeral as she requested. You are her one benefactor."

I nodded. Gran had no other family but me, I knew that.

"The service will be this Friday, do you think you'll be able to make it?" he asked in soft, measured tones. He obviously dealt with this kind of thing on a regular basis.

I wished I was as unflustered as he.

"I don't think so," I spoke through the tears, pulling on all my acting skills just to get through the conversation without completely breaking down. "I'm afraid I'm in the US and I don't think I can make it back in time." I wanted to go. I wanted to drop everything and run back to Thornleydale to find out that Gran wasn't gone, that she was still in her comfy chair by the window of Copse Cottage, knitting and watching the garden grow as the world rolled by. Just like she'd always been when I was a little girl. But I couldn't. No one could know that I was Janet Davey, and if I turned up to Gran's funeral then I'd be discovered.

"That is a shame. I can arrange for it to be online for you, so you can watch remotely. Is that something you'd be interested in?"

"Oh, yes please," I sighed and wiped my eyes. "That would be good."

"Okay, I shall put that in place for you. I'm sincerely sorry for your loss and if you don't feel up to this now I can ring you back at another time but there are just a few details I need to go through with you."

I held it together long enough to tell him my email address, confirm my full real name and birthdate, but I couldn't think past that.

"Your grandma's house is the majority of her estate. I will talk to you again tomorrow so we can decide what you want to do with it." Mr McAlister clearly realized I wasn't really with him and ended the conversation.

I couldn't believe it. Gran was dead.

I collapsed on the sofa and just cried. She was the one person in the world who loved me unconditionally and now she was gone. I was completely alone, with no help, no hope and no comfort. The world was baying for my blood over something that I'd done but hadn't meant to do. I wished I could just disappear—life was too difficult to continue. What was I going to do without her?

* * * *

The next few days on set I threw myself into my part. I acted my socks off. It was the only way to get through it. Cameron wasn't pleased with me but as the week progressed he yelled at me less, and by Thursday, the last day of filming, he was almost smiling. I wasn't. It was a struggle and only Matt knew why.

"Do you want me to be with you?" he asked in the limo, which moved on unobstructed as the journos had moved onto their next target. My infidelity held just a few paps on the doorstep.

"What do you mean?" I scrunched my eyebrows in confusion, bone weary and not thinking about the possible wrinkles that would come from that.

"At the funeral, tomorrow morning, do you want me to be with you when you watch it?"

"No, no, no, no." I shake my head emphatically. "Why should you? You didn't know her."

"No, but I know you. And I'd be a shit friend if I didn't offer."

"Matt, I appreciate it." I choked up, my throat tightened. "I really, really do but I don't know how I'm going to react, I don't know what will happen. I don't want you to see me melt down."

"Kat, sweetie, I've seen you at your worst several times in our working relationship. I doubt you'll throw anything new at me." Matt smiled gently. "You need some support, can't let you go through it all on your own. I know when my dad passed last year I was a wreck. If Trey hadn't been with me at the funeral I don't know how I'd have gotten through it."

I wanted to protest that Trey was his partner and so that situation had been completely different from the one I found myself in. But I knew there was truth in what Matt said. It would be awkward if I fell apart in front of him, but could I survive the experience on my own?

"Okay, Matt. It's going to be early, starts at seven in the morning. Can you make that?"

"Darling, I'm up earlier than that every day. 'Course I can make it." He gently scoffed.

"Thank you." I sighed and gulped the lump from my throat.

"You're welcome, sugar. I've got to look after you — after all, you're the one who signs my pay checks!"

I had to smile at his awkward attempt to break the atmosphere. As employees went, Matt was a superstar.

* * * *

I didn't like wearing black. I didn't possess a little black dress because it drained my color and made me look vampish. Also, it was all I'd worn back in high school. I tried to avoid repeating that particular look. So I'd bought myself a black blouse to go with the one pair of black trousers I owned. I felt as though I was going back in time, coating myself in darkness once more. I wasn't going to physically be at the funeral, but I needed to mourn, I couldn't mourn in my usual everyday clothes.

I felt as insecure and alone as I had as a teen but one thing had changed — I didn't have Gran to go to for comfort food and hugs. She hadn't been in my life for a long time, apart from the odd letter, but her presence back there in my old home town was in itself an anchor.

I hadn't slept well last night. I must have woken once an hour or more, afraid I'd wake late and miss it. Eventually I'd given up trying to sleep at five. Had showered, curled my hair in just the style Gran liked it and put on makeup. Just a little. I knew it was stupid, but I needed to look my best, do it properly for my gran.

Matt arrived half an hour early, with a cup of freshly brewed coffee in his hand.

"Thought you might need this." He stroked my arm after I took the cup from him. "And don't worry, Trey made it, not me."

The smile that stretched my lips was genuine. Matt was notoriously bad at putting together a good cup of joe. Trey had worked as a barista to see him through college, and as I sipped the bitter-sweet, milky cuppa I appreciated his years of practice.

I watched through a camera. It was obviously seated high up on the wall as I looked down on my old place of worship. The church was packed, but I could only see tops of heads and none of them seemed familiar. Thornleydale was one of those quaint British villages where everyone went to church on a Sunday whether they liked it or not. That was why there were so many in attendance, I was sure.

They had a new vicar, a young chap with short-cropped hair. I wondered if Reverend O'Reily had retired or if he'd passed away too. He was about a million years old when I'd attended church—he spoke slowly and methodically and his sermons were an instant insomnia cure. He was a bit deaf, too, so he never heard his congregation snore. Although Ms Swadlinhurst was known to 'accidentally' press an organ note partway through if anyone was snoring particularly loudly. She was a spindly old spinster with a wicked cackle. It depressed me to think she'd probably passed on too.

Ironically I'd wanted nothing more than to get away from my old life, but knowing that it no longer existed floored me. It was as though I expected it to be perfectly preserved like dried flowers—not my taste anymore but always there just in case I changed my mind.

Matt was good. He sat next to me on the sofa. He didn't speak, he didn't touch me, he was there, and that was all I needed. Just a body to be there with me so I wasn't alone.

The funeral passed in a blur. I couldn't believe that my vivacious grandmother was inside the dour and dark mahogany coffin. People spoke about her, told stories I'd not heard. There were badly sung hymns and rote-read prayers. Then she was gone, the coffin carried high on the shoulders of men I didn't know to a grave I wouldn't see.

That was when I decided what I was going to do.

"Thanks, Matt." I closed the laptop and turned to him. "I'm glad you were here."

"I wouldn't have had it any other way. Are you all right? Do you need me to stay on? I've got Clay on standby just in case." Matt seemed concerned but looked away from my gaze. I suppose he was aware that I was uncomfortable with him seeing me so undone.

"Get on with your job," I insisted with a flick of my wrist. "I'm actually okay."

He didn't look convinced.

"Seriously, I'm fine. Well, I'm not, but I will be. Honestly, Matt." Thank God for my training. I thought I was pretty convincing. "And the last thing Clay needs is more time on duty—his wife just gave birth a few weeks ago. No, let him have his day off. You get back to work—you don't have to worry about me."

"I always do that, whether I'm on duty or not. But I will go do my job. Gotta keep you protected and keep my man in expensive shoes."

Matt was a gorgeous man—if he wasn't gay I'd be interested in him. I was glad he had such a partner, though. He deserved happiness. In a world of false friends and shallow promises Matt was an island of reliable kindness.

Mr McAlister rang a few hours after the service.

"Ms Quinn, I hope you managed to view the service adequately?"

"Yes, thank you. It was good to be in attendance." Even though I hadn't really been and I still felt guilty about that. Yes, I had seen what happened but there had been an ocean between me and my gran's final send-off. I didn't think I'd ever be able to shift the feeling that I'd let her down. I shook my head and concentrated on the call. What did Mr McAlister actually want? I wasn't in the mood to deal with details but at least while I talked to him I wasn't condemning myself for being an awful grandchild or dwelling on past mistakes.

"I'm glad. Now, I just need to chat to you about your grandmother's house. It is in such a wonderful location and would make a fabulous holiday home and we know there will be a lot of immediate interest. I'm wondering how you'd like to proceed."

"Actually, I don't want you to sell it. I'm going to come home and sort it out myself." Where that decision had come from I didn't know. I just knew it was the right thing to do.

"Oh, well, certainly, but—and I hope you don't think I'm being forward in saying this—but is that actually wise?"

"Probably not. But you've just told me how perfect Gran's house is for a holiday home. Well, I need a break and where better than in a quiet corner of my home county, Yorkshire? Yes, Mr McAlister, I'm coming home. I'll fix up Gran's place and get it ready for sale."

"That is, of course, completely fine. Let me know if you need any assistance. I will be in touch about the rest of your inheritance soon."

I slept that night. Deeply and with sweet dreams of fields and trees, the summer sun beating down, the sound of happy children blending with the tweeting of birds and my gran's house in the background.

* * * *

"You're going *where*?"

"England. I need some time to myself."

"Oh." Matt looked a little deflated.

"I won't be there too long, a couple of months at the very most. And you'll be paid while I'm gone, don't panic."

"No, no, I wasn't worried about that, I was worried about you. Are you sure you'll be okay on your own?" He nibbled his bottom lip with a perfectly white tooth.

"Contrary to your popular belief, I am capable of looking after myself, you know." I pushed my hands onto my hips.

"So you keep telling me." Matt laughed. "I suppose this means I'm getting a paid vacation."

"The mansion still needs looking after, but yeah, I suppose so. Well, as long as you spend a chunk of that time here, making sure the silver is still in the right place and all that."

"Right you are, boss." He nodded.

"Now, would you be a dear and get my luggage from the loft for me?"

Having a hulking man around the place was good for many things, including reaching things down from awkward places.

"The where? Is this another one of your weird Brit jokes?"

I took some twisted pleasure in confusing Matt with his own mother tongue. It was amazing how different English was from the UK to the US.

"No, the loft." I pointed up to the ceiling. "The storage room at the very top of the house."

"The attic." Matt's face lit up with recognition. "Now you're talking."

Packing was a joy. I loved writing lists, imagining what I might need, where I might go and what I might do. It was the holiday before the holiday. However, packing to go back to Thornleydale wasn't pleasant. I had the urge to pack dark colors, drab clothes to mourn in, but I had to stop myself. It would be a dead giveaway that I wasn't just a celeb on holiday if I moped around in black clothes all the time.

In the end I came up with a character. She was a woman getting away from it all, revamping an old house and kick-starting a new life. Putting myself in her shoes made it easier to decide what to take with me. It made it easier to buy the plane tickets and book the cab to take me to the airport. It made it so much easier not to think, not to feel but just to do.

Planes were not fun for me. Even in first class I couldn't get over the fact that I was in a huge metal machine that was in the air. In the actual air. I always feared the world might work out how ridiculous that was and make the abomination plunge to earth. But, of course, I was a reasonable woman so I had to pretend I didn't mind. I had to play it cool and just internally hate every minute.

"Ms Quinn, would you like another glass of champagne?" the smartly dressed air steward asked, breaking apart my musings.

"Oh, no thank you, I've had enough, thanks. I would love a glass of water, though."

"Of course, of course." He nodded and took a step forward but then hesitated. After a few seconds he turned around. "I know I'm not meant to ask and I won't be offended if you say no but I've been your biggest fan since I saw *Seven Whiskers* when I was ten. Can I please have your autograph?"

"Yes, of course. I'll sign whatever you want when you come back with my glass of water."

"Oh, thank you so much!" The young man clapped his hands together gleefully and jumped in the air with a ballet dancer's elegance. "I'll be right back." He waved both hands in front of his face to stop tears or cool down his blushing cheeks, beamed at me then rushed off toward the staff cabin.

I chuckled and looked out of the window once more. Ryan Taylor's jaw would drop to the floor if he could see me now. He'd never believe I was rich, famous and adored by millions. *I* barely believed it most days. He wouldn't know it was me, though. My name had changed from mousey Janet to exotic Katrina—I'd lost the glasses for contacts and I'd grown into the ample curves I'd been blessed with from such an early age. My hair was mousey blonde back when I was a kid but as an actress it was permanently dyed, my favorite and most usual color being a deep, dark raven black. My style varied but I'd keep it mid-length so it was easily managed. I was voted the best butt in the world by one of the lad's mags last year. Yeah, that bully wouldn't even guess that Janet Davey had grown up into a hot celebrity.

"Ms Quinn, here's your water."

"Thanks."" I smiled. "What do you want me to sign?"

"Oh, would you mind signing this serviette for me? I don't have anything more glamorous."

"Of course, who do you want me to make it out to?"

Usually I'd be carrying photos of myself with me for just such occasions but not this time. I wasn't on a promotional trip—I didn't want to draw any attention to myself. So I signed the young man's serviette and posed for a photo with him that his fellow steward took with a camera phone.

Katrina Quinn on an airplane wasn't news—if it ended up on the net it wouldn't be the end of the world. I was flying into Heathrow. I spent lots of time in London but very rarely left the metropolis. I wasn't worried—no one would be expecting me to disappear into the wilds of the Yorkshire Moors. They'd just gobble up yet another photo of disgraced Katrina, giving the paps a new excuse to splash me across the tabloid pages. Once I was snapped at the airport they'd forget about me.

It was raining at Heathrow. The sky was dark and drab, the drops were large and cold and it suited my mood to a tee. It was late afternoon, the airport was relatively quiet and I got out without too much hassle. The Brit press were just as interested as the yanks in what I'd been up to but my hired British security team protected me from them and I got to my limousine with the minimum of fuss and fluster. Matt had thought of everything, he wanted to be totally sure I was safe even when I wasn't in his immediate care.

It was eerily quiet in the back of the long, black car. The interior smelled of wood, polish and affluence. The leather seat gave under my body and cradled me comfortably. I looked out of the window and watched the world pass by. It would take about three hours to reach my old home. I'd hoped to sleep but my body clock was fucked to buggery. I couldn't sleep. Those stupid questions just kept spinning around in my brain.

If Gran had been around she'd have helped me snap out of it. She always had something to say. Often it would be baffling at the time but in hindsight she had made a lot of sense.

"You get nowhere running," was one she had rolled out quite often. As a sentence it was pathetic but as advice, it actually stood me in pretty good stead. I had learnt to stand up to things instead of avoiding them. It had made my life easier. However, Gran was gone and I wouldn't be able to get any new advice from her. That was a depressing thought but at least I had the years of advice she'd given me already.

Chapter Four

Ryan Taylor

"Well, I'm not going," Eve pouted. "The nasty old biddy never had a nice word to say about me. First time she saw us together she told you to go find yourself something better."

I remembered and tried not to grin. Mary had been a very direct lady.

"But she didn't mean it, it was just her way," I placated.

"Well, whatever. I'm not going. I hate funerals, they're so boring."

I shrugged. What more could I have said? Clearly Eve was heartless.

"Fine, well, I'm going. Mary was good to me."

"Yeah, right," Eve scoffed. "She was just as nasty about you."

"I know." I nodded. "But she was right. Always right."

I picked up my suit jacket and flung it over my shoulder then walked down the corridor to the door.

Eve was muttering something but I didn't care. I blocked her out.

It was a sharp autumnal day. The sun was low in the sky, the night drawing in even though it was just mid-afternoon and ice still clung to patches of ground and bush. Winter was rolling in. I pulled on my jacket and wished I'd picked up a scarf instead of storming out without a thought. I was a bloke and even more emotionally retarded than most. How could Eve be so selfish? I wanted her at the funeral to support me. Of course I'd not said that in so many words, that'd show my weakness, but a woman who professed to be my soul mate, who'd known me forever, should have picked up on that herself. I went to her mum's funeral, and Muriel had hated me with a passion. But Eve had needed me, so all that had been put to one side and I'd gone.

Mary wasn't my relative. No blood connected us but she was Gran. I'd called her Gran back then, when I was little. She used to laugh each time I did.

"When did I adopt a new grandkid?" she'd chirp.

Janie and I would laugh and I'd say something silly, depending on the moment.

Janie. Gosh, she hated being called Janie. Her name was Janet but it seemed such a grown-up name for a kid. I didn't like it. I wondered if she'd be at the funeral. My heart ceased again, for the millionth time since I'd thought about it. Janet would surely attend her grandma's funeral.

What would I say to her? Could I even bring myself to speak to her? Would she want me to? I'd been such a bastard to her, would I just upset her more if I tried to talk to her? I was conflicted but even under all that, the boiling roll of guilt and grieving, I was excited at the possibility that she'd be there.

The church in Thornleydale had looked the same for a hundred and fifty years. A tall rectangular building topped with a tower, a clock, and bells that chimed out for weddings. Well, as long as old Mr Cranwell was capable of it, and he was heading into his seventies. The brick was silver-gray and stood out stark against the yellows and bronzes of the leaves still clinging stubbornly to the trees in the churchyard. The whole village seemed to be heading toward it. I bumped into Mrs Ebberson and her carer on the way. She was pushing her wheelie and wearing a black hat with a long, sleek feather at the brim.

"Sad day, Ryan," she said, "a sad day indeed."

"I know," I replied with a sigh, "but she did have a good innings."

"Aye, that she did, that she did."

I walked on past and bumped full force into a body.

"Oh, I'm sorry," the apology fell from my lips before I realized who she was. Then I cringed. I wasn't my aunt's favorite person—she insisted I called her Mrs Collins even though we were related, she was so desperate to distance herself from me.

"No problem." She didn't smile, just brushed down the arm I'd bumped into as though I'd made her dirty. "Oh. It's you, Ryan."

"Hello." I smiled stiffly. "How are you?"

"Bearing up, you know. Mark's coming up for Christmas, you should come over and see him. He's Managing Director now, you know."

"Oh, is he?" I feigned indifference for fear she'd go into detail.

"He is. How are you doing? Still in the manual trade?"

Even I could tell that was a dig.

"Yes, still doing my odd jobs, Aunty."

She hated being called Aunty and her nose crinkled up in disgust at the word quite satisfactorily.

"Have you got anything for me to do?"

"Not at the minute, dear, no, but I'll keep you in mind, I'll keep you in mind."

I slipped a hand into my inside pocket and pulled out a business card.

"Here you go, it's got my mobile number on it, the best one to get me on."

"Oh, wonderful, thank you."

I'd spent a lot of money on the cards, and I carried them everywhere with me to hand out to all and sundry. I don't think they ever got me any extra business but I was always hopeful.

"Is Eve with you?" she asked, looking pointedly around us.

"No." I coughed, covering my mouth for a moment to think of a viable excuse. "She's not feeling very well today."

"Send her my best then, Ryan. It must be so disheartening being out of work for so very long."

"It is, but she's still looking." I pasted on an optimistic smile. Eve wasn't looking at all. She would go to any interview the job center arranged for her but that was simply it. She'd gotten used to being looked after. I didn't think she wanted that to change.

At the church door the new reverend handed me an order of service and I headed to my seat. I'd not been to church in years. O'Reily had been the vicar in residence back then. Dithery old man, inclined to waffle. That was way back when I lived at home with Mum and Dad. I'd not gone after Dad had died. As a sort of protest. I had a bone or two to pick with God. But I found a seat at the back of the high-ceilinged hall of pews and cleared my mind of everything but Mary.

Gran.

It was a moving service. The new guy was very good and he certainly knew Mary well. He had several anecdotes that made the crowd mumble a chuckle. The whole church was packed with people. From the village, from her old days as a nurse in Wakefield, from the nursing home she'd ended her life in. There was no sign of Janet, though.

After the service I went over to the funeral director, who was well known throughout this part of Yorkshire for traveling to all the little villages and hamlets to do his duty. He'd been the guy who'd helped me bury my dad then my mum a month later.

"Hello, Ryan" — he shook my hand firmly — "it's good to see you but what a sad circumstance."

"I know, she was such a good woman." I nodded, then scuffed at the floor with my foot. Looking down I pushed out the question I was desperate to ask, "I didn't see Janie about, I mean Janet, Mary's granddaughter. She was here, though, right?"

Jack looked a little amused, which really didn't go well with his solemn top hat and tails.

"No, no, she wasn't here."

My heart sank. What reason would keep Janet from her gran's funeral? Surely she couldn't have passed away herself? That just wouldn't be fair.

"She looked in via the Internet or something — that was the weird wire rig-up we had going. Not sure where she was, but something kept her from physically being here."

"That must be hard." I tried hard not to smile with relief. *She isn't dead. Thank God!*

"I imagine so. Can't quite think of anything that would keep me away from my only relative's funeral, though."

"Wow, is she the only one left now?"

"Oh aye, buried Keith in Barnsley five year ago. She won't there neither. But that's not so surprising."

"I didn't know," I sighed. "God, all this talk of death is depressing. Want to come to the Fiddlers for a pint with me?"

"Wish I could, lad, wish I could. But I have to go to the interrin' then I've got to visit a new widow out Flockton way." He slapped my back heartily. "But thanks for asking."

I went directly to the pub—I couldn't face going to the graveyard and seeing that coffin dropped into the cold, hard ground, and I couldn't face going back to Eve either. She'd prattle on about something insignificant and I'd get angry with her. No, it was safer for me to be in the pub.

The Fiddler was quiet, so I got a good space by the roaring log fire and cradled my beer in the flickering light. I took a long draft of my bitter, letting the hopsy water trickle down my throat and the memories flicker across my mind's eye.

* * * *

Copse Cottage, 2007

"I can't believe it," I exclaimed, "it's that same fencepost that went when we were kids."

Mary had me down at the far end of the garden to mend her back fence.

"I know, it always seems to be the first one to rot away. Can you fix it?"

"I can, I've got some wood in my van. I'll get to it."

"Brilliant, how much will it be?"

"For you, not a penny," I responded. We were skint. Eve was still in work, but she was off on the sick and on minimal pay. Which she insisted on spending on herself. She wasn't even ill, not really. She was just sick of work and had gotten the doc to sign her off with depression. I wasn't happy about it but she didn't listen to my protests. I was struggling to pay all our bills but Mary was still family in my mind, I couldn't charge her.

"Oh, no, now, Ryan, I've got to pay you something," she chided. Her eyes sparkled just the same as they had when I was a kid. The wrinkles were more prominent and her hair was bright white, but other than looking a little frailer she'd hardly changed.

"Beef stew and dumplings, Mary. If you want to give me summat, give me that."

"Right, you're on. I've got some stew steak in. I'll set it going now and it'll be ready in a few hours."

I completed the fence repair job in just over an hour, but I returned to Mary's at five thirty on the dot. That was teatime from when we were little kids. She always kept to it.

"Hiya, Ryan, it's just ready to serve."

I walked into her corridor, the warm, hearty scent of stew embracing me, taking me back to my childhood. She led me straight into the kitchen and sat me at her table. I'd noticed a pile-up of magazines in one corner and some books in another, but I didn't mention it. The rest of the space was sparklingly clean.

She served me up the biggest plate of stew, laden with cubes of softly parting meat, chunks of potato and carrot, which was covered in the most delicious meat and herb gravy known to man. She gave me three of her dumplings—huge, white and fluffy they were, like tasty clouds that melted into a blanket of comfort on my tongue.

"Oh, Gran, you sure can cook." I moaned.

Mary laughed and shook her head. "Long time since you called me that, Ryan."

"I know." I paused in my demolition of her food. "Sorry."

"No worries, I'm used to it now," she chuckled. "Truth be told, it's good to hear you say it."

I ate some more, the silence jovial.

"How's Janie these days?" I asked, dipping up the last of my gravy with a chunk of fresh baked white bread.

"Oh, she's fine, just fine." Mary smiled. "She did great in university, passed with flying colors."

"Oh, good. I knew she would." I nodded.

Mary didn't tell me anything else. She was always tight-lipped when it came to Janet. Never gave me any details, just that she was happy and well, and working in America. But Mary would never tell me precisely. I'm sure Janet had given her instructions to keep me in the dark.

* * * *

It had been about six months before the funeral when I'd seen Mary last. She had been in Sunnyfields, the nursing home just outside Wakefield. They'd gotten a burst pipe in the middle of the night and the usual plumber wouldn't see to it. Mary had told them about me — it had been her room that all the water had run into — and I, of course, had gone to the rescue.

"Hello, Mary," I'd greeted her with a huge smile. She had been sat in the lounge with a cup of tea, wrapped in a white furry nightgown. Her skin had

51

been pale and taut, her cheeks hollowed and her hair wispy. I'd been surprised by how old she suddenly looked.

"Hello, trouble," she'd cackled, her eyes twinkling with mirth just like they always had.

"I hear you're the one causing trouble this time," I'd teased.

She shook her head. Just then the nurse on duty had butted in and led me off to inspect the offending pipe. After I'd fixed it, I'd hung around to fill in some paperwork at the desk. Just as I had been turning to go, Mary had walked toward me, hobbling with the use of her stick.

"Ryan," she'd called.

I'd walked over to her.

"I should be in bed—when Rowena catches up with me she'll be so mad—but I just wanted to say thank you."

"Oh, you're welcome, Mary, it was just a little job."

"No, not just for that. I want to thank you for looking after my Janie when she was so small. Her house was not a place of happiness, you know that, and you helped her escape from it for a while. You were a rascal, Ryan Taylor, I know that, but you were Janie's hero."

"Well, thank you, Gran." I'd swallowed the lump in my throat to fall into the boiling pit of guilt in my stomach. "It was my pleasure."

"I wish you'd not fallen out, you two. I really do. But I'll let Janie know I've seen you. Maybe she'll mend bridges with you while I'm still around to see it."

"Oh, Gran, you'll always be around."

I had laughed and she'd joined in.

"Now where's your room, let me escort you back. Then if anyone gets in trouble it'll be me."

"And you're used to that, now, aren't you?" She'd giggled.

I'd linked her arm and she'd leaned heavily on me as we'd shuffled back down the corridor to her room. She had weighed next to nothing but her smile was as diamond studded as it had ever been.

"Goodnight, Gran," I'd whispered just as she'd pulled the door shut.

"Goodnight, son," she'd replied.

I'd gotten back in my van and I'd cried. Big, heaving sobs. When had everything gone so wrong? I'd known about the tensions at Janie's house. I wasn't exactly clever but it was easy to see her mum and dad weren't in love. I never felt like I rescued her from it, though, we had had fun when we were together. Then in those teenage years between childhood and responsibility I'd deserted her. Left her to it.

I rolled home after the funeral and my eighth pint. I was more than a little tipsy — it was pretty late.

"Where've you been all day, you bastard? You could have called me, I've been worried sick."

"I was at the funeral." I shrugged.

"And the pub, I can smell it on you. I could have come with you if you'd asked."

"Didn't want you," I replied, my alcohol-addled mind too soaked to mask the honest answer. "I wanted to be on my own."

"Oh, you did, did you? Well, you can sleep on the pissing couch tonight then, you twat."

She twirled, or attempted to, and dragged herself back upstairs. She was as drunk as I was. I collapsed on the sofa and slept. I dreamt I was trapped in the bole of a tree that then morphed into the silk-lined interior of a coffin and as much as I yelled, no one came to help me.

* * * *

The insistent blaring of my phone alarm woke me at five thirty a.m. I must have set it at some point the day before. When I switched it off, one eye shut against the glare of the screen, the sound seemed to continue inside my brain.

It took a moment to realize where I was, what had happened and why I needed to be up so damn early. I pulled myself with a groan into a sitting position. That was so much effort that I was close to flopping back down and going back to sleep. But I had a big job on, several final demands to pay and Eve to avoid. So by sheer strength of will I got myself moving.

Thank God for twenty-four-hour supermarkets. Sometimes, in my line of work, I had to go to the specialist stockists and dealers, but if I needed black bin bags, rubber gloves and other such shit-shifting gear then the supermarket was the place to head to. I needed supplies and so I ended up in the domestic cleaning aisle of Tesco when most people would have still been in bed.

At first I thought I was hallucinating. There was probably more alcohol in my blood than was really wise for a man driving and planning a lot of heavy lifting for the day. But she didn't move, she was still there after I blinked a few times and pushed my trolley closer.

"No way, it can't be," I exclaimed.

She looked up, startling blue eyes staring fixedly at me.

"Dear God, it is, it really is. Oh, I'm so sorry, I'm babbling but I can't believe you're here!"

A teenaged Belieber had nothing on me. I was in complete fandom meltdown.

"It is you, isn't it? You're Katrina Quinn, aren't you?"

She nodded hesitantly.

"Well, bugger me. I can't believe it. What on earth are you doing here?" I asked, mouth agog.

She didn't answer, just stared at me and I just babbled on.

"Of course, you don't want to tell me, it's none of my business. Sorry, sorry. I'm just so surprised. Now, look, I'm sure you're fed up with this kind of thing, but could I get your autograph?"

I patted my pockets, pulled out a trusty business card and a pen.

"Can you sign it to Ryan, please? That'd be cool. I don't suppose I could have a photo with you…"

Her fingers brushed mine as I passed her the pen, and I felt like a deflating balloon, out of control and violently shrinking. Well, apart from one particular part of my body. Dear God, her touch was potent.

"No, no photo," she stuttered.

"Of course, no worries, just thought it was worth asking, you know, to prove I've actually met you."

She wasn't very talkative but that didn't bother me. I was babbling enough myself to keep up her end of the conversation too.

"I can't be seen in a photo with you," she exclaimed, rudely.

"No, fair enough, fair enough." It was incredibly early in the morning, no wonder she was blunt.

"There you go." She pressed the card back into my hand.

Her skin was so soft and pale, her fingers warm and dainty. I imagined them around my cock for a moment then shook myself from the fantasy.

"Thanks so much." I couldn't meet her eye—my cock was so hard and my mind so filled with wanting to fuck her I was scared of letting her see what a pervert I was. "Really, this is awesome. I better let you get on with your shopping but here's one of my cards, you might have need of my services, you never know." It was a punt but even famous movie stars need odd jobs doing now and then.

"Yes, okay then, I'll take one."

I passed her a card without making eye contact. I was still nervous she'd notice my hard-on bulging in my trousers.

"Thanks, Ryan. Have a nice day." Her accent was heavily American, which surprised me. I knew she'd lived in the US for a good long while but I'd imagined a Yorkshire accent would take a lot of losing.

"Thanks and bye." I waved like a complete idiot.

She waved back and I walked away. Looking over my shoulder I noticed she was taller than I'd imagined. Her curves were no less attractive, though. Especially her arse, which was perfectly cupped in a pair of faded jeans. What I'd give to do the cupping...

My trolley was already filled with the stuff I needed, which was good because I was completely incapable of thought after meeting her. I followed her around the shop at a discreet distance, occasionally catching her fragrant scent like a sweet shop from my childhood mixed with a top class department store.

I went to a different till from her and didn't follow her into the car park. I didn't want her to think I was a stalker! When I got into my van, I sat for a moment and stared at the autographed card. I remembered her touch and — bam! All I could think about was sex. My dick hardened, painfully mashing itself in the confines of my jeans.

I should have thought of something disgusting to get the erection to piss off so I could get to work but it had been such a long while since my cock had worked I had to take advantage of it while there was life in it.

I unzipped myself, checking carefully that no one was walking past my van. When I was sure the car park around me was completely empty I grabbed my hot erection and wanked. She was there, in the van with me in my mind's eye — it wasn't my hand that was pleasuring my cock, it was her cunt. Katrina was riding me, milking me dry.

The orgasm rocked my body forward — I hit the center of the wheel and accidentally pipped the horn. Luckily no one came running, and I got my cock under control and back in my pants. My blood was hot with arousal, and I zinged with a joyful energy I'd not felt for a very long time.

It was a sad reality that I'd been more sexually aroused by one brief meeting in a supermarket with a hot woman than I'd been by Eve in months.

It was shallow, I knew it, but past the natural urge to copulate, which I'd either fought or given into over the years, I wasn't interested in fucking my girlfriend. Her skin was orange from too much fake tan and her attitude stank. It didn't help that every day, just a little bit, I fell more and more out of love with her. I became less and less convinced that I ever had loved her. But she was my responsibility. I'd taken her on and what would happen to her if I left? Her drinking habit worried me. She would start on a bottle of wine at lunchtime and have finished two or three by bedtime. I had to try to rein her in. After all, I'd brought her to

Thornleydale when she'd wanted to go off and see the world. She'd sacrificed that for me. I was tied and bound so tightly in a life that I didn't like. How I wished it could have been different.

I tidied myself up and set the van running, then I noticed the time. I was going to be late.

Thankfully Frank, the guy I was odd jobbing for, was in a good mood. He just shrugged and pointed me in the direction of my workload. When I started shifting the broken furniture, moldering food and other miscellaneous nastiness that the gray bricked two-up two-down contained I realized why he hadn't been so fussed about my lateness. He didn't want to do the dirty work himself!

I dug in, determined to bury myself in work to stop thinking about how much my head hurt or, worse, remembering how I had felt in close proximity to Katrina. I didn't have time for another wank.

I did eventually take a break for some lunch, which I grabbed from the corner shop. I picked up a paper, too, as a headline on it caught my eye.

Paxton's New Squeeze.
Brian Paxton's quickie divorce came through just hours before he was seen out in a New York bar with nineteen-year-old supermodel Candice Dubray. Photos of the forty-year-old star's passionate affair with Seven Whiskers *star Katrina Quinn proved the undoing of his eight-year marriage…*

"Well, the cheeky bastard!" I exclaimed. He'd made a whole song and dance out of Katrina seducing him and how much he regretted it. Well, that had clearly been a crock of shit. He had been trying to get out of that marriage to have a go at some barely legal model chick. No wonder Katrina had escaped over to the UK — this new bit of news would intensify the media's hounding of her, I was sure.

Part of me was a bit jealous of Paxton's happy-go-lucky attitude. I was far too loyal to my partner. I was sure that if I'd taken a survey, most respondents would have seen nothing wrong with me leaving my drunk, selfish girlfriend.

What kept me with her? I'd asked myself that question many times. Janie had even asked me the same thing several times herself.

* * * *

College, 1996

"So why do you stay with her then?" Janie snapped.

"None of your business," I growled back. Not because I was offended at the question, more that I wasn't sure how to answer.

"Exactly. Think you could keep your large nostrils out of my business, please, for once. Just leave me alone." She turned and stormed off. I'd overheard her telling a friend that her dad had left. She was upset, sat outside the deputy head's office. I should have stopped and checked she was okay but no, I carried on to my lesson, and when I saw Eve at the end of the day I passed on the juicy tit-bit of gossip.

"No wonder, her mother is as ugly as she is. She's keeping it a secret, right?" Eve responded.

"Seems so, she was just whispering it to that cross-eyed bird she hangs out with."

"Then you need to tell everyone about it."

"Oh, Eve," I sighed. "That's nasty."

"So's telling lies. You told me you'd do anything for me. I want you to tell everyone about Janet's father running off and leaving her."

"Fine" — I huffed — "but I don't like it."

I told everyone I met about Janie's dad. I just hoped it wouldn't get back to her that it was me who'd started it all.

A sunny afternoon a few weeks later I was playing footie with the lads, and Keano hoofed it right into the bushes at the end of the front field.

"I'll get it," I yelled, feet already pounding. It was only as I gingerly parted the dense bushes that I heard the sobbing noise. When I was behind the cover of the hedgerow I found Janet.

She was scrunched up, knees to chin, and when she looked up at me I could see she'd been crying for quite some time.

"Oh, Janie, I didn't want to tell anyone," I gasped, still looking for the ball.

"Why did you then?" Her voice was level and emotionless, it was eerie.

"Eve."

"Of course," she sighed.

I was still looking for the ball. "I'm sorry, Janie, you know I don't mean it."

"Then why do you do it? Why do you stay with her?"

"It's nothing personal," I sighed. "I still like you, Janie, but I've got to keep in with Eve and that lot or I'll get bullied too." She deserved a bit of the truth after all. I didn't give her the chance to respond — I found the ball, picked it up and jogged back out to the field then continued to play footie. My mind wasn't on the game, though. I wanted so badly to go back and talk to Janet. To tell her she was still the best girl in the world and wipe those tears away from her cheeks.

It was a close run thing, I very nearly did it. Eve had me under her thumb but the thrall was wearing off. I had always had fun with Janie. Being with Eve was hard work more often than not.

I made the decision to run back to Janie, Eve be damned, and struck the ball hard away from me. I'd turned back toward the foliage when I heard a piercing scream and a lot of fuss being made. I turned around — my over-enthusiastic kick had booted the ball into Eve, knocking her flying.

"Ryan," Keano bellowed up the pitch. "Eve's hurt."

I had to race over and check what the matter was. She was clutching her ankle and howling.

"Better get you to the nurse," I said as I glimpsed the red swelling beneath her fingers. "Get you looked over."

She mumbled something I was sure wasn't complimentary but then flung an arm round my neck, hauling herself up onto her working foot.

"You did it on purpose," Eve accused.

"I didn't, sorry."

"I'm so embarrassed, my own boyfriend knocking me to the ground."

I just let her witter on. She was in pain and scared, which always translated into anger with Eve.

The nurse was convinced that she'd twisted it. She put ice on it and went to call Eve's mum to come and pick her up.

"Sorry." I put my arm around her. "Does it still hurt?"

"It's better now." She rested her head on my shoulder. "I shouldn't have shouted at you, really."

"It's all right."

And it was. I'd all but forgotten about Janie, for the time being.

Chapter Five

Katrina Quinn

The scenery became more familiar and the sky became greyer. Yorkshire seemed to have ordered its best drizzling weather to greet me. I suppose it was my own fault for heading back to the UK in November, just in time for the long dark winter of the cold. The stark greys and purples of the moors, flat yet rocky and devoid of green vegetation, took me back in time to when I'd just turned eighteen.

* * * *

The Road to Wakefield, 1998

I was leaving home. Dad had left a couple of years before and Mum hadn't been the same since. The last straw had come when I'd asked her if she would miss me when I went to university in the autumn. I was working up to my A levels and had my nose deep in my English textbook.

"No," she replied flatly. "I'll enjoy the solitude."

Even my mother didn't want me. I didn't scream and shout, that wasn't my way. I didn't argue with her. I finished my chapter of revision and told her I was going out to meet friends.

She should have known I was lying—maybe she did—because I didn't have friends. The only person in the whole village I used to visit regularly was my gran, whom Mum didn't visit often because she couldn't stand seeing her ex-mother-in-law anymore. I had my head down and I was going to get excellent grades, get to Oxford and get the hell out of Yorkshire. Away from the bullies and the sheep who followed their opinions. All that flew from my mind as distress took over the reins.

I packed a rucksack with a few clothes, my two favorite books and a light wooden box with my name inscribed in the top. Then I raided my piggy bank. My savings were swollen in preparation for my new start in college—pocketing it all I left the house with no idea where to go. I just needed to get away. I couldn't drive as I'd given up on the idea of taking lessons to save for university and thought it best not to get the bus as the driver would tell my mum exactly where I'd gone to if she asked. That was the downside of living in a small village where everyone knew each other.

I walked toward Wakefield, the nearest town. Luckily the sun was shining and the day was fair. It was early spring, so the moors were dark and brooding—just the very eager plants were trying to push their heads above ground. I walked past Gran's place quickly, in case she spotted me and came out to speak. Her house was on the road out of the village, caught in a little copse of trees that sheltered it from the wind and the rain. I walked on past the copse and out again into the desolation of the moors.

I kept to the main road. I was sure that if someone were to drive out looking for me they'd be able to find me, but I also knew that it was crazy to just walk off into the countryside and away from the paths. I had some knowledge of the area and in spring the fog could roll over quickly and with little warning. I didn't want to be lost in the wilds—a little sense still lodged between my ears.

I stopped to rest on a road marker that indicated there were three miles between me and Thornleydale, and a further seven to get to Wakefield. It was just after lunch and I started to realize what a stupid thing I'd done. A car horn peeped and a familiar moss green Jag pulled up beside me.

"Hey, Janie, what are you doing all the way out here?"

It was Ryan. When we'd played together as kids he'd always called me Janie—he said it was a far friendlier name than Janet.

"Oh, nothing." I shrugged. He might have called me by an old pet name but he and Eve, his girlfriend, had made my life hell all through senior school and college. If I told him I was running away I was sure it'd fuel a whole barrage of offense.

"I'm running away, Janie. I'm pissed off. Want to come with me?"

I stared at him, the low hum of his engine muting the sounds of nature around us. Was I hearing him right? How could I trust a word he said after the way he'd treated me? Eve had him under her thumb—everything he did to me was directed by her.

"Oh come on, Janie. We used to be the best of friends. We always said we'd travel, see the world together. Well, let's start right now. I'm sick of Thornleydale, sick of my parents and sick of fucking Eve. Let's go, Janie, leave that shit creek idyll to its own downfall. We'll go and discover the world."

"Okay then." The answer had leaped from my lips before I'd thought. It was a dream come true.

"Yes." He grinned, softening his face into the mischievous lines of his youth. "Jump in, then."

I walked round the back of the car then opened the passenger side door. I flung my bag in the back and took to my seat, after removing an empty can and crisp packet. The interior smelled of polish and elbow grease. It was Ryan's dad's pride and joy. He'd be pissed off when he found out it was gone.

"Right, buckle in, Janie. We're off for an adventure."

There was no conversation for a while. I sat in silence, taking it in. I was in Ryan's car, and he wanted to take me on an adventure. Ryan might have been the source of many of my problems through school but he was also my biggest crush. I just couldn't stop fancying him. He was my teenage idol. Messy dark blond hair that he had to flip from his face at regular moments, and ivy green eyes that sparkled with mischief. We'd been playmates as kids and the best of friends. I'd never seen him as anything other than my mate Ry until puberty had hit and suddenly, whenever I saw him, my stomach would feel hollow and would rattle as though it was filled with dried rice.

Ryan had gone from cute to handsome in his teenage years. Whereas I had gone from plain to chubby with visitations from acne and the greasy hair fairy along the way. My eyesight had worsened so I needed glasses and my curly hair would not be tamed by hair products. I was frizzier than a bear cub. So as

Ry joined the cool gang, I became the geek everyone laughed at. Including Ry.

"It's nothing personal," he'd told me once back in the first year of sixth form. He'd accidentally found me in the bushes at the bottom end of the playground crying. He'd just chased in after the football. "I still like you, Janie, but I've got to keep in with Eve and that lot or I'll get bullied too."

There was some kind of weird teenage logic there, but I never saw any indication that he liked me. He was as cruel as the rest.

"I'm hungry," Ryan announced, pulling me from my thoughts. "Shall we stop at the chippy for something?"

"Sure." I nodded. "I'm hungry too."

We pulled in at The Golden Fry. Ryan told me to stay in the car and he went out to get us some food. It was the chip shop just up the road from school, where kids would go for a sneaky bag of chips on the way home. It didn't feel as though we'd gotten very far on our adventure at all.

Ryan came back with a carrier bag in hand and two cans in the other. He passed them to me and started the engine again.

"I know a good lay-by to stop in not far from here. Don't want to be caught before we've even started, right?"

"Okay," I acquiesced again. I would have agreed to anything, I was that besotted with him. We drove through town and headed out on the A road toward Leeds. Not too far along Ryan pulled into a lay-by, quiet at that time on a Saturday, but frequently used judging by the amount of litter carpeting the grass by the side of the road.

Ryan took the bag from my hand and passed me a paper-wrapped parcel. We opened them and ate the cooling chips in silence.

"So, why are you leaving?" I asked, growing brave.

"Well, what reason is there for me to stay? My parents are pricks, they grounded me just because I was out late last night with the guys. I'm fucking eighteen, Janie. They need to treat me like an adult. So what I busted the tractor and ruined half a field with my late night drive out with the lads? I said I was sorry. Then Eve was just as unreasonable. Told me I needed to grow up! She was just jealous I wasn't out with her. She's so fucking controlling, Janie. I just want to break away, make a new start. Because where am I going otherwise?"

"Aren't you going to uni, then?" I asked, naïvely.

"Oh, Janie" – Ryan leaned over the hand brake and covered my hand with his – "you're so sweet. But surely by now you know I'm completely thick. I can't go to university. I'm just going to end up working for Dad."

"You... You... You... You're not thick," I stuttered, my body humming with his touch, my voice fighting to break through the earthquake of emotion. "You're really bright. And good with your hands. I've still got the jewelry box you made me for my tenth birthday."

"You still have that?" Ryan asked, eyes widening, mouth softening into a smile. His hand was still over mine, heating my fingers to boiling point.

"Sure, it's beautiful. Actually, it's in my bag now."

He scrunched his eyebrows in confusion.

"I'm running away too."

"No," he exclaimed, "really? Why are you running away?"

"Maybe you *are* thick, Ry," I scoffed gently. "Can't you guess? My dad left us, my mum's not been the same since and I'm the butt of everyone's joke at school. I can't take all that anymore."

I swallowed hard—a lump had formed in my throat. My skin felt electrified and there was a waterfall of tears pressing at the backs of my eyes.

"Oh, Janie, it's been tough for you, hasn't it?"

His strong, soft hand cupped my cheek, and as a tear slipped down he gently wiped it away with his thumb.

"I still think you're the best girl in the world," he whispered, his breath caressing my lips he was so very close.

"And you're not bad, for a boy," I replied with a wry smile, remembering back to the first argument we'd ever had. Ryan hadn't wanted to play pretend mummies and daddies with me even though I'd told him he could be a builder for his job and I'd let him play with my Lego. I'd run off crying and he'd followed me and told me he was sorry and that he thought I was the best girl in the world.

I had still been mad at him, so I had just said, "You're not bad, for a boy."

We'd laughed then, like six-year-olds do, and had gotten back to playing.

I snapped back to the present, his lips so close to mine, his hand on my cheek. I felt as though I was shaking, my whole body taken by a quake of shock and lust. His lips met mine and I stilled. Quiet peace reigned for a moment. I was at the pinnacle of bliss, everything was perfect and light. Then he moved his lips and the agitation returned. I burned deep in the pit of my stomach, my skin itched for his touch and I burned up, waiting for more.

He was my first kiss. I didn't know what I was doing but instinct pushed me forward. I reached out to grab at his biceps, needing to feel more of him—he kept me grounded. I'd fall away into a chasm of darkness if I let go. I wanted to know it was real. Could I get him to pinch me to make sure I wasn't dreaming?

Suddenly there was a harsh rap at the window and we exploded apart, cold chips leaping from my lap to the footwell. Ryan rolled down the window at the second tap.

"Ryan Taylor?" The deep voice of the policeman in high-vis jacket roused us from the moment.

"Yes," Ryan replied, dreamily.

"You need to go home, now," he said firmly. "You can either drive back of your own accord or I can take you in the car to the station."

"I'll drive home, officer," he replied, sounding much more serious. "I'll just drop Janie off at her place on the way."

"Certainly, sir." The policeman nodded. "I'll be following you, so no funny business, okay?"

"Okay."

Ryan wound up the window and shrugged at me.

"It could have been a brilliant adventure," he said, and switched on the engine.

We didn't talk on the way home. I didn't know what to say and Ryan had retreated back behind some kind of invisible wall. He dropped me off at my gran's and continued back to his.

For a long while I wondered if it had actually happened. It was such a bright memory, so sharp and in focus that I wondered if it had been just an intensely vivid dream. Ryan was back with Eve on the Monday at college and he wouldn't even look at me. I wondered if I'd flipped into an alternate reality just for those few hours—that I'd been shown what could have happened. It kept me going till the end of the school year. I got my grades and went to Oxford to study English and Drama. My life changed from that point on but I would always remember Ryan and that first blinding kiss, the only kiss that had ever shaken my soul.

* * * *

Gran's place hadn't changed a lot from the outside. Yes, the brick was more weathered, the window frames not as bright as they had been, but generally it looked the same. The garden was no longer neat and tidy, the grass was more natural than manicured and the bushes were encroaching on the moss-laden path. It smelled the same, though. The crisp apple and mulch of autumn that always signaled the start of hard labor. Gran would pay me handsomely to keep her gardens free from leaves. I used to spend a long time with a rake in the autumn but it gave me plenty of money for Christmas. If I'd left her garden like this, there would have been all hell to pay.

Of course, Gran hadn't lived at home for a few years—she'd moved into a nursing home after a fall and had liked it so much she stayed. I had spoken to her on the phone when she'd first gone in and she was telling me she couldn't wait to get out. A few weeks later we'd talked again and she'd been determined to stay. She'd made so many friends.

"I didn't realize how lonely I was, Katrina, but now I have so many people to talk to and I don't have to clean anything, they do all that for me."

It was bizarre to think of my very independent gran in a nursing home, but she had been happy, so I was happy. I'd ring once a week — until her hearing worsened — and she'd tell me all the gossip from the home and I was convinced it had been the right place for her.

I unlocked the door with a heavy heart and the limo driver helped me into the building with my luggage. I gave him a generous tip, and he thanked me zealously. I shut the door behind him and took it all in.

It was strangely comforting how familiar it all was. The mirror on the wall with the scrolled gold frame with the tiny crack in the bottom right corner. I'd knocked it off when I was just eight. I had been trying to show Gran the latest dance move I'd learned at ballet but it had gone a bit wrong and I'd crashed into the wall, knocking the mirror off its nail and causing the crack. I'd been completely mortified. Gran had just laughed it off and told me how proud she was of my improvement in ballet.

The small table beneath the mirror carried the same small wooden box and carriage clock that had always been there. At Christmas they'd be decked with tinsel and a jolly, slightly balding, old-fashioned felt Santa would stand between the two. I could still even smell the orange-scented polish she'd used to buff up the bannisters once a week for as long as she'd lived there. It wasn't all oranges and baking biscuits anymore. There was a damp edge of must that made me remember that this wasn't the same place I came to in my youth. It was just a house, a shell, not a home.

Running a finger over the top of the box I pulled up a fluff of gray dust. A mental shopping list started forming with dusters and hedge clippers right at the top. Walking into the front room made the list grow. I was going to need a skip. There was a clear space in the middle of the room with a chair, a TV and a footstool and that was essentially Gran's living room. It looked as though she'd just nipped into the kitchen to make a brew. If I blocked out everything else in the room I could pretend there was nothing different, but all around were piles of newspapers and magazines, boxes and tins, stacked and arranged neatly to cover over fifty percent of the floor space. It was almost impossible to ignore.

"Holy shit," I exclaimed and the expletives got worse with each room I entered.

Every room was filled with the same mix of books, boxes and magazines. Tins, clothes and all kinds of other weird stuff. Even the kitchen was piled high with magazines and books. Only the sink and the cooker were clear. I could walk between the towers, there were paths between the piles of things and the cooking and cleaning area, but only just. I'd thought it might take a few weeks to clear the house but I soon worked out it'd take a lot longer than that. I decided it would be an even longer process when I discovered that the water had been switched off along with the gas and the electric. After a few more expletives and a comprehensive rundown of who I could get to help — no one — I stopped panicking and decided to work out how to fix things myself.

Thank God for the smartphone. A quick look online and I discovered what a stop cock, stop tap and fuse box looked like. It took a mere three hours to find them all and switch things back on.

I should have booked in at the local hotel but I was stubborn. I also didn't want to announce my arrival to the world just yet, and booking in at Thornleydale's B & B would have had me the talk of the town in minutes. The only people who ever stayed there were family members of villagers who'd somehow managed to escape but came back dutifully for holidays and high days. It was not the kind of place a top-named celeb would find herself.

I thought about leaving Gran's and finding a hotel in Wakefield to settle down in for the night. I could come back in the morning and get on. It was very tempting. I could sleep in a clean room on a soft, comfortable bed and someone would make me breakfast in the morning. Problem was I didn't think I'd go back to Gran's after that. I knew if I left I would find it really hard to come back.

I should probably have slept in Gran's room. The bed in there was clear, if dusty, and the surrounding stuff didn't tower too close to where I'd have to lay my head. But I couldn't sleep in Gran's room. It just felt wrong, it wasn't my place to be, and it reminded me so poignantly that she was no longer there.

So I started to clear off the one in the spare room. It was piled high with records. I wondered as I moved them to the floor if there would be a player for them anywhere in the house. Gran must have had hundreds. Eventually I found the bed itself. I removed the blankets and sheets and replaced them with clean ones I'd brought. I added a duvet to my mental shopping list because one fleece blanket wasn't going to keep me warm for long.

I didn't know that my gran had been a hoarder but clearly she had. How many years of stuff was I looking at having to clear?

* * * *

I woke in the morning to birdsong. I wasn't impressed. I tried to ignore the tweeting but then the heating pipes started gurgling like an ogre with a sore throat. So I just got up.

I found a piece of paper and a pen and wrote down the mental list, adding in essential food items as I went. I found the location of the closest twenty-four-hour supermarket and set off for it in the dark, at a time in the morning I usually only saw if I'd been out partying all night.

But I was doing something and I was positive. It was going to be a good day. I'd get started at Gran's and it'd be therapeutic. I had myself buoyed along with such optimism that I was actually humming to myself as I wandered down the cleaning products aisle.

"No way, it can't be." A strikingly familiar voice broke through my hum.

I looked up from the two brands of bin bags in my hands and almost dropped them.

"Dear God, it is, it really is. Oh, I'm so sorry, I'm babbling but I can't believe you're here!"

I smile, more in hysteria than amusement. Ryan Taylor was the babbling man. He didn't look very different. His hair was cut shorter, there were bags beneath his gloriously green eyes. But his smile was the same, crooked and cheeky, and his voice was enough to make my stomach flip. I froze. I didn't know what to do. Of course, I'd been faced with fans before, encroaching my personal space and I would get rid of them easily. Sometimes I'd sign, sometimes I'd pretend to be French. Mostly I'd get away unscathed. But I was faced by the one man I was bound and determined to avoid.

"It is you, isn't it? You're Katrina Quinn, aren't you?"

I sighed and nodded. He had recognized me, but as a star, not as the real me.

"Well, bugger me. I can't believe it. What on earth are you doing here?" he asked, mouth agog.

I didn't respond. I couldn't, my voice was lost somewhere deep in the pit of my stomach, sloshing around in there with my wits and my composure.

"Of course, you don't want to tell me, it's none of my business. Sorry, sorry. I'm just so surprised. Now, look, I'm sure you're fed up with this kind of thing, but could I get your autograph?"

I nodded stiffly. I just wanted him to go away. My mind was spinning with questions that the old me was dying to ask. Janet wanted to find out what he was up to, where he worked—was he married and did he have kids? She wanted to know if he ever thought of her, if he'd ever felt guilty about the way he'd treated her. Could he remember the kiss they'd shared?

I pushed Janet down and played Katrina. *Why would he recognize me?* My eyes were startling blue now, with the aid of colored contacts. Not the winter cloud blue-gray that he'd recognize as Janet's. And no glasses. He knew how bad my eyesight had been, had teased me about it constantly, so he'd not expect to see me without glasses at all. My hair was jet black—the mousey brown that was my natural color hadn't been seen since I'd moved to America. I dressed more confidently, I'd grown into my curves and was a completely different woman. I ate healthily, my skin glowed with the benefit of two liters of water a day and a diet filled with fruit, veg and wholemeal carbohydrates. I walked taller, with better poise owing to hours of yoga each week. Even my voice was different—my accent was more American, my tone more even and confident owing to my stage training.

On the outside at least I was nothing like the Janie he'd once known.

He ran his hands over himself, conjuring up some dirty images in my brain where he did the same actions naked.

"Can you sign it to Ryan, please. That'd be cool. I don't suppose I could have a photo with you…" He passed a pen to me and our fingers touched.

My stomach flipped and my head swam.

"No, no photo," I stuttered.

"Of course, no worries, just thought it was worth asking, you know, to prove I've actually met you."

"I can't be seen in a photo with you," I replied in a blind panic. I couldn't have him hold a photo of me — what if he recognized who I was on closer inspection?

"No, fair enough, fair enough."

I smiled, I hoped gracefully, and concentrated on writing. My acting training calmed me and I focused on being Katrina more than I'd had to in years.

Ryan moved closer. His mellow musk surrounded me, seductive like an Arabian night with hints of cinnamon and smoke. I gulped and concentrated on signing my name.

"There you go," I gasped, pressing the card back into his hand. Still big, with long, lithe fingers, but the pads were rougher, from work and years lived. His touch still shook me to the core.

"Thanks so much." Ryan grinned. "Really, this is awesome. I better let you get on with your shopping but here's one of my cards, you might have need of my services, you never know." He was blushing, inspecting his toes bashfully. It was adorable. Ryan Taylor was nervous in my presence.

"Yes, okay then, I'll take one." He passed me the card with a brief smile. "Thanks, Ryan. Have a nice day." I deepened the American edge to Katrina's accent. I had to be careful not to reveal any of my Yorkshire accent to him.

"Thanks and bye." He waved stiffly.

I waved back. He strode down the aisle, looking back over his shoulder and shaking his head. When he disappeared around the corner I dragged in a long breath and glanced down at the bin bags in my hand. I couldn't concentrate. I could only see his face, feel the swathe of his fingers over mine. I was shaking with nerves, upset and held in lust.

Chapter Six

Ryan Taylor

"Hey, Eve, you'll never guess who I saw in the shop this morning!" I yelled as I pulled off my muddy boots in the hall.

There was no answer.

"Eve? Oh, come on, you're not still mad with me, are you?" When there was still no answer I cursed under my breath. "Eve, where are you?"

She wasn't in the front room or the kitchen, both of which looked like a marauding band of teenagers had recently blown through. I ran up the stairs and finally found her slumped over the toilet bowl.

"Eve, are you all right?"

She moaned, so I knew she wasn't dead.

"Are you feeling poorly?"

Another moan and a half-hearted wave of a hand.

"Shall I call the doctor?"

"No," she snapped, then frowned.

I imagined her head was pounding.

"No, it's just food poisoning or something. I'll be right as rain tomorrow."

"If you're sure." I sighed. I picked her up and took her to the bedroom, then I found a big bowl in the kitchen and placed it beside the bed. She was fast asleep and she stank of alcohol.

I knew she had a drinking problem, but I hadn't realized just how much of a problem until I started tidying up the mess downstairs. There were bottles everywhere. I knew we'd not been particularly tidy of late. I was out most days on my odd jobs and each day I came in I noted that things were piling up. Pots in the sink, newspapers on the coffee table and clothes in the laundry basket.

It was nine o'clock before I finished sorting out the house. After such a long work day I was completely knackered. I couldn't afford to order a takeaway—the money I'd earned in Wakefield would finish off the most urgent bill payments. I looked through the kitchen and, as there was hardly anything there, I sat down to a bowl of baked beans followed by tinned rice pudding straight from the tin.

I didn't have any work planned for the next day, so I didn't know where the money to buy some more food would come from. I slept on the sofa that night, not wanting to disturb Eve, but I didn't do much sleeping at all. Mostly I was worrying and wallowing. How was I going to pay the bills and fill the cupboards on my meager and unpredictable salary?

It seemed I'd slept barely a few moments before my phone ringing woke me up. I reached out to the table, winced as my neck protested at being pillowed by the settee arm all night.

"No job too big or small, what can I do for you today?"

"Hi, I'm renovating Copse Cottage and I'm finding it hard-going. Would you be able to come over and give me a quote for shifting the rubbish that's accumulated here?"

I held back a yawn as I listened to the answer—it was a woman's voice, vaguely familiar. "Sure I can. I'll be free in about an hour, is that convenient for you?" I scrambled upright with a grin on my face.

"Yeah, that'd be great, thanks." She sounded relieved.

"Cool. Can I take your name?"

"Yes, it's Katrina," I looked around for a pen, but I didn't find one, so I just repeated her name and hoped I would remember it.

"Okay, Katrina, I'll be there soon. Oh, and just so you know, I don't charge just for giving a quote."

"Okay, great. See you in an hour," she answered then put down the phone.

Katrina. Well, how weird was that, having bumped into Katrina Quinn the morning before? Maybe it was the same Katrina? Being only partially awake I'd not really taken in the accent of the person on the phone. In a wondering daze I dressed, jumped in the van and headed to Copse Cottage, which was Mary's old place. Someone must have bought it—and with that, another possible link back to Janie was gone.

Janie selling the house just seemed so unbelievable, though. She'd always been so sentimental. *How could she just sell up the connection she had to her childhood?* Maybe it was down to me and how badly I'd treated her. Maybe she wanted to forget it all. Guilt boiled up in my stomach, the lead weight of it lifting to my gullet then slamming back down to rest deep inside. The load I always carried—that I couldn't be rid of.

My life was full of regrets, but being such a bastard to Janie topped the list.

The morning was cold—it took a while for the engine to warm up. Mary's old place was on the other side of the village, easily walkable, but a handy man needs his van and tools at all times. Plus it was cold and I didn't want to trek across the village. I parked up on the road directly outside the old place. It was weird walking up to Copse Cottage knowing Mary wasn't going to be there. The garden was unkempt and the front of house showed that it had been unloved for a while. I knocked on the door and waited.

"Oh, so it is you? It was worth my while giving you my card then."

She nodded.

"I thought you were here on a holiday or something."

"No." She shook her head. "I'm taking up a new hobby, house renovation. I wanted to get out of the US for a bit so I found this one on the Internet and bought it."

"Like you do." I grinned.

She stepped back, and I walked into the corridor. It was just like it'd always been. Except there was no Mary.

"I was going to do it all myself but I discovered that wasn't going to be possible." She pushed opened the living room door.

"Holy crap!" I gasped. The room was packed with random stuff floor to ceiling, with barely space to move. "Geez, I knew Mary had an inclination to hoard but this is crazy."

"Did you know the last owner?" Katrina asked, with strained politeness.

"Yeah, I did. I spent a lot of time here as a kid — me and her granddaughter were mates."

"Oh, right. It didn't look like this back then?"

"No, not at all. Though I do remember poor Janie having to help her gran clear out once a year with a spring clean. Clearly that hasn't happened for a while, though. Is this the only room like this?"

"See for yourself," she said.

If anything, the other rooms were worse.

"So what do you think? Can you help me clear it?"

"Sure, no problem." I nodded. "It'll take a few weeks, but I've not got anything else on at the moment."

"How much will I owe you?"

"Well, I charge by the hour depending on the work. But as this is a long job I can do it to you on a day rate. How about a hundred a day?"

I waited for her to shoot me down. That was a ridiculous amount of money for an odd job man.

"Sure, that's fine. I'll pay you on Fridays until you've finished, okay?"

It was a surprise that she'd accepted without haggling. At last there was light at the end of the tunnel. Maybe I'd be able to afford to buy food and pay the bills for a change.

"That'd be great, thanks."

"When can you start?" she asked.

"Well, now, I guess. No time like the present."

"That's fabulous. I'm going to work in the kitchen — you can start in the front room."

"Sure" — I nodded — "no problem."

Maybe I'd stared at her too long, maybe she was a bit stuck up, but I did feel a bit put out being completely segregated from her. But then I'd never worked for anyone who even vaguely classed as a celebrity before. Maybe this was the way they operated.

* * * *

She was one hot woman, though. Even at the end of a day of hard labor, her sleek black hair fuzzed up and her black T-shirt marked with dust, she was stunningly beautiful. She was definitely a bit kooky, though. I had to preserve anything I found that seemed to be personal to Mary. She said she wanted to make sure it got back to the family. She was passionate about it. Most people would have just chucked everything away—I found it endearing that she wanted to preserve Mary's history. Even if she was colder than an iceberg when dealing with me.

I got back home about six o'clock.

"And where have you been?" she asked as soon as I came in through the door.

"Oh, I got a new job clearing Copse Cottage. My God, Mary was a hoarder. That place is stuffed full of junk. It'll take weeks to clear. But I'm getting a hundred quid a day, so that's not bad, huh? It should give us a decent wodge for Christmas."

"Why the fuck didn't you let me know?" she moaned.

"Oh, I'm sorry, love. You were feeling so poorly yesterday I didn't want to disturb you." Keeping my tone casual and lighthearted had worked well for me in the past, but my gentle words didn't seem to be softening her anger this time.

"You could have text me." Eve pouted.

"I should have done. Sorry, doll, it's been a busy day."

"Whatever." Eve shrugged. "I'm going out."

"Where?"

"Into Wakey with the girls from Bissons. It's their pre-Christmas do and they've invited me."

"But, love, we've got no money," I calmly pointed out.

"I have. Went to get my dole this morning," she gloated.

"Oh, great. Well, we need some food, there's nothing in. I'm going to be paid on Friday but until then I'm skint."

"Well, that's your problem. I'm going out. I need my money." She crossed her arms and glared at me.

"Charming." I growled. "I break my back trying to keep this place going and you can't even throw in a few quid for some bread and milk. You selfish cow!"

"What did you call me?" Eve pushed the center of my chest.

"Selfish cow," I repeated each word carefully.

"You're unbelievable, Ryan, you know that? You made us move here, you told me you'd always look after me. It was you who wanted to live in this draughty old, nasty house. Not me. Moving here made me lose my job and I've been depressed ever since. I'm staring at these same walls twenty-four/seven and the first time I get invited out into the world you want to deny me a bit of fun."

"No, Eve, no. I'm quite happy for you to fuck off with your mates, I won't have to listen to your incessant chattering. What I'm pissed off with is the fact you've been fucking drinking away all the money I'm bringing in. You're a lush, Eve." All the tension of the last weeks poured out of my mouth in accusations.

"Whatever." She shrugged. "I'm going out. I can't talk to you when you're like this."

"What? When I actually challenge you about your crap behavior? When I refuse just to give you my money? Well, fuck off out and if you don't come back I won't give a shit."

The next thing I heard was the slam of the front door and the clack of the letterbox as it swung with the force of impact. My tea that night consisted of three freezer-burnt fish fingers and one wrinkled old potato with green shoots nuked in the microwave.

I was starving when I woke up but there was nothing in at all. Something green and furry resided in the back of the fridge but it could have been a living organism, a fridge monster or something worse—I didn't want to try to eat it.

I did what all desperate souls do when they're completely skint—I looked down the back of the sofa then the sides and underneath the sofa itself. I was in luck—just behind one caster was a pound coin. Salvation. Eve hadn't returned from her night out before I left for work—it worried me a little but I was still pissed off with her so I didn't give it too much thought.

"Morning, Dilly," I called as I walked into the village store.

"Hello, Ryan, how're you?"

"Not bad, love, not bad."

"You off to a job?"

"Yeah." I nodded, looking around for cheap and filling inspiration. "At the old Copse Cottage."

"Oh, has Janet come back then?"

"No, it's that Katrina Quinn, from the films. You know she's originally from Yorkshire. She's renovating it as a holiday home."

"Well I never," Dilly exclaimed. She'd worked in the village shop as long as I'd lived in Thornleydale. She always wore a smile and quite often had slipped an extra sweet into my ten pence mix when I'd been a little boy. Everyone loved Dilly.

"I know, right? It's good for me, a few weeks work just before Christmas."

"Oh, yeah. It'll come in handy, especially with your Eve out of work. I've not seen her for a few days, is she all right?" Dilly sounded genuinely concerned.

"Yeah, she was out with the girls from the factory last night."

"Oh, right, I won't see her for a while then. Now, Ryan, I might be speaking out of turn…"

I picked up two Mars bars and plonked them on the counter.

"What is it, Dill?"

"Well, your Eve. She's been buying a lot of alcohol in here lately, you know, and, well, it's worrying me." She wrung her hands together and looked at the counter in front of her.

I nodded. Dilly picked up the bars and scanned them.

"Yeah, she's having a tough time of it. I'm working on it with her. It needs to stop."

"Good, good. I hope you don't think I'm a nosey old bat. That's a quid, by the way."

I passed Dilly the pound and, as she took it, I clasped her hand with mine.

"Dilly, you're the loveliest lady I know. Thanks for caring." I smiled. She really was. I was certain she didn't have a nasty bone in her body.

Her wrinkled cheeks pinked, and when I let her hand go she fluffed her gray perm with it.

"Oh, well, I've known you since you were a tyke, I don't want any harm to come to you."

"You're a star, Dill." I blew her a kiss then walked out into the late November drizzle.

It came to something when someone who made money from Eve's addiction found it essential to tell me about her problem. It was an issue I wouldn't be able to avoid much longer. I'd have to confront Eve about it properly, not just yell it at her in a bout of fury.

"Morning, boss," I chirpily greeted Katrina after demolishing both my Mars bars on the drive over to the copse. With all that crap in the house I knew I'd need to make some trips to the dump throughout the day.

"Hiya," she replied, less than chirpily.

"Look, I've got a delicate question to ask you. Basically, I could do with you paying me today. It's nothing personal, it's just you're new in town and I want to make sure I get paid. I mean, I'm sure you'll pay me—"

"It's okay, I understand," she cut in before I babbled any further. "I'll have to go out and get some cash—I don't suppose you'll take a card payment?"

"I'm afraid I'm not equipped for that particular transaction—you could run your card down my butt crack but I don't think it'd work." I winked wickedly. *That sounded smoother in my head.* I shouldn't have been flirting with my boss but I couldn't help myself.

"Right, well, cash then. I'll go out now for it." Katrina looked down to her toes and avoided eye contact. I knew I shouldn't have flirted with her.

"If you're sure—?"

"Yep, no problem. If you get on with the living room, I'll be back in an hour or so."

"Okay, boss." I disappeared into the front room and slapped my forehead. How dumb was I? At least she was going to go and get the money for me. I wouldn't have to eat the green mold-encrusted thing at the back of my fridge for tea. *Phew.*

I got down to work. It was just the kind of hard labor I hated—there was a lot of bending and stretching and carrying and sorting. *Give me firewood to chop any day than all this paper to shift.* It was just so monotonous. My mind started to wander as it wasn't particularly engaged in what it was doing. It was still weird to be in the cottage without Mary there. In fact, the few times I'd done jobs for her, it had been weird being in the house without Janie.

* * * *

Copse Cottage, 2004

"You know, Ryan, I should hold it against you, you know?" she stated one summer as she sat on the porch at the back of the house watching me weeding.

"Hold what against me, Mary?" I asked, mind on the task.

"You dumping our Janet."

"We were never going out, Gran," I exclaimed, the words trickling out over one another quickly.

"No, I know that. But you were the best of buddies and you mucked that up, lad. Broke her heart, you know."

"I know," I sighed, stabbing the fork into the ground with vigor. "I regret it, I really do."

"And so you should. You'd be miles away from here now if you'd stuck with my Janet instead of getting your head turned by that slut."

"Gran!" I exclaimed, not sure if I was more insulted on Eve's behalf or shocked at Mary using such language.

"Oh, well, it's true, Ryan. Don't come the innocent with me. That one's a wrong 'un. You messed up."

I didn't speak for a bit. Just attacked the dandelions in the flower bed. The summer sun burned down on the back of my neck and the sound of birds twittered gently through the thick atmosphere between Mary and me.

"I know, Mary. I was a stupid little boy. I hurt Janie and I regret that, big time. But Eve's stuck by me, moved out here to be with me after Dad died, gave up a life she'd dreamed of to be with me. She might have started out a wrong 'un but she's my girl now, and I love her. All right?"

"All right, son."" Mary nodded. "I'll never like her, but that's just me. I always thought you and our Janet would end up together. Even as kids you were like an old married couple."

"That's true," I chuckled, breaking the atmosphere a bit. "We definitely were."

I never felt totally comfortable at Mary's, I just felt like I wasn't whole. I was always with Janie there when we were kids — being there alone was just weird. Mary never brought up the subject again. That was her way — she made her feelings on the matter known then it was forgotten. But I felt guilty every time I walked up that pathway without Janet.

* * * *

Clearing out her gran's place without her was even more disconcerting. I wished I knew where she was and what she was doing. It just didn't seem like her not to be around for the funeral and to sell the house so quickly.

I heard the door creak open and slam shut. I didn't go out to Katrina and demand my money — that would have been crass. I continued tidying and thinking.

I had to accept that I didn't know Janie anymore. She would have been a completely different woman, like I was a completely different man. I lifted up another magazine about pristinely clean and fashionable houses — *I wonder if Mary got how ironic that was?* — and found an old photo album.

"Katrina," I yelled. "You need to come and see this!"

Chapter Seven

Katrina Quinn

I'd been back in the United Kingdom for less than a day and I'd already bumped into the one guy I was dying to avoid. Hopefully it was an isolated incident. I didn't want to deal with that tumult of emotion again anytime soon.

Back at Gran's I unpacked my shopping, and the first challenge was digging out then cleaning out the fridge freezer. Once I'd managed that, I had somewhere to keep my milk and I could make myself a decent cup of tea. Matt teased me that I just drank it to prove I was still a Brit, as my accent was being eaten away.

I wondered how Matt would be getting on without me. Admirably, I was sure. I sent him a quick text then looked up local skip providers on my phone. Not many would deliver to Thornleydale, but eventually I found a frank-speaking Yorkshire man who was willing to drop one off for me. I finished my last sip of tea.

"Well, Katrina, you better get on with it if you ever want to finish tidying this place up."

I sighed, dropping my tea cup into the sink. The sky was bright, the sun dazzling. I watched a squirrel scamper through the grass. That was something else I'd have to do. Maybe I could get a landscape gardener in to tackle the outside space. The garden was huge and led down to the copse at the back. So many of those leaves seemed to gravitate to Gran's back lawn. Well, my back lawn. I had to stop thinking of it as Gran's. It wasn't hers anymore. As she'd always said, 'You can't take it with you.'

I washed up my tea cup then continued to clean the sink and drainage area, before working down to the cupboards below. On my hands and knees under the kitchen sink pulling out old tins of Brasso and WD-40 I was overtaken by a memory from my time at university.

* * * *

Uni halls, 1999

I shared a flat with three other girls. We got on pretty damn well most of the time but there was one problem. No one seemed capable of cleaning up their own mess. I'd yell and shout and they'd agree to clean up. Occasionally they might even make a half-hearted start but every Sunday I ended up being the one on my hands and knees cleaning the kitchen floor. We didn't have a mop and bucket, and somehow we never got enough money together to buy one.

One Sunday morning, Claire, Mel and Julie were all in bed with Saturday-night-induced hangovers. I didn't go out a lot even in uni. With my issues from years of bullying and being the poorest of the house, I didn't have the money or the desire to go out.

"You don't need money," Claire would exclaim. "Just bat your lashes and rub your curves against a guy. He'll keep you in drinks all night." She had enough self-confidence to cover all four of us and the looks to match.

I wasn't so confident or so blasé about promising a man something I wasn't willing to give.

The kitchen looked as though we'd provided a three-course meal for half of Oxford and forgotten to wash up. I knew I should take a stand and just leave it, but I simply couldn't. I grumbled to myself the whole time, clattering and banging in the hopes of disturbing the alcohol-fueled sleep of the other girls. No one stirred, and I just got more and more irate. Just as I was putting away the dishes there was a knock at the door.

I was fairly certain it wouldn't be for me as the friends I had were the kind to arrange things well in advance. I grumbled to myself all the way to the door, pasted on a smile and opened it.

"Oh, hi, Janet."

"Hey, Sean, what's up?" I exclaimed. Sean was in my English class, we sat together and chatted a bit, but I didn't even know that he knew where I lived. I had no clue why he was there.

"Just wondered if we could hang out for a bit."

"Well, I'm in the middle of cleaning our shit tip of a kitchen, but you can come in if you like?"

"Yeah, sure, no worries." He shrugged.

I stepped back and he walked in, his long legs cased in light blue jeans cupping his arse tightly beneath his denim jacket. In the nineties, double denim wasn't so much of a sin. He looked good in it, too.

"How're you?" I asked following him into the kitchen.

"Not bad, you?"

"Pissed off at the other girls, but otherwise fine. How was your weekend?"

We continued to chit-chat as I set the kettle to boiling. My blood pressure started to even out, and I actually relaxed over a cuppa.

"I hope you don't mind, but I need to finish this floor, or I'll never be able to relax."

"I'll help if you like—two of us will get it done quicker. "

"That would be amazing, but, well, we don't have a mop, it's a hand job." I realized what I'd said and stuttered over myself, "I mean we have to get down on all fours and, you know, clean."

"Sure"—he smirked—"I understand."

My cheeks felt like hot coals and I tried unsuccessfully to get my mind onto the job in hand and away from the images to go with the words I'd just used.

"You know, as much as I'm enjoying the domestic chores, I didn't come here just to clean your kitchen floor."

I sprayed the floor and rubbed it with the kitchen roll. The lemon freshness released by my scrubbing tickled my noise.

"Really? I'd never have guessed. What else could you have possibly wanted?" I winked cheekily then continued to scrub. We were already halfway down the tiny room—Sean was by the cooker, I was near the wall.

"Well, that's the thing. I'm not sure how to put it."

"Oh dear, that sounds bad." I cringed.

"No, no, not bad." He sat back on his heels and sighed. "Okay, so if I say it quickly and I don't think about it, maybe it'll be all right. I came here to ask you to go out with me."

"Oh." I stopped wiping. My jaw dropped. "Me?"

"Yes, you," he confirmed.

"Oh." My brain had stopped working. I sat back on my heels too and tried to get my tongue around the word 'yes' that I really, really wanted to say but it seemed as though my tongue had swollen to the size of my mouth.

"Hmm, maybe I shouldn't have said anything..." Sean coughed.

"I'm trying to say something," I gasped. "But all cogent thought seems to have left me. Please don't go, I'd love to go on a date."

"You would?" He smiled and his face gleamed with joy.

My heart did a little happy dance from the sight of it.

"Yes," I replied. "I would."

"Excellent." He beamed and wrapped his arms around me in an embrace. I was glad to note that he'd dropped the wet rag first. I hugged him back, taking note of his broad shoulders and the hints of cinnamon spice that came through in his scent.

I moved back—I was going to say something about having to finish the kitchen floor before anything else—when he kissed me. It was just that unexpectedly abrupt but it was glorious. His plump and giving lips undulated against my own and after the initial spurt of uncertainty I kissed back with equal passion. I was overtaken by a flood of desire. I didn't want to stop kissing him—I didn't want to stop touching him. It felt so very good.

He cupped my waist as we kissed. His fingers crept up under the material onto my skin, the prickling sensation of his fingers on my flesh extended through my whole frame, tickling in such a pleasant way that I moaned into his mouth. He took that as encouragement and moved his hands higher.

I tried to readjust myself to do the same to him but when I moved forward I must have moved into the washed zone of the floor because in the next moment I was falling. Luckily, Sean was quick-witted and, by some feat of elasticity, I landed on top of him.

"Oh, I'm sorry—"

Sean just pulled my lips back down to his so I assumed I hadn't broken him with my clumsiness and just continued to kiss him. I was astride him and could feel the definite imprint of his erection on the inside of my thigh. It was a curious feeling, something completely new to me, and I wasn't sure what to do. I wanted to feel more. I wasn't a prude, and if sex was on the cards I was eager for it to happen, but I was stuck for inspiration— *What should I do next? Could I make a move or would that put Sean off? Would he think I'm a slut?* I had all these questions and more buzzing in my brain and getting in the way of the delicious signals of arousal that were coursing through my veins.

I don't know if Sean realized my quandary or if he was just a wicked young man, but as I fought myself over what to do next he took control and pushed me to the side. I screeched in a very unladylike way when my T-shirt hit the wet floor and started soaking up the lemon-scented water.

Sean just laughed and held me down. I think he liked the way I wiggled against him.

"You're so hot," he gasped, kneeling beside me, his body towering over me.

"And wet now!" I grumped.

"Oh, really?" He waggled his eyebrows.

I was confused then giggled when I realized what I'd said.

"Let me check," he whispered.

He boldly ran his hand down over my stomach and into the waistband of my jeans. I held my breath. This was it. This was something properly sexual and it was happening on the damp kitchen floor of my shared apartment. That bit didn't seem to register as I lost all focus. His fingers brushed through my pubic hair and the longest slipped into my slit and over my clit. My back arched as if controlled by that button and I pressed my breasts against his chest.

"You weren't lying," he breathed the words heavily, parted my slick lips and pressed a finger into me.

I gasped, felt my internal muscles clamp, and sought out his lips with mine. I needed to be completely immersed in him, in that moment. The moment someone first touched me in such an intimate way.

Sean kissed me with a passion that was dizzying — or maybe that was all the fumes from the kitchen cleaner? — and I didn't want him to stop. I'd masturbated, of course, had been doing so regularly for years, but his touch was different. He was testing me, finding out what delighted me, getting to know me in such an intimate way. I wanted to do something for him. But my hands were caught up, and all I could do was run them under his top and feel his tight chest. I rested a palm over his heart and felt just how fast it was beating. As fast as mine? Maybe not quite because I was spiraling into ecstasy. A familiar tightness coiled in the pit of my stomach and between his fingers and my clit. I knew it would take only a little bit more pressure to make me come.

I heard a door creak open and so did Sean because his hand whipped out from my pants and onto the floor behind me.

"God, if I knew this was the way *you* cleaned the kitchen *I'd* have agreed to do it for you," Claire quipped.

Sean sat up and smiled timidly. I followed, my cheeks emblazoned with leftover lust, and awkwardness heightened the heat that focused there.

It was quite possibly the most embarrassing moment in my university career, but I wouldn't have changed it for the world. It set the tone for the rest of my years there. Sean set free Katrina, even when I was still technically Janet.

* * * *

It was a pleasant side effect that every time I used a lemon-scented cleaner I'd remember that particular moment. My sink was clean and I could get on to removing some of the rubbish. How many magazines had my gran bought? I was pushing them into black bags and the dates were pretty recent but I was certain that the farther down the piles I went the older they'd be. It was boring and monotonous and even nineties pop on my mobile didn't help with my energy levels. The longer I was in the building, the more I was aware that Gran wasn't there. Memories cropped up all over the place—Gran had spent a lot of time in the kitchen. She'd baked the most delicious of things. I loved her custard tart the best, and if I went to stay there would always be one cooling on the kitchen table.

Well, as long as Ryan hadn't gotten there first. He had a habit of convincing Gran to give said pies to him. He used to come up with some wacky claims, and I think Gran gave in simply for the imagination in them.

There was the time his aunt had fallen down a well and desperately needed sustenance. Then there was the picky pet cat who'd only eat homemade custard tart. And my favorite was the disease he'd made up that needed an hourly intake of egg custard to combat. Gran always used to make another, just for me, but it rankled that my best mate kept nicking my treats.

I could barely see the kitchen table when I finished for the night. I'd worked non-stop all day and I just couldn't see the difference. Yes, I had ten bags filled and ready to go in the skip, and I could see the sink that sparkled quite prettily, but otherwise it looked just like it had.

It was as I thought of the skip that I realized I'd not heard it arrive. I went to look out on the drive but it was empty. It was late but I vowed to ring the contractor in the morning and give him a piece of my mind.

* * * *

"But you told me the skip would arrive by eleven a.m. yesterday," I gasped in exasperation.

"Aye, but there's been some bad weather and I've not been able to get one over there."

"It was bright and sunny all day yesterday," I snapped.

"Ah, well, the weather's very dangerous here on't moors. Of course, American ladies like yourself won't have a clue about that, but I won't hold it against you."

"I'm very aware of the special weather on't moors," I growled in my broadest accent. "I'm Yorkshire born and bred."

"I'll have it sent over today," he grumbled.

"Good." I slammed down the phone.

I went back to the kitchen and tripped over a filled bag. The curse words that issued from my mouth would have made a hardened criminal blush, and I continued to curse as I carried the bags out to the drive. Finally, when I'd shifted the ten bags I'd filled the day before I started on clearing some more space, it became obvious after just a few hours that if I was ever going to finish renovating the house I was going to need some help. Especially since there was neither sight nor sound of my skip.

I didn't want to admit defeat but I wasn't getting very far very fast. I'd barely cleared a quarter of the kitchen and I had a whole house to clear, clean and redecorate. But who could I get to help? I remembered the card Ryan had given me at the supermarket and went to the table in the hall where I'd left it.

NO JOB TOO BIG OR TOO SMALL,
I'M THE MAN TO FIX IT ALL.
Large van for removals, gardening tools and knowledge.
Whatever you need, give me a call.

At the bottom it had his number, and gas and electric safety details.

Could I ring him and hire him? My first instincts were negative. He might discover who I was, or I might do something stupid and let him know. I looked up other workmen, but none of them lived very close and those I rang were all busy and wouldn't be able to fit me in till after Christmas.

As my options dwindled I went back to thinking of Ryan. He could work in a separate part of the house to me. We'd barely talk and as long as I kept a good grip on my Katrina character it would be okay. In the end I rang him, heart thumping.

* * * *

It wasn't pleasant seeing Ryan on that doorstep. I was assaulted by memories and my heart broke anew. I had answered that door to him so many times when we'd been mates, best mates. But we were nothing more than strangers again and I couldn't let it become anything more. I knew I needed his help to get the house emptied but I was determined to keep as much distance between us as possible.

Chapter Eight

Ryan Taylor

I flicked through the album as I waited for Katrina. Most of them were of Janie, when she was a tiny baby right through to her teens. She was always a pretty, smiley girl. Of course I hadn't thought that at the time. All girls were stinky until I hit puberty.

"What is it?" Even Katrina's voice at the door couldn't distract me from flipping through the photos of familiar faces.

"Seems to be a photo album," I answered, distractedly.

"Oh, I'll definitely keep that." She walked closer.

I noticed her perfume again, sweet and tempting.

"For the relatives, of course." Katrina continued, "I'm sure someone will want it."

"Yeah, I guess it needs to go to her granddaughter, Janet. That's Mary's only living relative, I believe."

I would have loved to flick through the album with her. See her face light up, listen to her reminisce. The permanent guilt lump in my stomach heaved once more. I fought down the thoughts. What was done was done—I couldn't go back and change time, however much I wanted to.

"I'll ask the solicitor what to do with it." Katrina's reply was very dispassionate. Her reaction made me not want to give her the photos. It didn't seem right to give them to someone who didn't care for them.

I kept flicking through the pictures—there were a few with Mary in them, too, and it was sad to see her jolly smiling face knowing I'd never see her again. I became aware of Katrina's hand just above the top lip of the book.

"Oh, sorry." I shook my head. "There's lots of memories in these photos, and I kinda got lost in them."

I closed it gently and passed it to her.

"Is that it for now?" she asked.

"Yeah," I sighed and shook myself. "Right, back to the grindstone."

"Okay, I'll get back to it myself. Oh, but I wanted to check with you about a skip. I rang some guy and he was supposed to bring me one—"

"Fred Campion, no doubt. He's a right bugger. But don't worry. I'll get a skip for you. He just needs a kick up the arse to get him moving."

"Thanks." She nodded.

"No worries." I grinned but Katrina turned and left the room without even a smile.

I wished I could tell Katrina all about Janet and Mary, to give her some insight into them, but she didn't seem at all interested. Which was weird as she had insisted on keeping everything of personal value to pass back to the family. Strange woman.

I rang Fred and got him to bring the skip round. It was a usual trick of his—he'd keep a customer waiting until they threw extra money his way. He'd not get away with that behavior on my watch.

Just as I got back to shoveling crap into bags my phone rang. I wondered if it was Frank again but answered with my usual business patter just in case.

"No job too— Oh, hi, darling."

I didn't get through my spiel as I heard Eve's voice.

"Where are you?"

"I'm out on a job, should last a few weeks at least."

"Where are you?" she repeated with more grit in her tone.

"I'm at Copse Cottage, clearing it out. I told you, remember?"

"Are you with that American slut, then?"

"Eve!" I gasped, trying to keep my voice low. I didn't want Katrina overhearing. "I'm working for Katrina Quinn, I told you this already."

"And I told you I don't like you working for women and definitely not for that one. I want you to come home right now."

"I can't, you know we need the money."

"And you're in that place, you know I hate you going there, too. It stinks of the Janet woman, and what if she ever just turned up while you were there?"

"Come on, Janie hasn't been here in years. I don't know where she is but she didn't even make it to her gran's funeral. She's even sold the bloody place, so don't be ridiculous."

"But you're still there with a fucking film star, Ryan. I don't like it. I don't want you to work for her. I need you home here with me," Eve whined. I kicked at a pile of junk in frustration.

"Oh, Eve, shut up. You're such a jealous bitch."

"Don't you be so damn rude! I don't know why I try. You never listen to me anymore."

"Look." I lowered my tone, not wanting Katrina to overhear. "I'm sorry but I need this job. We need this job. We've got bills to pay."

I didn't want to be having it out with her on the phone with my boss within hearing distance.

"You're just saying that so you can get in that loose American tart's knickers."

I couldn't see her but I knew she'd have an arm across her chest and her bottom lip would be drooping down. Eve really knew how to sulk.

"No, I'm not just saying that to spend more time with Katrina Quinn. Look, I have to work — she could come to check on me at any moment. We'll talk later."

I clicked the phone down and hoped she wouldn't ring again. How could she not understand that I couldn't turn away work? I'd have to talk to her when I got home, there were clearly issues we had to address, but it wouldn't do me any good to overthink it beforehand.

Tucked in a flimsy cardboard box filled with old batteries, pencil stubs and various pins and fastenings I found a photo.

"Katrina!" I yelled again.

"Yes?"

"Come and look at this, it'll give you a laugh." It certainly made me smile. I remembered exactly when it was taken, too, about six thirty on Christmas Day, 1985.

"What is it?" She burst into the room with great energy. She clearly wasn't impressed with me calling for her again.

"Come here." I beckoned her over. "Look at this." My voice was raised with amusement.

"Another photo, eh?" She seemed barely interested. "I'd better put it with the others in that album."

"Yeah, of course, but you've got to see it first, it's got me in it."

"Has it?" She was still seriously uninterested.

Maybe I was being a bit like an enthusiastic traveler giving hours of description to each of his holiday snaps to friends who really couldn't care less.

"Yeah, it's from when I was little," I pushed on, desperate to tell the tale.

Finally she shuffled closer until she was stood shoulder to shoulder with me looking down on the old, yellowed rectangle in my hand

The photo had captured two young kids—me and Janet—against the background of an old, spindly Christmas tree. Covered in tinsel and bright colored baubles—the tree, that was, not us. We were smiling at the camera. We were wearing matching jumpers.

"Now isn't that a bobby dazzler?" I chuckled.

"Yeah," she laughed, though it sounded a little forced. "Which one's you?"

"The one on the left!" I nudged her elbow. "You cheeky mare. I know my hair was long back then but I couldn't put it up in a side pony."

I remembered the moment the photo had been taken really vividly.

* * * *

Copse Cottage, 1985

It was Christmas—I went up to Gran's at teatime to get my present and eat the buffet at Mary's, as was my tradition. In my opinion it was by far and away the best bit of the festivities. It was a typical British Christmas Day. It was raining. I ran all the way to

Mary's in my duffle coat, the hood pulled over my head. I panted as I rang the doorbell.

"Merry Christmas!" Janie exclaimed as she opened the door.

"Merry Christmas, Janie. What are you wearing?"

"Cool, isn't it? It's my Christmas present." Janie did a twirl in her thick-knitted, dark yellow-colored top.

"It's a super jumper. Love the color. Is tea ready yet?"

"Yes." She giggled. "But Gran says you've got to open your prezzie first."

Janie led me into the living room where I greeted Mary, and Janie's mum and dad, Keith and Barbara, then I picked up the present left under the tree.

"Oh, wow," I laughed. Gran had knitted me a mustard yellow Arran jumper too.

"Put it on, son, and pose for a photo. Our Keith gave me a camera for Christmas and I want to use up the film."

I put on the jumper and posed by the tree next to Janie in her matching one. We beamed at the camera, pure amusement in our eyes, because Gran couldn't work out which button to press for the longest of times.

* * * *

I'd been quiet for a long while and Katrina was shuffling from foot to foot.

"That Arran jumper was toasty warm." I laughed. "And we thought we were so cool in them."

"Cool? In mustard yellow?" She shook her head in amusement.

"It was the eighties. It was a pretty cool color for that time, I seem to remember!"

"If you say so," she tittered.

It lightened her face considerably, and I actually felt as though we had a bit of camaraderie going. Then I met her gaze and suddenly it all dissipated.

"I guess I'd better get back—"

"That's Mary's granddaughter, Janet," I continued, hoping to keep her with me a little longer. "We were best mates back then. That's why Mary knitted us those matching jumpers."

"Are you sure she just didn't have a lot of ugly wool to get rid of?"

She was making fun of me—I didn't care at all, I was enjoying the interaction.

"No, she was a lovely lady was Mary. Really thoughtful, and I loved that jumper. Janet loved hers, too. We wore 'em all the time. People started calling us the twins. God, that was a long time ago."

"Yeah, obviously." She yawned, pressing a delicate hand to her mouth.

"Anyway, I suppose we'd better get on. Here's the picture and I think there's a few more in this box."

I scrabbled through and passed the other dog-eared photos to her. I wondered if they were of Mary's family because they were so old and I didn't recognize anyone in them.

"Thanks, I'll put them with the others."

"Yeah, 'course. Actually, could I have the mustard jumpers one back for a bit? I'd like to get a copy for myself. I'll bring it right back once I've scanned it, I promise."

I didn't have any photos of Janie and me, and I wanted to keep hold of that memory to revisit it at a later time.

"Ohhh, Ryan, I'm not sure—"

"I know it's your property, Katrina, but it's a fond memory. I've not got much to remind me of them days anymore."

"Okay," she relented, "but bring back the original tomorrow."

"Sure, tomorrow. No problem. Thanks, boss, and while you're in here, I'm pretty much finished. Which room should I move to next?"

"The dining room, I guess. I just found the door from the kitchen into it, too."

"Awesome. Well, I'll join you in the kitchen in a minute. Do you think I might get a brew on my way through?" I winked cheekily.

"Hmm, I suppose there's a possibility of a cup of tea for you, you've been working pretty hard after all." She smiled.

What a smile. I'd do anything to see more of it.

"Great. A brew and a pretty lady, two of my favorite things."

"Charmer." She waved her hand dismissively and turned to leave. Well, clearly my flirting was a bit rusty. I'd have to try harder.

A heavy rap at the door made Katrina jump. I looked out of the bay window and saw the one person in all the world I wanted to avoid.

"I'll get it," I yelled, sprinting across to the door then down the corridor.

"Fine." Katrina followed me out but walked toward the kitchen. "Let me know it it's for me."

"What are you doing here?" Eve screeched before I even got the door wide open.

I tried to placate her, knowing full well that Katrina was just down the other end of the cottage One door between her and the very loud Eve.

"I'm working, love," I replied.

"Yeah, that's what you tell me," she spat—literally spat.

I wiped my cheek and tried hard not to let my smile slip. She was still wearing her night things and slippers. She'd walked across the village dressed like that. *Dear God, we'll be a laughing stock.*

"I'm clearing out the house, it's full of stuff." I kept it light and to the point, knowing that anything could set her off.

"You're here with her, aren't you? That slutty, home-wrecker bitch." Her face screwed up with the effort of putting the sentence together.

I had never fancied her less.

"Eve, please," I gasped, "she's only in the kitchen." I realized too late that that hadn't been the best thing for me to say.

"Oh, is she? Well, I'd like to talk to her. Taking my boyfriend from me!" Eve stumbled forward, as if to push past me.

"Eve, you're not making sense, darling. Come on. Let me take you home—" I reached out to take her arm but she shook her head viciously.

"No, no, I want to talk to Katrina. Find out why she loves other women's men so much. She's got some cheek coming here."

"Eve, please."

She tried to push past me but she didn't have the strength. I just stood my ground, hoping to God this conversation wasn't carrying down the corridor.

"I told you I didn't want you working for her. Her of all people."

"I know," I whispered, "but it's good money—she's paying me almost twice my usual rate."

She shrugged.

"Look, let me take you home, we'll talk."

"I miss you," she whined, suddenly the rigidity of anger leaving her, so she slumped into my chest.

"I miss you too. Hang on a minute." I turned my head and shouted down the hall, "Katrina, something's come up. I'll be back in a bit."

"Okay," she called.

I don't know if she added anything else because I'd already rushed out of there as quick as Eve would let me. Which wasn't terribly fast. She was dangling onto me like moss. I got her up to the van, piled her in one side then had to lean in to fasten her seatbelt.

"Ryan," she whispered, as I clicked the belt buckle home.

I looked toward her and she kissed me. Wet, sloppy and alcohol infused. I pulled back, smiled nervously, and shut the car door. I was boiling with anger but I knew that shouting at her would do no good. I needed to get her home, away from Katrina. How much of the altercation had she heard? I hoped not much.

"I got some good news," she hiccupped, as I jumped into the driver's side of the car.

"Oh yeah?" I buckled up and started the engine. Eager to move.

"Mm, I got a job. Back at factory."

"Really?" I looked at her, stunned.

"Mm." She nodded then held her stomach.

I hoped she wouldn't be sick.

"New guys in, needing more staff. I know the ropes so I'm rehired. Good, innit?" She put both thumbs up and smiled freakily then hiccupped.

"You'll have to sober up then, love," I replied, not convinced she was even telling the truth.

"I can do that, no problem." She held her stomach again and, even though the air was chill, I rolled down the car window.

"Don't you dare throw up in here, Eve," I snapped.

"I feel poorly, Ryan. I feel so poorly."

I was torn. Did I slam my foot down and race back, or did I take it slow and steady not to shake her up? I went with slow and steady—it was less likely to get me arrested and, although she heaved a few times, she waited till she'd gotten out of the van to throw up. All over our front path.

I herded her toward the house once she'd spewed. I struggled with her and my keys but finally got her in through the front door.

"What did I tell you about that woman, that bird? No, not bird—cat. She's a cat." Eve giggled.

I shook my head. How much had she drunk? She was ridiculously pissed. "I think you need to go to bed, love."

"No." She shook her head, and fell over. Luckily she was near the bannister and managed to grab hold on her way down. That prompted more raucous giggling and a struggle to get her upright.

"I'm mad at you," she slurred as I pushed her up the stairs, my hands braced on her arse.

"And I'm mad at you," I replied flatly.

"You're off with that slutty slut, slut, slut. All the time. In that old house. Without me. You don't like me anymore."

I didn't answer that, couldn't trust myself. She hiccupped.

"Look, we'll talk this over when you're sober, but I'm not giving up that job. It pays way too well to turn my back on."

"You don't like me," she repeated at a high whine.

I pushed her into bed. She waved her arms around and screamed like a tantrumming toddler. I left her to it and, just like a baby, a matter of minutes later she was asleep.

I hung around for a bit, in case she woke. The bowl I'd left next to the bed was still there, so if she needed to erupt again she could. She slept, I watched. Where was the fresh-faced young girl I'd fallen in love with? Granted, I was sure I wasn't the same. I'd aged. We had all aged. But Eve wasn't the same. Back when I'd met her she'd been a bitch—a complete bullying bitch—but she'd had a softer side that I'd seen more and more as the years passed by. That's what had kept me with her. At first it had been her beauty and the call of my teenage hormones, but later, when she gave up her dreams to stay with me and help me to pursue mine, it became something more.

I cast my mind back to an earlier time when I'd discovered something surprising about Eve.

"Don't tell anyone, or I'll kill yer," she'd growled.

"Okay, okay," I'd laughed, "I won't tell a soul."

"I can't sleep without him, you know? Don't tell anyone, though, right?"

"I won't tell," I had said, solemnly. "I promise. I slept with my teddy for years."

It had been the first time we'd slept together, literally slept together. The first night in the lodge and she'd revealed this dog-eared and tatty old bear, a brown and gray matted ball of thread. She had to have it close to sleep.

She still had the bear with her now. Sat on her bedside table. Herbert was his name. It was those little things that had deepened my love for her. The vulnerabilities and insecurities. But they were buried in her drinking problem now. There was no personality to her as long as she was drinking. She was just a yelling, smelly ball of angst.

How could I break through it? We'd been together for fifteen years, possibly more. Way back when I must have loved her. But as I cleaned up her puke off the drive I found it hard to pity her at all. She was a shell of the woman I used to love. After finishing that disgusting job I checked on her again and she was still sleeping. I would have to go back to Katrina and face the music.

It was amazing how many times Eve had gotten me into trouble with a boss, or even fired.

I had lost my paper round because I'd dumped them all at the end of the street and gone fishing in the stream with Eve when I was fifteen. When I'd been in college I had worked at a clothes store in Wakefield, and Eve had gotten me fired there, too. She'd called my boss a twat, and I had laughed. To be fair, I had already been on a warning for being repetitively late but, again, Eve had been involved with that. She had a way of distracting me from the time.

I think Mary was right. Eve was a bad'un. But how could I turn around and desert her after so many years together? If I threw Eve out, where would she go? She had no family left and no money of her own. I couldn't do that.

I'd have no one to come home to, no one to provide for. The thought scared me, but there were good possibilities that could come from it. I wouldn't have any ties. I'd be able to do what I wanted to do. A glimmer of excitement wriggled in the pit of my stomach — what could I do if I had no responsibilities?

* * * *

"Katrina?" I called her name as I walked back into the house. She'd not shut the door behind me. She was obviously getting used to village life.

"Ryan?" her muffled response came from the kitchen.

"Yeah." I opened the kitchen door and walked in to see her on her knees scrubbing at a cupboard front. My gaze lingered on her denim-encased arse. What I'd pay to see it naked.

"I'm so sorry about that," I said when I realized I'd been staring for a bit, possibly too long. "Eve can get a bit worked up sometimes."

"Oh, don't worry, it's fine. She's just worried about her husband working with a home wrecker like me." She didn't look round from her task.

The venom of her words stung. "Jeez, no." I shook my head and crouched down beside her. "Eve's not my wife. She's my girlfriend, and I don't think you're a home wrecker at all."

"Well, whatever. It's fine. I'm used to it now. I've been called a bitch in several languages you know."

She looked pointedly at me and I cringed.

"Oh God, you heard that?"

"Yep, I heard it."

"Bollocks," I cursed. "Pardon my French. Katrina, I'm really, really sorry."

"I'm sure you are," she retorted, "but what's done is done."

"Do you want me to leave?" I clutched my hands together and waited to be told to go fuck myself.

"No, I don't. I need you to get this house cleared but I can't be doing with your girlfriend coming and screaming the odds at me every damn day."

"I'll keep her away." I met her gaze. "I promise I will. She was a bit tipsy today, she's had a hard time of it lately and she's not normally like this. Well, she doesn't normally mither me on the job. And she won't now because she's got a job herself."

"Ryan, just keep her away, please. I've come over here to renovate this house in my home county to escape the press and the media and the accusations." Her sadness played across her face.

I felt all the worse for upsetting her. She had enough on her plate without my drunken girlfriend calling her names.

"Sure, sure. I understand. I'll keep her away." I reached out and squeezed the top of her arm before I had thought about it. The heat of her flesh against mine set my heart pounding.

"Thank you," she whispered, so low I barely heard the words.

"Hey, looks like you're pretty much done in here?" I commented to change the subject before she changed her mind and decided to fire me.

"Yeah, just cleaning down the sides and it's done."

"It's a lovely room—brings back a ton of memories for me. I ate really well in here. Really well. Mary's custard tart was the best. God, the lies I told to get hold of them."

I chuckled. She shifted uncomfortably.

"Sorry, I'm boring on again. I'll get back to work."

Chapter Nine

Katrina Quinn

Ryan sat next to me watching as I cleaned. A few times I was sure he was going to say something, but I tried my best not to look at him, and after a few moments he took the hint, stood and left. I was relieved to stop scrubbing. As the cupboard door probably was too. I'd buffed it to within an inch of its life.

I could understand Ryan's meander down memory lane because once the room was uncovered it looked just like it had when we'd been kids. Yes, there was a new color of paint on the wall—Gran had gotten fed up with the magnolia when I was back in college. She'd gotten it updated to a pale green and added some new accessories too, but by and large it was the same place I'd spent such a large part of my childhood in.

The large wooden table was pushed up against the wall, half collapsed. It came out to its full stretch at Christmas when the extended family would gather around its buffed mahogany surface. Even the old spiky brass clock sat on the wall in its usual place. Stuck at five thirty, the time Gran always served tea.

That confused all my American friends. The fact that tea to me was a meal in the evening *and* a drink.

On the windowsill sat the egg cup I'd made when I was five. Bobbly, rough and painted the most garish shade of yellow I had been able to get my kiddy hands on. It had sat in that same spot from the moment I'd brought it home for Gran. She'd cherished it, even though it was too small to actually contain an egg.

She would stand in front of the sink and stare out over the garden, a placid joy covering her still face. She was truly happy at Copse Cottage. It was where she was meant to be.

* * * *

Copse Cottage, 1991

One day, back when I'd just started secondary school, I burst in on her and one of her peaceful moments. She was stood looking out over her garden by the sink, a strainer of potatoes on the side beside her. I ran in wailing.

"What's up, my dear?" she crooned, patting me on the back. "Let's sit down, shall we?"

Gran sat me at the kitchen table and put a handkerchief in my hand. She didn't believe in tissues and always had her hanky with her and a spare one just in case.

She covered my hand with hers and let me calm down. She didn't keep asking me what was wrong — she waited for me to pull it together enough to speak.

"Right now, tell me the problem, Janet."

She squeezed my fingers. I gulped down the nervous lump in the back of my throat and I took the plunge.

"Ry doesn't want to be my friend anymore." I sniffed. My eyes stung from all the tears I'd shed.

"He doesn't?" Gran exclaimed. "Well, why ever not? You've been friends since you were babies."

"Because I'm not cool, Gran, and he wants to be cool."

"Well, he's got that wrong—really wrong. You're the coolest eleven-year-old I know."

Gran only knew two of us—me and Ryan—and I'm not sure she even knew what cool meant, but the words soothed me.

"Thanks, Gran. I miss him, though." I sniveled and more tears fell.

"You will, dear, you will. He's been a part of your life for a long time now. But you've got to let him go his own way. He's growing up and he's made a huge mistake but you've got to let him get on with it. You're far too brilliant to be left on the sidelines moping over him."

I nodded. She made sense but I don't think she understood how my heart was breaking. I'd lost my best friend, but he was still around being cruel and indifferent.

"Now, I've got some scones I baked earlier here, would you like one?"

I nodded again. Gran was the comfort food queen. We didn't talk anymore about my problem. We ate scones and chatted about this and that. She was good at putting stuff into perspective.

* * * *

Everywhere I looked, memories assaulted me — the hooks on the back of the door where we hung our coats in the winter, the light brown and orange vinyl on the floor, the fleur-de-lys pattern still present though rubbed and scuffed in areas of high traffic.

The large jars on the shelf... Empty of contents now but they used to be laden with biscuits and sweets and dried fruits. How I loved Gran's biscuit jar. Whenever I needed a pick-me-up, she'd reach in and pull out just the right kind of sweet, crumbly treat to make me feel better.

Or she'd make a cottage pie for me, heavy on the creamy, mashed potato. Gran was the very best at comfort food. Treacle pudding, heavy and sweet with a blanket of unctuous custard, or thick and cheesy lasagna with homemade garlic bread that dripped with herby butter.

Just thinking about those delicious treats made my heart cease, not literally — although I had consumed a whole lot of saturated fat and sugar back then — but with emotion.

I'd cleaned up my diet when I'd gotten into acting. It was important for me to leave the old world of Janet behind and that included the yummy snacks and comfort food treats. I avoided faddy diets, knowing they'd do more harm than good in the long run. But I gave up processed foods and took to eating vegetables and fruit as though they were going out of fashion. My water intake increased, I cut out fizzy pop and even managed to cut my caffeine intake down to just a couple of cups of tea a day.

The food change wasn't enough and I took up yoga. The gentle exercise toned my curves and tightened my posture, and the meditation did wonders for my state of mind. I became much happier within my own skin once I got control over what I ate and changed the wobbly bits I was never happy with into tighter, more purposeful curves. I knew I'd never be a size zero and I wouldn't have wanted to be but I'd learnt how to make the most out of what nature had given me.

There were ways to hold yourself when on camera to show your best features and hide your flaws. I knew them all. Although it seemed useless information for this situation. I wasn't interested in making myself look good. I was mourning and every moment I spent in Gran's old home added to the weight of grief in my soul.

I closed my eyes and just breathed. A technique I'd learnt back in university to control my tendency to panic. I had really made the change from Janet to Katrina back then.

I had been with Sean for several months. He was my first and I wouldn't change that for the world, but our break-up was messy and it was my fault.

Sean was selfless, gave me so much encouragement and helped me out of my shell. Unfortunately it had back-fired on him. I hadn't thought about it too much at the time, clearly.

* * * *

Student Union Bar, 2000

I was out with the girls on a Friday night, drinking and dancing and wearing a cute little dress that cuddled close to my curves. I'd have never bought it by myself but Sean had encouraged me to get it. He helped me embrace my shape, helped me overcome the hang-ups I'd inherited from high school.

I danced into a guy that night. I danced into him and kissed him. He was hot but I didn't even know his name. It was only a kiss but it was hot and steamy and observed by one of Sean's mates. It was the end of a relationship. I was heartbroken and didn't know why Sean couldn't forgive me for just one kiss. I was young, I was naïve and after that incident, newly single.

I kissed a lot of men in many, many clubs. It wasn't my finest hour but it started something for me. I realized that the curves that had made me stand out in a bad way in secondary made me stand out from the crowd in a particularly good way. My curves were something to embrace and love, not curse.

I moved out of the house share in year two of my studies and moved into a tiny apartment of my own in the student digs. I dug in and got serious about my studies. Well, for the first few weeks anyway. Then I was distracted by Ben in the room over the corridor from mine. He was just like Ryan. Same eyes, same hair – but just a shade lighter – and same attitude. It didn't matter how much I tried to forget him, Ryan was always close to my mind even when I didn't want him to be.

Ben became my new Ryan. I wanted him. In some twisted way I thought if I could get Ben it would be a two-fingered salute to Ryan and all the years of heartache he'd caused. Problem was, Ben was a player. He flirted with me – Lord, I practically rubbed up and down his leg like a territorial cat every time I saw him – but I couldn't get past that flirting stage. I thought maybe he had a girlfriend, making him reluctant to take things further, but when I found out he didn't, I did a particularly audacious thing to change that.

I broke into his room. Well, technically I didn't. He'd left it open. Well, I'd distracted him so he hadn't pulled his door all the way closed. I'd leaned against the door jamb pushing out my chest, in a top with a low scoop neck. He'd been distracted by the view and hadn't finished shutting his door. Just winked at me and walked off.

I slipped into his room, kicked my way through the dirty clothes and pulled the duvet over his well slept in sheets and stretched myself out on his bed.

Naked.

I waited there for him, I knew he wouldn't be long. It was a Wednesday and he just had the one lecture. He came back just as I was starting to question the soundness of my plan.

"Oh, wow, I didn't order takeout," he quipped, closing the door behind him and kicking off his shoes. "But now I'm feeling really hungry."

He dropped his bag onto the floor and pulled his T-shirt over his head. I just watched as he slipped out of his jeans and boxers. He strode over to me as I leaned on one elbow and admired his long, lithe frame. I was nervous until he pushed me down onto the bed and held me there.

"I think I'm dreaming," he whispered between kisses. "This can't be real."

"Oh it is," I gasped, running my hands down his back to grip his tight buttocks. "Very real. Feel."

I arched my back and pressed my breasts to his taut chest. I was sparking with desire at every point his body touched mine. He wasn't gentle or loving, but that wasn't what I wanted. His every touch was purposeful, fueled by lust and used to whip up the same frenzied desire in me. He took the condom I held in my fist and sheathed himself. Ben kissed me a while longer, let me run my hands all over him and feel his strength, then he plunged his covered cock into me and took what I had on offer. He fucked me hard and wildly — I loved being out of control. Being used. I was thrilled to be with him. I was on a mental high and although I didn't come I still felt amazing when he did.

That was a truly fantastical moment but it was only a moment. We went back to flirting across a corridor and nothing more. He eventually got himself a steady girl, and I realized he wasn't Ryan and was not the man for me. But that fuck marked another step in my journey from Janet to Katrina. I realized I didn't need a Ryan to make my life work. I started to file him away as ancient history. He'd always be in the back of my mind but from that day on I labeled him as a past chapter and moved on to fresh, new pages.

* * * *

I opened my eyes, centered once more. Feeling more Katrina but it was hard to maintain that, with reminders of my childhood everywhere I looked. The sadness boiled up without warning — the deep, aching pit of emptiness that the death of Gran left inside me opened up and began to envelop me. I was just about to reach the level of maudlin that brought me to tears when I was rescued by the dramatic entrance of Ryan, skidding and slipping with a squeak on the shiny floor.

"Oops, sorry," he laughed, catching the door handle. "I've just been outside and it's a tad wet.

I could see the evidence over his shoulders and down his back, the edges of his jeans dark with soaked up water. Must have made my shoes a bit slippy."

"As long as you're okay, that's the main thing." I smiled, glad that he'd distracted me.

"Nothing broken! Now, let's get started on this dining room. It's three o'clock, so there's a few useable hours left yet."

"Are you okay to carry on? I meant to ask before, but I forgot. Don't you need to go to your— Be with your—erm, poorly girlfriend?" I hated Eve, yes but she was clearly majorly intoxicated and probably needed adult supervision. Ryan probably just about qualified.

"Oh hell no." He shook his head vehemently. "The best thing I can do right now is stay away from her until she cools down, sobers up and gets to being a bit reasonable, like."

"Oh, okay."

"But thanks for thinking of me. I'm still completely mortified that she's kicked up such a fuss right here, under your nose." His cheeks were flushed red, like they used to be when I caught him doing something naughty.

"Water under the bridge." I waved dismissively. "Let's get back to business."

I'd been determined to keep a huge distance between us but after my emotions had been so rocked I felt like I needed someone around. Just having a person with me made it easier not to break down and sob.

"Right then. Let's open this door."

Opening it wasn't the trouble. Getting past it into the dining room was. The rest of the house was uncluttered compared to the packed arrangement of magazines in there. Maybe it'd been the place where she'd started her collection.

"What on earth was Mary planning to do with all these?" Ryan chuckled. "I knew she was a bit of a hoarder, but never imagined it had got this bad."

"I don't know, but we better start moving all this crap. You take stuff out. I'll put it in bags."

"Right, yep. Okay." Ryan put his hands on his hips and cocked his head to the side. "It's like flippin' Jenga. One false move and I'll be buried under an avalanche of vintage paper."

"Maybe start at the top? She can't have piled them to the ceiling…"

I was wrong, they were piled up incredibly high in places. Luckily, though, at the doorway they didn't stretch that far and Ryan managed to dig out the top few inches of magazines with little trouble.

The partnership was working, except every time Ryan passed me more papers my hand colliding with his sent wildlife dancing about in my stomach. Usually it was just butterflies, but the movement was more intense — I imagined hedgehogs, even a few deer might have been involved. I didn't want to keep being excited by him, so I started grabbing only the very ends of the bundles he offered me. Which was fine while the piles were just papers but when he passed me a load with an old scraggy book in the middle the heaviness pulled it down. Papers scattered toward the earth in pages as the book plummeted with a crash.

"Bugger," I cursed and fell to my knees.

"Sorry, I must have fluffed the pass," he apologized, dropping to the floor in front of me.

"No, I think it was me. I didn't realize we were playing rugby."

I giggled and his hearty guffaw mingled with it. Just like the old days. That scared me. I panicked and wanted to get him away from me as soon as possible. I hadn't known it was possible to swing between such extreme moods so fast.

"I reckon we best call it a night," I insisted. "I think I'm getting too tired to concentrate."

"Yeah, time is marching on." He looked at his watch after stuffing a handful of yellowed pages into the bin bag. "It's nearly six anyway."

It was rather clichéd, like a scene from a corny romance, but we both reached for the same stray magazine and ended up bumping foreheads.

"Oh, I'm sorry." He pulled back. "Are you all right?"

I nodded, but he still ran his fingers over my forehead. His touch sent tingles down my body, to my toes and back again.

"No bump." He ran his hand down my cheek and rubbed at it with his work-hardened thumb. "You'll live."

I couldn't breathe, I'd forgotten how to. My brain had stopped working and the only part of my body in gear seemed to be my pussy. I longed to press myself against him, to pull him toward me, onto me, into me and I didn't care that it was dangerous and deeply inappropriate.

He coughed and moved back, clambering to his feet.

"Yes, I better go, better go. I need to see... Eve, yes, Eve." His cheeks flamed red and his eyes dropped with guilt.

I sprang to my feet too. Agitated like him, there was no doubt my cheeks glowed just as bright. I felt them burning. Damn, that had been too close for comfort. What would have happened if I'd kissed him? Would he have recognized my style? I'd had an overlapping tooth removed when I'd first gone to the States to flatten out my smile. Had it changed my kissing technique too? I inhaled deeply and tried to push the questions back into the depths of my mind.

"Yes, of course. Well, I'll see you in the morning then." He coughed.

"Yep, I'll be here at eight but I'm going to get the skip emptied, so it might be a bit before I come in't house." His Yorkshire accent thickened.

"Okay, well... I'll see you when I see you."

He tied the bin bag up and carried it off down the corridor over his shoulder. Like Santa with presents for the naughty boys and girls.

Chapter Ten

Ryan Taylor

"You spent how fucking much?" I yelled.

"Oh, honey, don't shout at me." She pouted. "I've had a long shift in the factory."

She was stretched out on the sofa, staring at the TV.

"You're going to have to have many more to clear this debt. How in the hell did you spend eighteen grand and why didn't you tell me?"

"I meant to." She shrugged. "I just forgot."

"Just forgot? Just forgot? Well, you clearly hid the damn bills from me for months, too. They're demanding three grand by the twentieth of December or they're going to take me to court. Me! I've not spent a penny of it!" I ripped open my overalls and shook myself out of them.

"I know, I'm sorry. I'll work hard and help pay it." At least she sounded a little bit sheepish.

"Fuck, Eve. You've done some stupid shit in your time but this takes the biscuit." I threw off my work boots and wiggled my aching toes. All I really wanted was a bath. I'd been working hard, trying to banish my frustrations. I'd made a grave mistake, nearly kissed my bloody boss and the atmosphere between us was chilly to say the least. I just had to keep my head down, and was thankful that she'd not already sacked me. Between almost snogging her and Eve's yelling the odds, we'd not ingratiated ourselves with the star.

"Don't you have anything to say for yourself?"

She shrugged, kept her eyes trained on the lively, orange, yelling people on the TV.

"Fuck's sake," I exclaimed.

It was so frustrating. She was all for a big bust-up fight when it was her who had the issue but if I was angry, more often than not she'd just deflect and ignore the issue until I gave up and sulked. And I was good at sulking.

"Right, fuck you then." I shot up out of the chair and stamped into the hall. "I'm going to the pub." I didn't even pause to pull on my coat, I just stormed out of the house and slammed the door behind me. My anger staved off the cold until I got into the warmth of The Fiddlers.

"A pint of mild and a packet of cheese and onion crisps, Michael, please."

"That'll be eighty pounds and ninety-eight pence, Ryan."

"You what?" I must have heard him wrong.

"You heard me, Ryan." Michael was a funny sort, the kind of beer-bellied, red-nosed publican you could have a joke with, but unusually his face was stony, his glare icy.

"What for?" I asked.

"Three pounds for your mild, ninety-eight pence for your crisps and seventy-seven quid to settle your tab."

"My tab? I've not got a tab!" I snapped. "Michael, come on, stop joshing around."

"I'm not, mate. Your Eve was in here the other night, said to put her drinks on your tab after your card wouldn't work."

"My tab?" I pulled in a deep drag of air. I felt lightheaded with anger.

"Yeah, she said you wouldn't mind, since it were your card that wouldn't work."

I chuckled dryly—if it wasn't happening to me it'd be funny.

"Oh, she did, did she?" I shook my head.

Michael continued to look unimpressed.

"Right, right, fine."

I took the money Katrina had paid me out of my pocket and counted out nine ten pound notes.

"How the hell did she manage to rack up that much in one night?" I sighed.

"Oh, she wasn't on her own." Michael rung it into the till and popped open the draw. "She had help."

"Of course she did!" I exclaimed.

Michael just nodded, and palmed my change out before offering it to me. He'd not picked up on my sarcasm, but then he wasn't the pointiest cocktail stick of the bunch.

At least having to pay Eve's tab out of my earnings meant I didn't overdo the alcohol. It made me think, not drink. Three grand is a lot of money to anyone but I had no savings and several other bills to pay, too. Drinking my money away wouldn't help. Even if I worked solidly for a month for Katrina I'd just make the required amount and at my normal odd job rate it would take forever.

I had three weeks. The figures just didn't add up, but in the end I decided that my only course of action was to save, save, save and hope. If I paid the credit card folks something, surely they'd be sort of happy with that?

The pub was quiet. I was thankful, not in the mood to make small talk. The pint disappeared all too quickly but my money worries prevented me from ordering another. I walked home, slowly taking in the familiar surroundings.

I loved Thornleydale. It was so beautiful and tranquil, and it was all I'd ever known. I'd never left Yorkshire and I didn't see any real reason to do so. Except back when I was a teen—then I'd wanted to break free from the place. I'd found it boring and staid and I hadn't been able to wait to get out and see the world.

But the world was cruel and expected things that my safe little community didn't. When I was a kid that had been a mystery to me. With a few years of experience behind me I realized the comforts of my home village. So I stayed.

It was still weird walking up the path toward the lodge and not straight to my childhood home. My sister had sold that on years ago to Mrs Letheridge and her husband. They were a strange couple, very unapproachable. Her husband had passed away a few years after they'd moved in, but Mrs Letheridge still lived in what I consider to be my home all by herself. She must have rattled around the place. The poor old dear could have been dead and moldering up there for all I knew. I stopped that line of thought, it was far too morbid for that time of night.

It pissed me off that I didn't have the old house. When Helen hadn't moved in I'd been sure that she'd let me have it but no, my greedy sister had sold it on at the height of the housing boom and probably made more than a pretty penny from it.

I have to give her some credit, though — grudgingly, anyway. When Dad left me nothing in the will, Helen had taken pity and let me have the lodge, otherwise I'd have been homeless. It wasn't that generous of her as it had lain disused for decades and had needed lots of work to make it habitable. I knew I shouldn't speak ill of the dead but that sister of mine never did me a straight up favor. There was always a catch.

I had made the lodge cozy for Eve and me. Not that she appreciated it. I could count the number of times Eve had said a genuine thank you to me on one hand. She was not terribly expressive.

"But I have to travel so far to work," she'd whined. "It'll take an hour on the bus."

"I know, love. But we can't afford to buy in Wakefield and this little place is ours."

"Can't you sell it?" She'd stomped her foot. Something she did with regularity.

"No, I can't. Even if I did, we'd barely get a deposit on a house in the city."

In the end she'd agreed to move in with me. I'd still had my grand vision and I'd sold her a life of Riley once my fleet of handy men took off. Okay, I didn't have Dad's money but I could go to the bank and get a loan. I was determined to make my vision a reality but it never happened. Eve was sacked for being late day in, day out, and I had to work to support us. I couldn't go leaping into an uncertain business when I was struggling to pay bills and feed us both. The recession certainly hit me hard.

Home didn't seem half as attractive as it should have. I was tired, mentally and physically, but I didn't want to sleep with Eve, I could barely even look at her, so it would mean another night on the sofa.

Gravel crunched beneath my feet, the moonlight bathed the fields and hedgerows around me. My life was shit, with problems piling up, my future uncertain, but the air was clear, the moon beautiful and for a moment my soul was light.

Eve wasn't in the house, I looked everywhere. No note, no text of explanation. I probably should have worried but I didn't. I just got into bed and slept.

* * * *

The next morning she still wasn't around so I went to work.

"Morning." I didn't even look up at Katrina when I walked past. "I'll get on with the dining room then."

"Sure." Her reply was emotionless, she clicked the door shut and headed upstairs. *They say misery likes company, don't they? Well, they know nothing about me.* When I was miserable I wanted isolation, so I worked incredibly hard that day and didn't once interact with Katrina. There was no friendly offer of a brew, or kindly word as we met in the corridor. I kept myself away from her and she didn't go out of her way to seek me out, either.

Being locked in my mind wasn't a fun place to be. The anger and frustration I felt at Eve slowly eroded away and turned into self-doubt. Maybe it was all my fault. Surely a responsible man would have checked his card statement each month and caught on when he'd not had one for a while.

So much of the crap in my life was my fault. Once I'd kicked myself around mentally for not checking up on my credit card I sought out other things to beat myself up about and there were plenty. Why hadn't I reached out more to my sister while she had still been alive? I'd ignored my only relative for years, on Eve's demand.

But then my track record with relatives was shit anyway. And friends, well, I'd lost the one decent friend I'd ever had before I'd even started shaving. My trips down guilt alley always ended up in the same place with the same person. The front drive of school, pulling Janet's hair at the behest of Eve. From there on in, a cruel clip show of all the nasty things I'd said and done to her would play in my mind.

* * * *

Secondary School, 1996

"Why did you punch her, you moron?" I bumped into Janie in the corridor, by the woodwork room. It was the quietest area of the school.

She tried to duck past me but I stood firmly in her way until she stopped in her tracks and sighed.

"I punched her because she called Gran something I won't even repeat. She doesn't even know my gran. She's not from Thornleydale."

"That's no excuse for hitting her."

"No, it isn't. I feel a bit bad about it, actually." She looked up into my eyes and I could see the regret there. "Violence really isn't the answer but she pissed me off and punching her full on in the face felt very satisfying at the time."

"You bitch," I growled stepping that bit closer to her, invading her personal space. "You've hurt my girlfriend. She's got a black eye."

"I'm sorry." She looked down at her toes, her body slumped. All the fight just seemed to leak out of her.

"So you fucking should be. You're twice the size of Eve—you're the bully here."

"Oh, I'm not." Her spine straightened and she looked at me again. Her usually placid light-blue eyes tossed to a darker, more sinister blue. She prodded her finger into the center of my chest three times violently then held it there. "I'm really not. She hasn't said one nice thing to me since the day we started at this school. She has made the last four years of my life a misery and not just that." Her accusing finger dropped slowly to her side. "She nicked my best friend in all the world. I'm not the bully here."

I knew she was right, so I did the only thing a stupid, mixed up fifteen-year-old me would. I insulted her.

"No, you're just a fat, lonely loser who's jealous of my girlfriend. Now leave her alone, right? Or you'll have me to answer to."

I turned my back on her and walked away. I hated myself, then. When I remembered the disturbing color of her eyes, the red rims around them and the lines of real sadness on her face. I never wanted to hurt her, I'd always been her knight in shining armor.

* * * *

I was a complete and utter fuck-up. My thoughts were dark and melancholy as I continued to clean up without thinking. I could have been shoveling diamonds into the black bin liner, I wouldn't have noticed. Life kicked me in the balls so often I'd developed a strong sense of optimism but sometimes I just couldn't summon the energy to smile. Sometimes my life dragged me down into a dark pit of despair it would take time and effort to climb out of.

I looked out of the window into the gray, wet day that seemed to echo the way I was feeling. The murkiness of my thoughts had leaked out into the weather.

Even as a kid I'd had dark moments and Janie had always been there to drag me out of them. I had sometimes even managed to rescue her, too.

* * * *

Thornleydale Primary, 1984 – 1985

"Don't you do that!" I stretched out my body, tried to make my four foot nothing height seem menacing.

"Or what are you going to do, little boy?"

Carl Johnson, ten years of age and the biggest kid in the school, looked down on me. He must have been at least a hundred feet tall.

"It's not right to hit girls, Carl, and that girl is my best friend." I stood my ground, Sheltering Janie's body with my own. She was sat with her back against the schoolyard wall, sobbing.

"Well, I'll hit all the girls I like," he said, scruffing up my hair with his big, intimidating hand. "And I think you'll be the next one I punch."

"Run, Ry!" Janie gasped. "Don't let him."

"No," I replied, holding my ground. "I won't leave you."

And Carl Johnson, junior school bully, punched me in the gut and sent me flying backwards into Janie. Luckily one of the dinner ladies saw and rushed over to sort him out.

"Oh, Ry, are you hurt?" Janie asked.

I'd fallen on top of my best friend and slid to the floor beside her. She wasn't at all concerned about herself.

"I'm all right," I coughed. "Are you?"

She nodded. "Thanks for standing up for me."

"Always, Janie. I'll always protect you."

If only I'd followed the words of seven-year-old me, but within a few months I'd put her in danger yet again.

"Gran! Gran!" I yelled, my eight-year-old legs running as fast as I could push them. "Come quick!"

"Hells bells, Ryan, what's the matter?" Mary turned from the sink, a part-peeled potato in hand.

"Janie's stuck," I gasped. "She sent me for you, come quick."

Mary dropped the potato and ran out behind me, not stopping to take off the bright, orange floral pinny or her slippers.

"Where is she?" Mary asked, as I ran down to the bottom of the garden.

"Erm." I was reluctant to say, even though I knew I had to take Gran to the incident itself.

"You've been playing in the ruddy copse again, haven't you?" she sighed.

We'd approached the back fence and clearly Mary had put two and two together.

"Yeah," I admitted. "I'm sorry, I said we should, but I didn't mean for Janie to get hurt."

"I know, son." Gran rustled my hair with a sigh. "I know. Lead me to her."

I pushed through between the fence posts, in the gap that a broken one had created. Gran followed.

"Good grief," she panted, easing herself through the tiny space. She was a slim lady but it was a challenge for her still. "I'm getting too old for this malarkey."

We went straight to the big oak. Janie and I played there all the time. It had a gnarly hole in the side of the trunk where we'd hide sweets and treats.

"Help."

I heard Janie's high-pitched voice before we reached the right bit of the copse.

"Oh, please help."

"We're coming," I yelled back. "Gran's here."

It was just behind the big oak where the disaster had happened. We didn't usually go that far into the copse because although Janie didn't mind disobeying her Gran by a few yards, more than that brought her out in hives, so she said.

"Oh, my darling," Gran cried. "How on earth have you managed to get yourself in there?"

Janie was inside the bole of a tree.

"Ryan did it and said it was well good, so I climbed in to look but I'm taller than him."

"I'll grow," I muttered, ever sensitive to the fact that she was taller than me by three inches.

"And I got stuck and I can't get out." Janie sobbed.

"Now, now, pet, don't fret, don't fret." She tried for a little while to help maneuver my shocked best friend out of the hole but she was well and truly wedged inside.

"Reet, Ryan. You'll have to go into my house and dial nine-nine-nine. Explain the problem, tell 'em you'll need the fire brigade and maybe th'ambulance too."

"Got it," I yelled then scampered back the way I'd come. My heart thumped nineteen to the dozen. Janie was stuck and it was all my fault. I had to put it right—Janie was the most important thing in my whole world.

The phone call was easy. The waiting by the road for the fire crew wasn't. It felt like ages but it was only a matter of minutes before they arrived. I had to direct them around another way to the old, dead tree. It took about ten minutes of tramping through the copse to get my bearings, then I got them to the tree pretty quickly. They set about assessing the situation, kept Janie talking then went to get cutting tools. Tears pricked my eyes and I hopped from foot to foot anxiously. Guilt tied my stomach in knots and closed up the back of my throat. I shouldn't have let her try to get in—I knew she'd get stuck but I thought I'd be able to get her out.

"You did good." Gran squeezed my shoulder and made me jump.

I'd been so lost in my thoughts I'd forgotten she was there.

"You came for me, you called nine-nine-nine, you did good," she said to reassure me.

"But I shouldn't have let her go in there in the first place." I sighed, a tear slipping down my cheek.

"You might have led, but she decided to follow. Don't fret your head too much, son. You'll think twice before playing in the copse again, now, though, won't you?"

I nodded.

She pulled me into her side and gave me a brief cuddle. "Janie's not hurt, she were just a little panicked that's all. Firemen will have her out in no time."

It wasn't quite as easy as that, but the firemen did free Janie and she was okay, just a few minor scratches. As soon as she was released she ran over to me and hit me hard in the arm.

"Ryan Taylor, you are nothing but trouble," Janie scolded then pulled me into a tight embrace. "But I do love you."

"Eww," I responded, backing out of the hug. "Glad you're all right, though. You're the best girl in the world."

"And you're all right for a boy," she responded, like she always did. The laughter that followed was healing. I was so happy she was free.

* * * *

I'd been an awful protector and a terrible friend. I hoped that she'd found someone to properly take care of her, even if that left a bitter taste in my mouth.

I got home that evening to Eve, cleaning the kitchen. It was quiet disconcerting actually.

"Hi, Ryan. There's food in the oven. If you just clean yourself up it'll be ready in ten minutes."

I was so surprised I didn't say anything, just nodded and ran upstairs to change. The kitchen had been cleaned, the bed made and laundry piled into the washing basket. It was as though I'd stepped into an alternate reality. All the fire of my anger had burned itself out. I didn't want to argue or fight. I'd had enough angst.

"Look," she said, over tea — which happened to be a supermarket lasagna with garlic bread. "I'm sorry, I'm really sorry, Ryan. I don't want to argue with you anymore, okay? I'll do what I can to help you pay off my debt and we'll work it all out together, okay?"

Anger still bubbled in the pit of my stomach. I really wanted to give her a piece of my mind but decided to take the road of least resistance in the end.

"Okay." I nodded. What was the use of dragging up what had already happened? There was no sense in that. The problem was, as much as I pretended it was all fine with Eve it really wasn't. Deep down resentment churned.

Chapter Eleven

Katrina Quinn

The next week was long and difficult. Ryan cleared the dining room and I went upstairs to work on the guest room, the one I was sleeping in. We communicated only when we had to and that interaction was painful. I should have rejoiced — I didn't want Ryan to work out who I was — but it was distressing to have him blank me. Worse than his flirting, in fact.

I was trying so hard not to think about him, or Gran, or the past, but then I found something that blew that plan out of the water. My suitcase was tucked up behind a box, near the bedhead. In it were my overnight things back from when I'd been in college. I would leave that one suitcase at Gran's so that when I went to stay my stuff would already be there for me. Gran would wash everything I'd worn then put it back in the old-fashioned suitcase under the bed.

In it I found my old pajamas, a vibrant red jumper that Gran had knitted me. It was a staple present, a jumper. Some were okay, others were complete disasters. The red one was warm and not too garish so I'd gotten a lot of wear from it. The clothes were a blast from the past, but then it got even worse. I found something I thought I'd lost.

A box.

* * * *

Janet's house, 1990

"You're old," Ryan said, deadpan.

"No I'm not. Just because I'm ten and you're still nine and you're jealous." I stuck my tongue out.

"Whatever, you're old." He laughed.

"You coming to Gran's later? She's doing a buffet and a cake."

"I'm there." He waved his legs, banging his heels on the wall. We often sat on the front at my mum's house in the summer. We could watch the world go by and we didn't have to go inside and face Mum or, worse still, Mum and Dad.

"So what did you get from your parents?" Ryan asked.

"I got an Etch-A-Sketch."

"Oh, nice." His eyes lit up.

"I'm not allowed to bring it outside." I quickly followed up, "Mum says it cost too much to let you break it."

"Pfft." He shook his head. "Did Gran knit you something?"

"I dunno, not had her gift yet. I'll get it when I go round."

"I've got you something."

"No way," I gasped. "You never buy presents for anyone."

"Well, I won't give it to you if you don't want it." He shrugged.

"I do want it, what is it?" I bounced up and down on the stone.

Ryan reached down to his feet, picked up the black bag with bright, light-blue zigzags over it.

He opened it up and sat with it on his lap.

"Ry," I whined, "stop teasing me. What is it?"

"All right" — he grinned — "here you go."

He passed me a parcel wrapped loosely in brown paper.

"Careful, it's a little heavy."

I felt the weight and the angular sides as I took it in my hands. The paper crinkled as I pulled it down to reveal a light wooden box. In the lid my name was inscribed in curling letters.

"Wow, it's beautiful."

"I made it," he said, "in Dad's shed."

"It's gorgeous." I opened the lid and inside there was more.

"Oh, Ry, it's your lucky penny." I picked up the misshapen penny and flipped it in my fingers.

"I know. Well, I'm so bad at keeping things and you're so good at it. I thought you'd like it — to remind you that, you know, I'm still alive."

The penny had been misshapen in the fire that had burnt down the far corner of Ryan's house. He'd been in the room when it had started. He had only been six. I'd seen the smoke and had run to tell Gran, who had rung the fire brigade. I had been there when the fireman had carried Ryan down over his shoulder. He'd fainted but he had something clasped tightly in his hand.

It was the lucky penny. Misshapen in the heat. It had burnt his hand—he had the scar all through childhood.

* * * *

It might still have been there. I hadn't looked at Ryan's palm close enough to notice.

That box was where I kept all my treasured possessions. Even when Ryan had been a complete bastard to me at school I'd go home and open the box he'd made for me and I'd take out the items one by one and remember our friendship. Having it back haunted me.

Everything was still there—the thread of mustard wool that had come from his woolen jumper. He'd ripped a huge hole in the center of it scrabbling through the copse and had had to get rid of it. The conker he'd won several battles with, stringed and still as rock hard as ever. The pencil he'd whittled into the letters of his first name and mine, and his favorite marble, the one with a green eye in the middle like his.

I slammed the box shut and shoved it back in the suitcase, back under the bed.

I think that was what stirred my dreams. I was looking for him, he was lost and although the location changed, from a large school to a forest, I could hear him calling for help, like when he was in that fire— and I couldn't get to him. And I'd see Gran. She'd not recognize me and I'd wake up several times crying.

I kept all the old stuff in the suitcase under the bed. I figured it was the safest place—Ryan wouldn't look there. When I had finished clearing the back room I called him to help me shift all the bags that had piled up in the landing down to the skip.

"How's the dining room?"

"Pretty much cleared," he replied, face deadpan. It was disconcerting to have him so emotionless.

"Oh, good. I've just finished in the back room so I'll start on the larger front one next."

"Great."

I started to drag a filled bin bag down the stairs.

"I'll do these, you carry on in the bedroom."

"Are you sure?" I asked.

"Sure I'm sure." He squeezed out a smile.

"Look," I sighed.

He turned around part way down the stairs.

"I know we've not known each other long and I just employ you, but you've been really off with me of late, is it something I've done?" I shouldn't have asked, but I would have much preferred to duck the flirting than have him mad at me.

"No" – his face softened – "no, nothing you've done. It's me, just me."

"Right, well, can I do something to make it better? Do you need to have some time off? I mean, we've been working day in and day out for, what, close to two weeks now –"

"No," he was insistent, an edge of hardness to his voice. "No," his tone softened. "Really, I'm much better being here."

"What's the matter, Ryan?" I asked gently. Now I looked at him closely I could see he was hurting.

"Nothing, Katrina, it's nothing – but thanks, for, you know, asking."

"Yeah, no worries. Just let me know if I can help at all."

"Well…" He paused for a few moments then shook his head. "No, no, I don't think you can. Thanks anyway. I'll get these sorted and I'll try to be less arsey from now on."

"It's okay" — I smiled — "I've been just as bad myself, I'm sure. We'll call a truce?"

"Sure." He grinned then went to carry on down the steps but stumbled, tumbling down the last few, the bag of rubbish slapping him in the face.

"Oh, bloody hell, Ryan. Are you all right?" I dashed down the stairs and maneuvered around him.

"Ryan," I called again, absolutely petrified. "Ryan, are you okay?"

"Findelridel faffnaffer."

I lifted the bag off his face and he took a deep breath.

"I hit my head but I'm okay."

"Can you sit up?" I crouched beside him, and when I saw he was struggling to get upright I slipped my hands under his arms to help him.

"Oooh that's nice," he purred, then giggled like a little girl. "But it doesn't part tickle."

He'd definitely given his head a good bump.

"Let's see where you bumped your head." I reached out and ran my hand over his forehead, a definite lump forming on the right. "Oh, that's nasty. I'll get you some ice."

"Okay, cutie." He giggled again.

It was a weird sound coming from a grown man but it was something I'd heard a lot when we'd played together as kids. It ripped at my heart. I took a deep breath and ran to the kitchen. In the freezer I found a pack of frozen peas that might have been well past eating stage but they'd make a decent salve for a bashed head.

When I got back to the stairs, Ryan wasn't there.

"Where are you, Ryan?" I called. I looked in the front room and glimpsed him on the front lawn, zigzagging with the refuse bag.

"Ryan! Ryan, come here!" I yelled. "Before you do yourself a mischief."

"Oh, shut up, Janie-wanie."

I stood in stunned amazement, then he fell over. I ran over to him.

"Oh, my head," he groaned. "Katrina, I feel sick."

"Oh, dear, I think you might be a little concussed." I sighed with relief. Clearly he was less than compos mentis.

"Mmm, maybe."

"I'd better take you to A & E—you've had a nasty fall."

"Oh, I'm sure I'll be fine. Sure, I'll be fine, sure I'll be— What was I doing again?"

"You're going to hospital with me."

"Are you ill?" he asked, stroking my arm.

"You could say that. Come on."

"Okay, I will do when I work out which leg I need to move first."

It was a trial getting Ryan into a taxi—he kept wanting to get into his van but I couldn't let him drive—he could barely steer a sentence let alone a vehicle. He asked me several times in the back of the taxi where we were going, called me Mum a couple of times then lay his head on my shoulder.

"Ryan?"

"Hmm?"

"Ryan, come on, don't go to sleep now. I can't let you, not until you've been checked out by a doctor."

"But I'm tired, sweetie."

"I know you are, but we're almost at the hospital and you need to stay awake." I jiggled my shoulder and he folded his arm over my body.

"Ryan, come on now," I gasped, panic growing. "You can't sleep."

He made a strange gurgling sound in the back of his throat and shifted his hand right over my breast.

"Ryan," I gasped. "What are you doing?"

"Keeping myself awake." He moved quickly — before I could move or take it in, his lips were on mine.

I was stunned into indecision. My body was all for deepening the kiss, my hands were itching to run into his hair and add pressure to our kiss, my back wanted to arch and push my breasts farther against him and my mouth was ready to thoroughly explore his. However, my mind was completely against all of it. My mind held onto the facts. Apart from being seriously mentally incapacitated by his fall he was also the one man in Thornleydale who could work out who I was by my kiss. So I pushed him back.

Luckily, the taxi pulled up just then, and I got to bundle Ryan out of it and into the hospital foyer. He seemed to have completely forgotten the kiss. However, I hadn't. I felt as light on my feet as Ryan. I vibrated, my skin hummed and felt the urge to scrub at it, to stop it reminding me how good it had felt to have Ryan's arms around me.

He was seen quickly by a triage nurse — they didn't mess about with head injuries. After some tests and the administration of some painkillers he was ushered in to see a doctor.

"Well, Ryan, you're going to be okay but you do need to take it easy until the dizziness wears off. No more heavy lifting for a few days."

"Right." He nodded then winced.

"Thank you, doctor, I'll get him home." I smiled with relief.

"Just one more thing, Ms Quinn." He smiled, running a hand through his salt and pepper hair. "Could I have your autograph?"

I hadn't thought about anything but making sure Ryan was okay until that moment, then I realized that running into a busy hospital was not particularly conducive to keeping a low profile. I bought a hat and scarf set in the hospital shop and wrapped myself up so that most of my face was hidden.

"Ms Quinn?" A nurse came over to me as I pushed Ryan toward the main doors. I got ready to sign a quick autograph. "Don't go that way, there's photographers by the door. Follow me."

The nurse led me back the way we'd come and to a side door that explicitly said that it shouldn't be used by members of the public.

"Go out here. The back of the taxi line's just to your left as you exit."

"Thank you so much" — I smiled broadly — "I really appreciate it."

"No worries, I think it's wrong that they're allowed to harangue people here. It's not right, not right at all."

"Thanks again, nurse," I called.

Ryan smiled absently but waved anyway.

It was a short wheel to a taxi at the back of the rank. No one looked up and paid any attention to me. I could just see the photographers in the distance and my heart thudded until we had gotten into the cab and he pulled off, heading back to Thornleydale.

"Right, Ryan, I guess I better take you home."

I wasn't looking forward to it. The day was drawing on and I was fairly certain Eve would be waiting for him.

"Will Eve be in?"

"Eve?" Ryan looked confused.

"Yes, Eve, your girlfriend."

"Oh, Eve." He nodded. "I dunno. She's been doing a lotta shifts at the biscuit factory lately."

"Have you got keys to let yourself in?"

He nodded. "In my pocket."

"Good."

I had to hope she was out.

"She's been trying to make up for being a total prat. She maxed out my credit card, you know, without telling me. There was I, not using it, thinking I was being good and not needing to pay it and she was buying a fuck ton of booze and hand-fucking-bags on it."

I just let him prattle on. Well, to be honest, I couldn't stop him prattling on.

"My credit limit was fifteen thousand pounds. I've got very good credit. Never been in debt and being the son of my father helped. Now I'm somehow eighteen thousand quid in debt and totally screwed all because of that bitch." He sighed heavily.

I thought he'd stopped talking. I didn't say anything, I couldn't. I didn't know how much of what he was saying was true. The doctor explained that basically his brain had been shaken about and so it was a bit mixed up and would be for a few days. Memories, recall and even just manners would be shaken up for a little while. It seemed that no permanent damage had been done but the symptoms could persist for a few days.

"She's fucked up my life consistently, you know?" Ryan laid his head on my shoulder again.

I immediately tensed up.

"I don't know why I'm still with her. Well, I think maybe she's my penance. I think I have to put up with her as punishment for being such an arse to my old best friend, Janie."

I didn't relax, I didn't breathe, I couldn't move. What was he going to say? I wanted to change the subject, to get him away from talking about me, but my mouth wouldn't work and just a little tiny bit of me was curious to hear what he said. Dangerous.

"Janie was great. We were the best of friends as kids. Got into so much trouble together. She just was the best person in the world. But I fucked up. Let me teenage hormones get the better of me. I was so mean to her in high school and college. It hurt me, it really did, but I wanted Eve and I was thinking with my dick. Well, clearly, because I totally flunked my exams, too."

"Well, we're nearly finished with the house," I chirped, desperate to change the subject.

"And I'm still with the bitch. I don't know why. I guess because I chose her over my best mate—the best girl I've ever known, in fact. I've stuck with Eve to see if she can prove she's actually better."

"I mean, there's just the main bedroom to do and what you've got left in the dining room and then I can get on and renovate." I kept talking about the house in the hopes that he'd catch up with me eventually.

Ryan lurched up and waved a finger at me.

"Janie would never have run up a credit card bill. Janie wouldn't be a wine-soaked drunk. I miss her so much, Katrina, I really do. I wish I knew where she was so I could tell her that."

I looked at him and nodded.

I'm Katrina, I'm Katrina, I'm Katrina. I had to cement my character — I couldn't let even a glimpse of Janie show through. It wouldn't end well.

"Oh, Katrina. It's such a mess." He sighed and settled his head on my shoulder again.

"I think a good night's sleep will set you straight, Ryan," I said with a stilted but I hoped soothing tone.

"I think so too." He yawned. "Thanks for looking after me. I know I'm not quite right at the minute. My head is all fuzzy-wuzzy. Glad you're here to look after me. I really like you, you know."

Chapter Twelve

Ryan Taylor

I didn't remember much from my slip down the stairs, just that I'd almost asked Katrina to lend me three grand. I hadn't, though, I'd just fallen down and bumped my head. We had gone to hospital and it had all been a little fuzzy. I remembered kissing her but I wasn't sure it was real. Her lips had been so soft and plump, her pressure so perfectly arousing. It had felt weirdly similar to the time I'd kissed Janie, so I must have dreamt that bit.

Katrina had been incredibly good, though, got me home and into the house. Eve hadn't been in, thank God. She'd even gotten me upstairs and into bed. When I'd woken up the next morning I'd moaned at the state the house had been in. Katrina had brought me home to a shit tip. I was working all day and Eve was too, so no one was doing housework. It was disturbing how disgusting a house could get after a few days of neglect. Contrary to doctor's orders I got up and got tidying. I found a note from Katrina on the bedside table.

"Don't come into work for the next two days. You need to recover. See you Monday."

We'd been working every day to get things cleared. Katrina wanted to have it done before Christmas, but me missing a few days would knock the plan back. I tidied in fits and starts but it wasn't until lunchtime that I started to worry about Eve.

I found my phone and checked the messages. The last from her was the night before.

Going out with the girls, back late.

Back late? That was an understatement. I continued to putter around, then at two o'clock my mobile rang.

"Hey, I just wanted to check how you're doing." It was Katrina.

"Oh, hi, boss. I'm better today, thanks. I could come in and—"

"No, no. You need rest." She was insistent.

"But you wanted to get everything done for Christmas."

"I know, but we'll do it. I'm working away here today and once you're back in we'll be good to go. No problems."

She sounded confident. I wasn't completely taken in by it.

"Well, if you're sure..." I wanted her to say she needed my help—I needed to get back to doing something with a purpose.

"I'm completely sure. Now, are you all right? I feel responsible as you were working with me when you had your accident."

"I'm all right, I promise. And don't worry, it was my own stupid clumsiness that caused this bump. Not your fault at all," I assured her. "You should always look the way you're walking when stairs are involved."

"Okay, well, I'm sure your girlfriend's looking after you, so I'll let you get back to recuperating."

"Actually, Eve's still not here. Oh, and I have to apologize for the state of the house. We've both been working so much lately—"

"No, don't worry. It's okay. Do you need me to bring you anything?" Katrina took a deep breath. "I could bring stuff over if you like."

"Well, that's generous of you, but I'm okay, thanks. And Eve could be back at any moment and we both know she's not your biggest fan."

"You can say that again." She chuckled. "Well, okay, then. I'll leave you to it. Just shout if you need anything."

"Yeah, sure, and thank you for looking after me last night."

"It was the least I could do, Ryan. I'll let you rest. Bye now."

I'm glad she put down the phone when she did because I was close to asking for eighteen grand—surely a celeb like her would have that kind of money. It'd be peanuts to her and would solve all my problems but would probably cause many, many more. I was glad I hadn't blurted that question out.

* * * *

A key in the front door woke me up. I must have nodded off on the sofa.

"Eve?" I called. "Is that you?"

"Yeah," she replied. "What're you doing here?"

There was a scuffle and whispers.

"I had an accident at work, I texted you. Bumped my head. I've got to rest up for a few days."

I strained to hear what Eve was saying, but her voice was too low. I thought there was another voice too, but I couldn't make it out.

"Who's with you?"

"Oh, no one," she chirped. "It's just some annoying door to door salesman." She shut the front door and walked into the corridor. "So what happened?"

"I tripped over myself and fell down the stairs. Bumped my head."

"God, are you all right?" She popped her head round the door jamb.

"Yeah, got a bump, but otherwise good. A little dizzy still. But where there's no sense there's no feeling, eh?"

"Oh, poor baby. I'm just going to get changed then I'll come back and soothe you."

She was acting weird but I was still drowsy and fell back asleep as I waited for her.

When I woke up Eve was hoovering.

"Hey, sweetie, sorry, did I wake you?"

"No, it's okay." I stretched. "I shouldn't sleep all day anyway."

"You do whatever you need to, darling," she crooned.

"I was worried about you, why weren't you here this morning?"

"Oh" — she waved a hand dismissively — "it all got a bit crazy and I drank a teeny bit more than I should have, so I just kipped at Carol's."

"Okay. You could have let me know, though."

"My damn phone died and you know I'm incapable of remembering phone numbers. I'm sorry, sweetie."

"It's all right." I smiled. "I understand."

Eve was attentive and sweet. She finished the tidying, cooked a meal and cared for my every whim. Something niggled at me about that but my poor, severely juggled brain couldn't focus so I let the niggle go, relaxed and let her look after me.

For the first time in months we went to bed together. We snuggled close, not just because it was damn cold and we couldn't afford to turn on the heating but because we wanted to. I was sure that deep down I loved Eve, I didn't know why, and sometimes I wished I didn't but there was something about her, something that pulled me back to her after her many transgressions.

"I've missed you," she whispered, I felt her breath on my lips as we lay face to face.

"I've missed you too." I reached out and pulled her to me and our lips met, we kissed. My body responded. It was intense and fast burning. I gasped, she moaned, we burrowed through winter layers of pajamas and jumpers to hot, soft flesh beneath. The foreplay was short and to the point, nibbles and caresses, nipple tweaks and boob squeezes that led to gropes in pants and fingers in and around genitals.

I was absorbed in the lust, joined with her in our desire. When she sat astride me I thrust up into her with equal passion when she drove down. We were together as one. The sexual tension built, our sex noises blended, and when I exploded she yelled out her pleasure too. We curled up together and slept. In sync for once, we didn't wake until Eve's alarm rang in the morning.

"I'm going to go in to work," I said, as she rolled out of bed, eyes still mostly closed.

"Aren't you supposed to be resting?" Eve yawned, stretched and shivered.

"Yes, but we need the cash and I need to do something. If I sit in here staring at the four walls again I'll go mad. "

"Don't overdo it, okay?" she threw over her shoulder then headed to the bathroom.

* * * *

I felt refreshed as I walked over to Katrina's place. The world was crisp and crunchy, ice and frost glistened everywhere, the trees dangled with it, diamond laden with the cold. Christmas trees were cropping up in people's windows—December was rolling on at quite a speed.

"What are you doing here?" Katrina exclaimed when I knocked on the door.

"Currently I'm freezing my balls off so I'd love to come in and get to work if you don't mind?" I replied through chattering teeth.

"Come in, then. But I told you not to come for a few days. You need to recover."

"I'm recovered, honestly. I'd go mad sat at home for another day. It's better I'm here."

"Ryan, are you sure?" Her tone was serious but had a soft edge of concern. "I don't want you to overdo it."

"I'm completely sure, I promise."

"You'll have to work in the bedroom with me because I need to keep an eye on you."

"Oh my, who's going to say no to that?" I winked.

Her mouth dropped open and she slapped my arm. Her cheeks flashed red so prettily, I wanted to stroke them.

"Behave." She giggled. "You know what I mean. And if you feel at all woozy you will stop what you're doing right away, won't you?"

"Yes, boss." I nodded.

"And you won't do any heavy lifting today."

"Right, boss."

"And you'll let me know if you feel unwell?"

"Of course, boss," I droned.

"Well, come on then, let's get on with it."

The bedroom was less packed than the other rooms, though that wasn't saying much. Clearly Mary had had to sleep in the room so she had left just enough gap to get from the door to her bed.

"She was definitely a well-read lady," I stated as I piled more magazines into a bin bag.

"Indeed. She must have read every magazine on the market for years. And there are books in that corner too."

"She was very clever, was Mary. I suppose her life here might not have been challenging enough for her. She could have made a lot of her life, but she was too involved with her family."

"How can you be too involved with your family?" Katrina snapped. Obviously I'd hit a nerve with her.

"I suppose I don't quite mean it like that. She put her family first, always. Her husband, who was a bit of a prat, if truth be told, and her son, who was also a rum'un. Not everyone would have taken what Mary took and hung around. But she loved her family, and her granddaughter especially. She probably used these books and magazines to escape from the mundaneness of life once she grew up. Me and Janet were a handful as kids, constantly pulling her gran into our make-believe shenanigans. I think we kept her well occupied, well, until we hit our teens anyway."

"What happened then?" Katrina asked, pulling a suitcase free from the surrounding flotsam.

"Oh, well, we went our separate ways, really. We went to the same school but got different sets of friends, you know? We kinda lost touch."

"That's sad." She fiddled with the old-fashioned catch and the retro blue-green case popped open.

"Yeah, it is. I regret it. I miss Janet a lot, we were such good friends. But then I met Eve, fell completely in love so, you know, I'm conflicted."

"Well, the past is the past, I guess," Katrina responded, distractedly.

"You're right." I flipped through a dog-eared Mills & Boon book then flung it in the rubbish bag. "I can't change it now. But if I could have my time again I'd have done things differently."

"I think everyone would, given the choice."

I pushed a few more paperbacks into the bin bag and looked over to Katrina who was stroking something woolen and mustard-colored against her cheek.

"Wow, I remember that jumper." I gasped. "Mary wore it constantly when Janet bought it her for Christmas one year. God, she loved that thing. She'd knitted us some the same color—you remember, right? I showed you that photo."

Katrina nodded. I saw tears in her eyes.

"Are you all right? Has something upset you?"

"I'm fine." She gulped, more tears trickling down her cheek.

"No, you're not." I moved my arse up the bed a few inches and put my arm over her shoulder. "What's the matter?"

"Nothing, nothing." She wriggled and tried to dislodge my arm from around her. "Really, I'm fine." The last sentence had come out as a whine and had ended with a sob.

I held on, my heart thumping, my dick interested in her soft curves. I tried with all my mind to not think about that and embarrass myself.

"It's definitely something." I kept my voice low—I hoped it was soothing. "But you don't have to tell me what, if you don't want to."

"Thanks." Katrina sniffled and rubbed her face with the back of her hand in a most unladylike manner. "It's just, this jumper. My gran had one just the same color. It brought back memories, that's all."

"Hell, yes. I think everyone's granny had one," I chirped, arm still around her.

My lips had joined in with the rebellion. They wanted to push themselves against Katrina's mouth but I knew that would be a very bad idea indeed, so I kept them occupied by talking. "Mary loved this one, well, you can tell, it's well worn, and it's got them navy patches on the elbows. She was not impressed the day me and Janet used it to cradle the cat we found on the side of the road. It'd been hit by a car and we needed to keep it warm."

"Ha, she shouted a lot." Katrina chuckled and sniffed. "I mean, I bet she did. My gran would have."

"Oh yeah, she did. But she still helped us get the cat to the vets in the town. Even adopted it once it was fixed up. But I got a flea in my ear over taking that jumper off the line and not one of her vests."

Katrina laughed and rested her head on my shoulder.

"She was a great lady. Well, sounds like it." She coughed. "Wish I'd met her."

"The best. Mary was the best—and Janet too, actually."

"Sounds like it."

"Hey, what's these? More books?" In the suitcase were some photos and letters, but among them were three old, faded books.

"Oh yeah." Katrina let me pull out the books then snapped shut the case.

"Poems. Emily Dickinson and another two volumes. These look well old."

"They do, don't they?" Katrina took one from me. "They might be first editions even."

"Hang on." I took out my mobile and typed the name into Google.

"Bloody Nora, look at this." I showed her the page I'd found. The books we'd found were displayed there with a price tag of over nineteen grand associated with them.

"For these?"

"Yeah, apparently they're dead rare. They printed just five hundred of the first editions."

"God, well, yes. I better put them somewhere safe. They belong to her family really."

"You're just going to give them away?" *How could she give so much away without blinking?*

"Yes, well, they're not mine, are they?"

"But they kind of are," I argued. I couldn't believe something so small, something I had in my hands, could get me out of all my debt. "You bought the house and its contents."

"I know, but they are clearly precious, the family should have them back. The amount they're worth just isn't relevant."

"But you could seriously do a lot with that kind of money. It'd change my life if I had it."

"Well, exactly, that's why they should go back to their rightful owners. When I've finished renovating I'll contact the solicitors, get all this personal stuff back to the lady's family."

"I guess. Where you going to put them?" I tried not to sound too interested but I really was. Obviously close to twenty grand was nothing to Katrina. She was a bloody millionaire. Would she miss the books if I took them?

"I'll find somewhere." She put them back in the suitcase and carried it out of the room.

The rest of the day I fought with myself over those books. Three books, simple and plain. They wouldn't be missed, would they? If I had them I could clear the debt, might even have enough left over to have a half decent Christmas.

Eve rang me when I was on my lunch break asking when I'd be home. I told her about the books but she didn't seem interested at all. In fact, she seemed massively distracted.

I continued mulling it over after lunch. It wouldn't have been stealing because Katrina didn't need the money and Janet wouldn't know they were here. It would be just like taking home a couple of the old romance paperbacks with me. A perk of the job, not stealing.

"Right, Ryan, I'm calling it quits for today." Katrina sighed. "I'll see you tomorrow."

"Okay, love. I'll take a few of these bags down to my van then I'll shift the rest tomorrow."

"Well, if you're sure you'll be up to it."

"Oh, I'll be fine. These bags are light anyway and I'm feeling much better today already. I'll see you tomorrow, then."

"Yeah, see you."

I walked out into the landing and picked up a few filled bags. As I came past the spare room, the one I knew Katrina was using as her room, I looked in and just under the bed, peeking out from beneath the old flower-laden blanket, was a flash of retro sea green.

Chapter Thirteen

Katrina Quinn

I wish I'd sent him off somewhere else in the house but, truly, I was worried for his health. He shouldn't have been back and working, and I sure as hell didn't want him collapsing on me again. He'd only been off a day—that couldn't have been long enough to fully recover. So I kept him in the bedroom with me and hoped to high heaven that he'd not tell me anything else I didn't want to know or make any attempts to kiss me. I wasn't sure I could've resisted.

Ryan didn't seem affected by his concussed confessions and kiss attack—maybe he'd forgotten all about it. Lucky him. I'd been unable to think of anything else! His lips on mine, his arms around me, so familiar and so different. So soothing and so disturbing all at once. It was as though I'd found home, as though all my questions had been answered, and I'd had a glimpse of somewhere I fitted in, where I was meant to be. I remembered that first kiss we'd shared when we'd nearly run away and I'd felt just the same then. I'm where I'm meant to be when I'm with Ryan.

But it was an illusion. Ryan wasn't interested in me. Maybe in Katrina but not me. Not plain Janie. He'd told me that so many times, so many cruel and twisted times. He couldn't have changed his mind. Yes, he'd told me he'd loved me in his concussed state but how much could I read into that, really? I couldn't. One comment versus several years of hate. It gave me a glimmer of hope, but nothing more.

It seemed that the room shrank as he sat beside me on the bed and dug into the piles of romance books Gran had hoarded. I'd felt freer when the whole room was still filled with crap. I turned my back to him, trying to pretend he wasn't there, and I was succeeding until I came across a suitcase containing a mustard jumper.

I'd bought it for Gran at Christmas in the late eighties and she'd worn it constantly from then on. It had cost me the majority of my saved pocket money that Christmas. It was an all the rage, chunky Arran with a cowl neck—Gran had seen it on someone in church and had commented how much she liked it. I'd had to get it for her, and she'd really appreciated it.

I couldn't help the tears from falling. This jumper was the most personal thing of hers I'd found and it went straight to my heart. I couldn't convince Ryan that I was okay and he put his arm around me to comfort me, making me feel all the worse. He looked into the suitcase and found the books. I'm just glad he didn't look at the photos and letters as they were all from me. Letters from America to Gran. He'd be able to work out who I really was if he read them.

He seemed incredibly concerned with how much the first editions were worth. I wasn't because I'd bought them. A birthday gift for Gran's eightieth. I knew she loved Emily Dickinson's work, and I wanted to get her something that she'd cherish.

I took the books and jumper and piled them back into the old suitcase then shoved it under my bed out of the way. I couldn't think about it anymore. As soon as I could I got rid of Ryan and continued rooting in Gran's room without him. I couldn't believe that it was the last room to clear. Yes, the gardens still needed work but Gran's room was the last to be cleared. Once it was empty, Ryan could stay outside and I could renovate.

* * * *

The next morning I gave a local estate agent a ring.

"I've not quite finished the renovation but I'd just like an idea of how much to market the place for once it's finished."

"Of course, of course. Well, I'm up Thornleydale way on Monday, I could pop in about two o'clock?"

"That's perfect, thanks."

Just as I finished on the phone Ryan knocked.

"Morning, boss, I'm going to get the rubbish cleared before we do owt else."

"Sure" — I smiled — "no problem."

"They're predicting snow to hit tomorrow, so we need to get this cleared while we still can."

"Oh, right, yes."

"Okay then, well, I'll load up and get going."

He sped past me and I shrugged. Something was weird about him but I couldn't put my finger on it.

After he whizzed past me again, hands filled with rubbish bags, I jogged upstairs and back into Gran's room out of his way. It seemed that I'd not have him around for very much longer. I was hoping he'd undertake the landscaping but that would keep him outside and away from me.

Talk about mixed emotions. I was split down the middle between two visions of Ryan. In one he was the hotter, older version of the Ryan I had been mates with as a little kid, and in the other he was still the bastard I knew from high school using me for some kind of evil end. My hormones, my emotions were invested in version one but my brain was more inclined to believe the evil version. I didn't have much evidence to support the second view but I just couldn't forget all those years of nastiness.

Ryan clunked up and downstairs for a while then yelled up to tell me that he was going out. I continued piling books, magazines, handkerchiefs and other such random items into black bags. It seemed to me that Gran had kept things she cared about inside containers. Anything outside of them was flotsam and jetsam. Her favored books were in bookcases — volumes of classic poetry, *Jane Eyre* and *Pride and Prejudice* knocked covers with James Bonds and Cadfael mysteries. Those were the tales she'd revisit time and time again.

I felt bad with every bag of stuff I threw away. Gran had needed someone and I'd been too wrapped up in my own world to see it. I'd gotten a letter from Gran a week or so after her eightieth.

Dear Janet,

Thank you so much for the thoughtful present. I love Emily Dickinson and those old books are truly delightful. I hope you're keeping well. Sorry you couldn't make my party. I know why, but I do miss you. Don't you think we could meet somewhere, though? You wouldn't have to come here, maybe we could meet in Leeds or even Manchester. I could get a lift to the train station, spend a night in a hotel. It would be fabulous to see you, you know. The best kind of present.

Anyway, think about it. I had a lovely party – the ladies from church put on a buffet and all the village attended. I'm a lucky lady indeed. Even Ryan came. He's turned into quite the nice young man, you know. His girlfriend is an acquired taste, but he helps me out a lot. Mows my lawn and such for a complete pittance. It was a shame you two ever fell out, you were such good friends. I know he was a mischievous monkey but he always had good intentions.

Anyway, less of my old lady ramblings. Please think over my offer, I'd love to see you.

Love,

Gran x

I hadn't gone to see her. I hadn't been able to get out of my filming schedule at the time and when I'd finished that movie I'd gone straight on to the next and soon she'd just stopped asking. I think she'd gotten to a point where she couldn't get anywhere else, she wasn't mobile enough. I was such an idiot to miss out on the opportunity when it arose but I had been naïve and believed that every film would be my last.

I'd been working for an hour or so when I heard a knock at the door. I ran down to answer it.

"It's bloody brass monkeys out there." Ryan shivered when he came back in. "Brr. Not surprised it's going to snow."

"I'll make us a brew then we can get on." I smiled.

"Oh, you're a Godsend." He followed me through to the kitchen.

I flicked on the kettle.

"Are you going back to America for Christmas?" he asked, pulling out a chair from the dining table.

"No, I'm not," I replied. "Nothing to go back there for yet. I start filming a new movie at the beginning of January, though, so I'll be going back just after Christmas."

"Oh, you going back to Leeds to see relatives then, while you're over this side of the pond?"

"Nah, I'll just be here on my own. I've got no family left now, I'm afraid." I wished he'd stop asking personal questions. I was trying to keep a distance from him.

"Oh, that's sad."

"Well, it is the way it is. What'll you be doing for Christmas?" I hoped that directing a question back at him would deflect him from asking me any more.

"At this rate, nothing much. I've got to pay every penny I earn to pay off this ridiculous debt." He sighed.

"Isn't Eve working now? Won't she help with the bill?"

"You'd think so, wouldn't you? But she's getting an absolute pittance considering all the hours she's putting in."

The kettle clicked. I poured water onto the tea bags and stirred then put the lid on the old brown fired teapot to let it brew.

"Well, I might be able to help you a bit there. I hired you to help me clean out the interior but, as you know, the exterior needs some TLC, too. Do you reckon you could tidy up the front and back for me?"

"Sure." He nodded. "I reckon so. Should only take a few days, all told. It'll be easier to do all the hacking now while it's cold and the foliage is off most of the trees and bushes and things."

"How much would you charge me?" I poured a cup of tea each then added milk. Carried it over to the table and laid a cup before him.

"Well, it'll be cold and it's much more physical work, especially if the ground's hard as nails. So it'd be more than I charge for the interior work."

"I'll give you a grand. How's that?" The poor guy needed the money. And I knew he'd do a good job. I didn't mind paying out for good work at all.

"That'd be great, yeah, thanks."

"Will you start on it as soon as we finish Gran— I mean Mary's room?" *What a slip to make. I have to remember I'm Katrina, not Janet!*

"Yeah, as long as the snow's not too deep I should be able to." He blew gently on the contents of his cup.

"Excellent, thanks."

We fell into silence as we sipped. The sky outside the kitchen window was an ominous shade of dark and gloomy. Wet stuff was going to fall from the sky and if it was cold enough then it was going to fall as snow.

"So you'll be selling this place, then, I guess?"

"Yeah, that's the plan. I'll have my fun renovating it then I'll sell it on, for profit, I hope." I nodded. "Got someone coming to value it on Monday, in fact."

"Excellent. I bet it'll sell well. It's the prettiest location in the whole village in my opinion."

"It is beautifully located," I agreed.

"Will you do more renovations on other properties then?" he asked.

The warmth of the cup in my hand and the scent of sweet, earthy tea enveloped my senses in a comforting blanket. So I just kept answering his inquiries. I was at peace for once.

"I don't know. I suppose it depends if I make money and if I'll get the time to do them between films. I'll definitely view them first, though."

I chuckled and Ryan smiled.

"You got plenty of flicks lined up for the New Year, then?"

"I'm not allowed to say." I grinned. "I'd be in trouble."

"Oh, yeah, of course. I wasn't trying to pry. Have you enjoyed your foray into the world of real estate?"

"Sort of." I laughed. "It's been more work than I anticipated but it's been good to do something different for a change. I get sick of pretending to be someone I'm not sometimes."

"I bet." He sipped at his brew, large hands wrapped round and interlocked. "Anything gets a bit repetitive when it's all you do day in, day out."

"Does that mean you don't enjoy your job anymore?"

"I never really did." He sighed. "I had plans to go into business, run my own company. A firm of electricians and gas men that would go out to all the isolated villages, and do the jobs the big city guys wouldn't touch. But it never panned out, so I got stuck being an odd job man. My dad was big in electricals, you see, so I learnt a lot through him. I'm an electrician, gas safe, I can make things from wood, I can keep a garden clean and tidy, but don't ask me to plant anything for you. I did loads of chores as a kid and a teen and I still seem to be doing them now."

"Maybe one day you'll be able to follow your dream." I sipped my tea. I felt sorry for him. He'd always wanted to inherit his dad's business.

"I doubt it, Katrina. I'll never get the capital together and my credit is now shot to buggery. I'll be stuck doing this till the day I die, I think." Ryan sighed, ran his fingers through his hair then knocked back the last of his drink. "Anyway, best get back to work before that snow comes down."

"Good plan. If it does snow overnight I won't expect you to come in tomorrow."

"If I can, I will. I need every penny I can get right now."

"I'll pay you the day even if you don't make it in," I insisted.

"No, I don't need charity." He stormed out of the kitchen.

"I didn't mean it like that," I shouted after him. He ran upstairs, and I slammed down my cup then followed him.

"I mean we get paid even if the movie's rained off or delayed for some reason. I just thought it should be the same for you. To guarantee you'll work for me, you know." I stepped into the bedroom and looked over at him, digging away and throwing things away as though his life depended on it.

"I didn't mean to be offensive." I put the full bottom lip wobbling, heart-felt, heart-string-pulling act on. I guessed it worked.

"Sure, I know, sorry. I'm just being a wanker. Thank you, it's good of you to offer to do that for me."

I thought he was going to say something more or ask me something but he just shrugged and kept on cleaning.

By the end of the day the bedroom was cleared. I still needed to clean down the sides and sort through the wardrobe and chest of drawers.

"I'll take this rubbish with me in the van and I'll dump it when I can," Ryan said.

"All right, thanks, Ryan. So I'll see you tomorrow… Or not. Depending how it goes."

"Brilliant, yeah. I'll bring my gardening equipment with me."

"You can see yourself out, right? I just want to keep going with this, try to get all the cupboards and stuff emptied, too. I'm desperate to start the actual renovating."

"Yeah, no problem. I'll see you tomorrow, all being well."

"Sure."

As the project neared its end I contemplated not seeing Ryan again and it hurt. He'd opened up a lot to me of late and it was almost like old times with us talking about anything and everything. It was good to have someone to chat with.

And of course there was the kiss. If I'd thought my attraction to Ryan had lessened over time, that kiss had proved that to be untrue. I couldn't stop thinking about that interlude in the back of the taxi. In the shower, eating a meal, lying down to sleep — whenever I wasn't thinking about something particular my mind fixated on that kiss and the heat of Ryan's body against mine.

So I tried not to stop for too long. I just kept working to keep busy to distract myself from the pleasant yet scary feelings that I was developing for Ryan.

* * * *

It was later that night that I discovered the suitcase filled with the books, Gran's jumper and my letters to her had disappeared. I was going to sort through it, keep the bits I wanted and file the books away to sell once I was back in the States—but the whole case was gone.

"The bastard," I yelled, slamming my hand down on the bedside. "The fucking bastard."

Who else could have taken it? I was convinced it could only have been him. I grabbed my phone off the bedside cabinet and stabbed at his number.

"You are a complete idiot," I snapped when he answered his phone.

"I beg your pardon?"

"You're an idiot. If you'd just asked I'd have lent you the damn money you needed, I'd have worked something out so you could have worked it off. I'm a fucking millionaire, after all."

"Katrina, is that you? What's the problem? Why are you so angry?" He sounded genuinely bewildered.

"Like you don't know!" I raised my free arm and dropped it back to my side, bunching the fist.

"I don't— What's the matter?"

"The books, they're gone," I snapped, "and you're the only person who had access to this house today."

"The books? What books? Oh, the books. Shit. They've gone? Are you sure?"

"Of course I'm bloody sure, the case has gone and its entire contents." I shook my head. "Look, I know it's you. I'm disgusted, but I understand why you did it. Please just return it before you do something you regret. If you do, I might be able to forgive you and keep you on. But if it's not returned don't bother coming back to work."

"Katrina, I didn't take it but I'll do my damnedest to track it down." He sighed.

I could hear the panic in his voice, clearly because he'd been found out.

"Don't lie, Ryan. Just bring it back."

I threw down my phone and paced up and down shaking my head and growling at myself. How could I have been so stupid? I didn't care about the books but if Ryan stopped to look at the letters and photos he'd find me out.

I couldn't sleep so I continued cleaning. I went through Gran's clothes, trying hard not to breathe in too deeply, the scent of her on her clothing making me choke up with the memories. The snow had arrived and the wind whipped it in flurries outside the window as I cleared off Gran's dressing table.

It looked as if I'd be snowed in. Not for the first time, but it certainly wouldn't be as enjoyable as the last.

* * * *

Rocky Mountains, 2010

It was *Snow Mountain* I was filming. One day a snowstorm hit and we couldn't film so I was confined to my trailer and bored. After a few hours there came a loud and demanding rap on the door, and when I opened it, David Stretford stood there, hunched under the oppressive snowfall.

"What the dickens are you playing at? Come in, come in."

I stepped back, and he jumped up the steps, letting me slam the door behind him.

"I'm bored." He sighed. "To damn tears in my trailer on my own. Thought you might be too."

"I am a bit," I admitted. "Do you want a cup of tea?"

"Tea? Fuck no. Do you have coffee?"

I nodded. "Milk? Sugar?"

"Just milk, thanks." He threw off his jacket and dropped onto the sofa.

I was in awe of David, an established Hollywood star and intensely handsome. *Snowy Mountain* was only my second film and I felt terribly inadequate. It was a new type of role for me, in a new place, with stunts and prop work that scared me. David was a good man, though — did all he could to help me relax.

He was easy to work with and even easier on the eye. Dark hair and eyes that shimmered as much as his perfect white teeth. I was completely in his thrall. Even though he was a bit of a diva, I still admired him.

"So what are you up to in here, my English rose?"

"Nothing much." I shrugged. "Just watching a bit of telly."

"Telly," he chuckled. "You Brits say the funniest things."

"I'll have you know it's you lot who do weird things with our language," I replied with a chuckle. "It's called English for a reason, you know."

"Well, sure. We just took what we were given and improved on it."

"Cheeky bugger," I exclaimed. "I'd watch what you're saying or you might get a surprise in your coffee!"

"Good point — English is such an awesome language."

We sat and chatted, flicked through the TV channels and relaxed in each other's company. After a while I stopped thinking of him as David the star and just thought of him as Dave the bloke.

"You're a special lady, Katrina." He sighed as the last of the natural light dissipated.

"Well, thank you. You're pretty wonderful yourself."

I thought he was being silly again, as we'd been silly for most of the afternoon, but when I looked at him his face told me otherwise.

"No, seriously. Most of my leading ladies I won't give the time of day to — they're vain and vapid — but you, you're fun and clever and fucking gorgeous, too."

I blushed and looked down, not sure what to say.

He tipped up my chin with his finger and made me look into his eyes.

"Oh, now don't tell me I've rendered you speechless."

I nodded against his finger.

"Hmm, well I'll have to take advantage of this sudden stilling in your lips then."

He leaned forward and brushed my lips with his. I didn't move, I barely breathed, and he pressed harder against me, mashing his mouth to mine. It was as though my reluctant engine had finally turned over. The machinery of arousal ground into action and I wrapped my arms around him and pulled him closer.

It was a little later when his shirt was removed and my bra had been flung into some far corner that I realized I was half naked with one of the most coveted men in the world. Millions of women swooned over this guy and not only was I getting to play at kissing and caressing him in the movie, but I was also getting to do it for real.

He was good, really good. We spent the rest of the day together on my sofa, over the table — he made use of a spatula in a way that expanded my horizons and pinked my butt cheeks — and we ended up in my bed.

"You're insatiable." David kissed my neck, just in the crook beneath my chin, as he lay cradled in my arms.

"Oh, I don't know, I'm pretty sated right now." I stroked his hair and looked out of the window to the clear, night sky. "It's stopped snowing."

"Maybe we'll be shooting tomorrow then, damn. I was hoping to stay shacked up in here with you."

"I'm feeling awful poorly," I purred. "I think I might have the flu."

"Funnily enough, I'm developing a cough." He hacked out the fakest cough ever.

"We should stay here in quarantine together for at least a day or two so we don't pass it on."

"I agree."

"Good."

It was an exciting and entertaining few days but once we got back to filming, we slowly parted. It wouldn't work, we both knew that. We had great chemistry but that does not a relationship make. *Chemistry, the bane of my life.* It'd have been so much easier if I'd gotten a number at birth so that when I met the other person with the same number we'd be the perfect match. That'd be that—love, marriage and happiness for ever after amen.

But no, I and every other human was cursed with the gift of chemistry.

Chapter Fourteen

Ryan Taylor

"Eve!" The sound climbed from the back of my throat, vibrated through me and filled the whole house.

"What do you want? I was just going for a bath. It's been a fucking long day and they want me in at six again tomorrow."

"What've you done?" I asked, walking up the stairs. "Confess to me now and we'll take them back and make it all right."

"What?" She shook her head. "What do you mean?"

"Oh come on." The words shook in my head as it moved from left to right. "That was Katrina on the phone."

"What did she want? Why's she got you so riled up?"

"Katrina has sacked me, Eve, and not because of anything I've done. Although I was stupid enough to tell you about the books this afternoon."

"The books? You mean them expensive poems? I've lost you, though. What've they got to do with anything?"

"Eve, are you truly trying to play the innocent here? The books have been stolen. I told you she'd just shoved them under her bed in the old sea-green case and now it's gone."

"It's gone? Fuck." Eve's eyes widened and the color dropped from her cheeks.

"Yes, but you already knew that. Now where is it? Where've you hidden it?" I tore into the bedroom and ripped open the wardrobe door.

"Ryan, stop it," she screeched. "Please, it's not there."

I ripped out her dresses and kicked around her shoes until she grabbed hold of my shoulders and pulled me back.

"I didn't take them," she whispered. "I promise you, I didn't."

"Eve." I let out a shuddering breath. "Just stop it, stop it now. She says if I take the case back we'll forget it ever happened, she'll employ me again. She's going to pay me a grand to do the gardens at Mary's place. If I can get the credit card company to give us a few days' grace, I'd be able to pay them off with that thousand, Eve. Well, the first installment anyway. So come on, own up."

Eve shook her head.

"Eve," I growled. "Come on. Fuck, I know we've done some dumb shit over the years, we've done some stuff that's been closer to illegal than I'd admit in a court of law, but we've always done it together. Stupid, mad, irresponsible, whatever. But we've always done it together. Together, Eve. I can't believe you'd do something like this and betray my trust."

"I haven't, Ryan." Eve gulped. "I didn't steal it." Her eyes were wet with tears, but I couldn't believe her.

"I only told you. Only me, you and Katrina know about those books. She won't have stolen them, they're her own—"

"Maybe she misplaced it, put it somewhere else and forgot?" Eve sounded desperate.

"Don't be stupid. She'd have thought of that before ringing me."

"She might not have—"

"Shut up, Eve. It's not her, it can't be her. I know her, you don't. I know her and I like her, actually. She's a fucking good boss and I'm so pissed off at you right now because I didn't steal those books and I'm getting the blame for it. And you're lying to me. Lying. To. Me."

"I'm not." The quickness of the response didn't ring true.

"You are lying. Don't talk to me until you're ready to confess. In fact, don't even talk to me then. Just put the case somewhere I'll find it and I'll take it to Katrina tomorrow."

I turned around and headed down the stairs then out of the front door. It was only when I was in the center of the village green that I realized I was up to my ankles in snow and I wasn't wearing a coat.

I tried to work out all the options open to me. Basically, I was fucked if Eve didn't come clean. And it had to be Eve. She'd rung me when I was having my lunch to find out when I was going to be home. And I had told her what we'd found. It was exciting, I'd wanted to share it. I'd almost wanted her to tell me to nick it. It was easy money just waiting to be made.

But she didn't, she hadn't even seemed really interested, and now she'd gone and done something stupid on her own and I wasn't sure I'd ever be able to trust her again. All the problems we'd had, all the upset she'd caused, I'd always known that we were in it together. Inseparable. Her working on her own disturbed me. We'd been arguing a lot at the time, but that didn't worry me so much. It was part of our relationship — it'd always been up and down, from hatred to love in a blaze of passion and sexual tension. I dealt with that, it was part and parcel of being with Eve. Although the passion and sexual tension had been missing for a long while. Maybe things were changing.

"You know, Ryan, I'll never change," she'd told me once after hitting me over the head with one of my mum's most precious vases.

"I know, love. I'm a thrill seeker, that's why I love you."

It had to be. I'd always loved danger and adventure. I loved Janie but I had to drag her into anything even vaguely dangerous kicking and screaming. Eve, however, seemed to thrive on not knowing what would happen next. She had dragged me into trouble more times than I could remember. However, I was sure that it was Janie's common sense that had kept me alive a time or two.

"But if I jumped in there now it'd be such a rush, I'd be down at the sea within minutes," ten-year-old me had said looking at the swirling, shifting black water of the swollen river. It had looked like fun to me. Something like the rapids at a swimming pool that would pull you along and fling you around at speed.

"You'd be dragged under and you'd be dead in seconds, you moron." Janie had sighed, placing herself between me and the river.

I'd looked at her, then round her to the swirling gray. I'd tried to think of something good to say, something compelling.

"But I can swim dead good, I'd be fine."

I'd failed miserably.

"No," she had snapped, grabbing my arm, "you'd be dead, Ry. Dead. Don't you dare do it, don't you dare."

The tears in her eyes had shown me that she believed what she had said.

"All right." I'd humphed. "But you're such a spoilsport."

"Yeah, well, you're alive because of this spoilsport. Now, come on, Gran's baking today. Let's go and see what."

A self-destructive gene was often blamed in films and things for a bad guy's urge to kill or steal or aim for world domination. I wondered if I had one. Since being small I'd thrown myself off things and under things, pulled dog's tails, explored dark, twisted parts of the woods, eaten berries off trees—and endured the resulting intestinal distress—and basically dug around in shit that wasn't good for me.

Maybe that was all that held me to Eve. That urge to destroy myself. Walking back toward the house I looked around me. Thornleydale was my life, had always been my life, but was it just a trap? I was expected to be a certain way here. If I went to London I could be a different man—Manchester even, New York or Dubai. Anywhere else in the world I could start fresh. Lose the label and become the man I might have been if I'd been able to run away that day with Janie.

If Janet had still been in my life I'd not be up to my neck in a sea of crap. Janie wouldn't have run me into thousands of pounds' worth of debt. Janie would have looked after me. At the end of the lane I turned around and headed toward Mary's house. It was the one place in the world where I'd ever been accepted with open arms. I knew Katrina was pissed off with me, but she was simply the new owner of the old place. It still contained all the most comforting memories I possessed.

Dad never wanted me at home, Mum just wasn't mother material. I couldn't blame her—she was bullied into having me and my sister Helen by Dad. She didn't do mothering, though. It just wasn't her. The only time I'd ever gotten positive approval from home was when I'd done what Dad had wanted me to do, and I tried, I really tried, but most of the time I failed. So in the end I'd decided it wasn't worth the hassle.

But no matter how much I screwed up, Mary and Janet had welcomed me back with open arms. I knew they weren't at the house, that Katrina was and if she saw me she'd probably call the police, but I wasn't thinking. I needed the comfort and that place was the only place I'd ever been welcomed in my whole life.

Down at the bottom of the garden was a break in the hedge and just on the garden side of that Janie and I had made a den. We used some old concrete slabs and a few old pallets. And the slates that had fallen off my dad's shed. Well, maybe they had been pushed but he could never prove that. It was a little cozy, as it had been built for two children, but it was relatively dry and it still felt like a refuge from the world.

Katrina was a good woman and the fact that she thought I was a thief—that I'd steal from her— tied up my insides. She was a stunning woman, beautiful. Of course I thought with my dick when around her, what man wouldn't? But past that, I really liked her. She reminded me of Janie in a way. I mean, not how she looked. But some of her mannerisms, her humor and her heart. She was a good woman and a great boss.

Which probably explained why Eve would do such a thing. To make sure I didn't stay pally with her. Eve was paranoid, completely convinced that one day I'd leave her. Clearly the Hollywood movie star was a threat.

"Stupid cow," I cursed.

I watched over the house. I couldn't see any lights on but I knew Katrina was in there somewhere. The snow was coming down heavy and no one would be getting out of Thornleydale for a while. The cold seeped into my bones, I shivered, but I didn't think of moving. I had nowhere to go.

* * * *

Copse Cottage, 1988

"What are you doing here?" Janie exclaimed as light dawned on Gran's snow-covered lawn.

"I was s-s-s-sleeping." My teeth chattered.

"Ryan, you idiot, you could have died out here! Why are you— Never mind. Come on, we'll get you into Gran's, warm you up."

She helped me ease out of the den, took off her hat and scarf then put them on me. She slipped her mittens onto my hands. They were all bright pink, but I didn't care. I was grateful of the warmth.

"Have you been there all night?" Mary asked when Janie pulled me into the kitchen.

I nodded.

"Ryan," she sighed. "Oh, my dear, misguided boy. You could have stayed here."

She shooed me through into the living room and pulled her rocking chair up to the fireplace and sat me on it. Janie made me a steaming hot mug of tea and Mary stoked the fire.

"Do you want me to tell your dad where you are?"

"No, no." I shook my head violently.

"They'll be worried sick."

"They won't." I pouted, crossing my scrawny arms across my body. "They don't care about me."

"Oh, darling, I'm sure they do. But okay then, you can spend some time here getting warm then you'll have to go home."

"I'm running away, Mary. Don't make me go back home." My bottom lip wobbled, and hot tears scalded down my still cold cheeks.

"Oh now, now, now." Mary stood from stoking the fire, winced, then wrapped an arm around me. "It'll all be all right. Whatever happened, I'm sure it's not that bad."

I sobbed into her arms and she held me close.

"You're just a little boy, Ryan. Little boys get into mischief now and then and adults shout at them. But adults shout because they're worried and want to keep their children safe. I'll make sure your dad doesn't shout at you anymore, okay? But you will need to go home."

"I know." I sniffed. "But I don't wanna."

"Oh, my dear, you'll soon find out that growing up has a whole lot to do with learning to do things we don't want to do." She reached into her cardigan pocket and pulled out a flower-dusted hanky. "Blow your nose, sweetheart. You don't want Janie to know you've been crying."

A few moments later, in came Janie carrying a hot water bottle and dragging a duvet behind her. I shoved the wet hanky down the back of the seat.

"I got 'em, Gran."

"Oh, good girl." Mary took them off her, placed the red rubber container on my stomach then covered me with the duvet.

Janie walked over and sat on the sofa. "You feeling warmer?"

"Yeah."

"Good."

We talked, played word games and laughed. I thawed out and felt at peace. Not for the last time did I wish I lived with Mary. But she was good to her word — she took me home and made sure Dad didn't yell at me. He waited until she'd left to do that.

But Mary's was home for me then. Always would be, no matter that she was dead and gone. She was the epitome of love. Her and Janie.

* * * *

Wakefield Secondary, 1991

"Who did it, Janie? Which boy was it?" Mr Franklin, the head, asked as he stared down his nose at us all.

We looked at Janet, all of us first year lads shaking in our oversized blazers. It was well known that Mr Franklin was harsh on newbies and a pussy cat by the time you made it to the last year. If you made it to the last year. I'd already been hauled into his office twice. Once for making a dinner lady cry and the other time was because I'd broken the windscreen of the science teacher's car with a cricket ball. I didn't even play cricket.

I had dropped a lighted spill into Janie's bag. It hadn't been near her at the time but it had burnt all the contents to a cinder. I hadn't been expecting that, daft as that sounded. I hadn't realized that her bag had been open. I'd just thought it'd singe the outside. Janet knew it was me. I knew she'd seen me. I was about to be expelled.

"Mr Franklin, I don't know, it all happened so fast." She shook her head and looked to her toes.

"I know, my dear, but these jokers were closest to your bag, so it must have been one of them. Just try to recall what you saw so we can bring the culprit to justice."

Janet looked at me. I tried not to let my emotions show. She would dump me in it. We'd only been in school a term and a bit, and already I'd discovered Eve and started being nasty to Janie. I'd made her cry on three occasions I knew of.

"I don't know, Mr Franklin. I... I... I didn't see him properly. I can't say."

"All right, my dear, thank you for trying. Now, you go back to lessons, I'll sort this out."

All five of us got lunchtime detentions for a fortnight but I wasn't expelled because Janet wouldn't rat me out.

A similar situation happened in the fourth year. I wasn't being a bastard to her that time but she caught me rifling through Miss Livingstone's drawers. I was looking for Eve's mobile phone, but, of course, Janie didn't know that. For days afterwards I was poised to be pulled in and accused, but I never was so Janie must have kept quiet. Even though I called her names, even though I made all my friends call her names, even though I made her life a misery at every step.

* * * *

I had done all kinds of stupid things just because Eve wanted me to prove that I loved her above everything else. I had back then, or at least I thought I had. It had become clearer the older I'd gotten that I wasn't in love, because love didn't leave you feeling guilty and hollow. I wanted to sit in the den all night, to freeze there, to give Eve something to mourn but I couldn't. Out of the whole mess I found purpose. To get rid of the woman who'd held me back for so long and to find out where my best friend in the entire world lived. I had to find Janet and tell her just how sorry I was.

She would probably tell me to fuck off but at least I would have apologized, tried to make it right again. When I got back home, Eve was gone. No note, our suitcase was missing from the wardrobe and there was no indication that we'd had the argument we'd had. I rang her, but she never answered.

Cold and angry I looked through the kitchen and found half a bottle of vodka. I wrapped myself in several blankets, unwilling to put the heating on with the upcoming bill in mind, and drank myself stupid. Well, more stupid. When I reached the bottom of the bottle I decided it would be a good idea to ring Katrina.

"Katrina, it's me, Ryan. Look, I'm sorry. I did tell Eve about the case and the books and stuff. It was stupid of me but it was such a good story, I couldn't help myself. And I think she's taken it. The suitcase and the books. I went mental at her, Katrina, I did. But she won't confess she's got it. But I'll get it out of her and I'll get your property back to you, I promise. Please don't sack me, Katrina, please don't." At that point I sobbed like a child. How pathetic. "I need this job, I need the money. I have to pay my debt and if I don't... God, I don't know what I'll do. And I like you, really like you. Not just want to shag you. Shit, that was coarse, but you must have blokes telling you they want to fuck you all the time, you're fucking gorgeous. But, Katrina, I like all your other things too, not just your tits and arse. Your brain and your heart and all that squishy emotional stuff. I feel sick knowing you think so badly of me. I didn't steal it, Katrina, I promise I didn't. I'm sorry, please forgive me."

I clambered up the stairs and passed out on the bed.

* * * *

The next morning my head spun and my stomach rotated in the opposite direction. I was being torn apart from the inside out. Eve wasn't home and I remembered the phone call I'd made. I threw up, washed up and looked out over Thornleydale village. Snow had fallen all night, my van was ensconced up to the top of the wheel rims. We were snowed in and I didn't know where Eve was.

I tried her phone again, but she didn't answer. Next I rang every one of her friends written down in the household address book but no one had seen her or heard from her. I wrapped up warm and headed out into the white blankets of snow. No one else was out—no one else was daft enough to be out. I made a quick pass around the village but when my fingers and toes went completely numb I decided it was fruitless. I was sure Eve wouldn't be out anywhere— she was lying low at some friend's house, waiting for me to forgive her.

She'd be waiting for a damn long time. Walking through the village square I saw Katrina coming out of the shop. Indecision hit. I stopped in my tracks. Part of me wanted to go over and talk to her. Maybe face to face she'd be able to see that I was telling the truth. I walked toward her, but then I stopped. Maybe she'd hit me, maybe she'd scream at me. Having a famous woman shout 'Thief!' at me wouldn't do my reputation any good. And it might have seemed that only me and her stood there in the center of the cotton wool-wrapped village but it would be overheard.

I stood, hesitating for so long that she saw me. I tensed but Katrina didn't yell, she simply turned up her nose, shifted her stride and turned away from me. Without a word she made me feel like shit. When I got in I rang round all of Eve's mates again, left another message on her mobile and felt my fuse burn shorter and shorter. I checked how much money I had saved from working with Katrina. Just short of two grand. It wasn't nearly enough to settle the credit card bill. There was nothing in the house worth selling, no one I could go to for a loan. Not the banks, I'd tried that. They'd laughed me out of there even with my well thought out business plan. There was no one personally known to me who'd give me that kind of money either, and if they did, well, what good would it be? I'd just be in more debt, unable to pay that. It would be more than a vicious circle—it'd be a downright fatal one.

What would happen if I couldn't pay the bill? I didn't really know, but, whatever it was, it was bound to leave a huge dent in my credit score and I could kiss goodbye to any ideas about ever owning a business of my own. I was at the lowest ebb I'd ever been at and I had no one beside me. No Eve, no Janie, not a soul. I was alone and miserable and couldn't see how that could possibly change.

Chapter Fifteen

Katrina Quinn

"You do know we wouldn't be able to put this lovely home on the market in its current condition, don't you?"

"Oh, I know. I need to clear the carpets and redecorate." I nodded. It needed freshening up to get a decent sale.

"No, Miss Quinn, that's not what I mean. Look at the light switches and plug sockets — they're the old style black ones. I believe, then, that the wiring isn't up to standard. The whole place is going to need rewiring. I mean, you can confirm it with an electrician, but I assure you it needs doing."

"Really?" I sighed.

"Yes, really. And you mustn't decorate until it's done or you'll just end up decorating twice."

"Oh," is what I said — my brain was silently spewing curse words.

"We could put it on the market like this, but you're not going to get much for it, if anything. The market for this kind of property is rich—city types wanting a country getaway. They don't want a project—they want something they can move straight into. The rewiring won't be cheap, but the few thousand outlay will get ten, maybe even twenty thousand extra on your sell price."

"So, I have to have the works done if I want to sell the property?"

"Yep, that's the top and tail of it. I've got the number of a local guy, he's reasonably priced and comes well recommended." Grant, the estate agent, passed me a familiar-looking business card. On closer inspection, it was Ryan's.

"In this weather, you're not going to be able to get anyone in from outside and Ryan's the only guy in Thornleydale qualified to deal with electrics. If you want a quick turnaround, he's your man."

"Well, thanks. I'll get this sorted out then I'll invite you back when all the works are done."

"Great, I look forward to it. This house, when it's finished, will sell very well, I'm sure of it."

I saw Grant out then slumped onto Gran's rocking chair. I couldn't hang about. I only had until the New Year to finish the place as my agent had secured me the leading role in the big fantasy adventure film I'd been coveting. It was incredibly exciting and I was sure that the positive publicity from getting the role would wipe out the infamy of my last.

So I had to finish the renovation in just over two weeks. And to do that I had to get the place rewired. And to do *that* I had to re-employ Ryan. What other choice did I have? I didn't need the money from the sale, but it was ingrained in me not to do a half-hearted job. Gran would have bent my ear if she'd even known I was contemplating underselling her house.

The snow had blocked in the valley. I'd have to contact Ryan, there was nothing else for it. Even though I wished I didn't have to, especially after the drunken voicemail he had left me. Did he really want to shag me or had that just been the beer talking? Part of me wanted to ask. The sensible part was telling me not to be so stupid and leave that topic of conversation well alone.

"Hi, Ryan, it's Katrina."

"Hiya. I just want to say I'm sorry. I was going to talk to you on the green earlier but you walked away and I thought you might be busy and I didn't know what to say but I want to say sorry. I'm really sorry and I didn't take the case, I promise I didn't, but I was stupid to tell Eve about it and—"

"Take a breath, Ryan." I stopped the wittering in its tracks. "The whole house needs rewiring before I can sell it on. The estate agent tells me you're the only man in the village who can do it."

"Yeah, that's right. I did notice they were the old style switches when we were working, but I wasn't sure if you'd want it all rewiring or if you'd leave it to the new owners."

"Apparently I have to, to sell the place. So I need it done and I need it done now. I've got to be back in the States just after New Year."

"Well, if I work every day I can get that done, I reckon. I've got all the kit in my van. Just hope I've got enough wire, I'll not be able to get out for more any time soon."

"Okay, well, come over as soon as you can, but, Ryan, I will be watching you like a hawk."

"I understand. I'll be there in half an hour. I'll have to carry some kit over, the van's going nowhere in this snow."

"Bye." I put down the phone, my heart thumping rapidly. A mix of nerves and excitement juggled around in my stomach, and I paced up and down the hall in agitation. I shouldn't have felt excited that Ryan was coming round. He was a thief. The Eve story was clearly a cover. Maybe she had gotten in and done the stealing but they'd have been in it together. That pair had been inseparable back in school and I could barely imagine it would be any different now.

"Pull yourself together," I snapped out loud. "Jeez, it's only Ryan and he's just here to work. Get that into your thick skull, woman."

I stormed into the kitchen then flicked the kettle on. Tea was the perfect solution to any kind of agitation, although Americans didn't see it that way. How that nation had survived so long I didn't know.

Following Ryan around would be a necessary evil. I couldn't trust him any longer and, although there wasn't much left of value he could steal, that didn't mean I could let him off scot-free. He had to know he was in the wrong and that I was angry with him, completely pissed off at him and scared. He hadn't indicated that he'd looked at anything else in that suitcase but what if he had? If he'd found out that I was Janet I didn't know what I'd do. It would get out to the world that I wasn't who I said I was but the very worst thing would be Ryan knowing that I'd lied to him. That I'd purposely kept him out of my life for so long.

I sat in the front room and looked out to the garden and street, well, what I could see of it. Snow was still swirling and everything was covered in a white sheet as though the whole outside world had been put away for the winter. Any kids in the village would be loving it. No school for the foreseeable future, maybe even until Christmas.

Not that I cared about Christmas anymore. It had been a great spectacle when I'd been a kid — Gran did an amazing Christmas Day dinner and an evening buffet that made the table groan under its weight. But being on my own meant I barely bothered with Christmas. Matt would put up a Christmas tree in my hallway and hang lights in the tree outside. We'd exchange presents and I'd get a few cards from folks at the studios, which I'd reply to with the same big box of bumper Christmas cards I've had for years, but otherwise it would pass relatively quietly. I'd avoid Christmas parties all I could and would spend Christmas Day studiously ignoring the fact that it was Christmas Day and that I was all alone again.

* * * *

Copse Cottage, 1999

Gran wanted us to help put up the Christmas tree in the bay window for all to see, on the opposite side to her TV. Sean had come home with me because his parents were off in some African country doing missionary work and Sean hadn't wanted to go out to visit them there.

He was really useful, he could reach the top of the six foot fake spruce to put the angel on and he was great at twiddling Christmas tree light bulbs until they worked. Of course, we ended up very sexually frustrated the time we were there. There was just no way we could have sex at Gran's, it just felt wrong and there was always someone around.

But on Christmas Day, I slipped a note into Sean's hand as I went over to Mum's to take her present from Gran. We'd spent a few hours with her in the morning, but she still insisted on keeping to herself even though Gran invited her for lunch every year.

Sean met me at the back door at ten fifteen—Gran was always in bed by ten—and I led him down through the garden to the very bottom, just before the hole in the fence that Ryan and I had ensured was always there as our doorway to adventure.

"It's not big, it's not particularly warm but it is private."

Sean was underwhelmed by the sight of the rickety den I'd built with Ryan when we'd been kids. It was pretty good as dens went, and I defended that fact.

"It's still standing and I built it with my best mate, oh, ten years or more ago. I've brought some blankets, we'll be perfectly snug."

"Well, needs must." He sighed. He wasn't very enthusiastic.

Once we'd gotten in, gotten under the blankets and I had let him feel that I had nothing on under my dress, things heated up quite nicely. I'd always dreamt of having sex in the den with a hot guy, though granted my fantasies had been firmly fixed on someone else through my formative teenage years.

It was not the most comfortable fuck I'd ever had but it was thrilling. The cool breeze caressed my thighs as I moved above him. It was easier for me to get on top, even so my head pressed up against the ceiling when I sat up straight and drove his dick into me. We didn't take off our clothes, just revealed the necessary bits. Sean lifted my dress up the back of my butt as he held onto my arse, intensifying our connection. Just as our orgasms peaked it started to snow and flakes fluttered down onto my exposed flesh, making me shiver and moan.

We sat snuggled together in post orgasmic bliss, our clothes tightened up around us as we watched the snowflakes fall unhurriedly to the ground. It was a magical moment, when I captured the joy and excitement of Christmas for one last time.

* * * *

Ryan's knock on brought me back to the real world. I took a deep breath, put down my cup then headed to the door.

"Cor, it's colder than a snowman's nuts out there," Ryan exclaimed and flew inside in a flurry of displaced snow. His toolkit was held in front of him like a battering ram.

"Hello," I replied.

"Hi." He smiled, putting down his toolkit and the roll of wire he'd had hung over his shoulder.

"Would you like a brew?" My British manners kicked in on autopilot.

"I'd love one. Then can you show me where the fuse box is? I'll need to know exactly what I'm working with, you see."

"Sure, no problem."

Ryan followed me into the kitchen and I poured his tea from the pot. He took a sip and we stood in silence. It was that kind of absence of conversation that hung like a physical weight around my neck. I felt so uncomfortable but I couldn't think of what to say.

"Shall we go find the fuse box? I can drink and walk then I can get straight to business." He broke the silence.

"Sure, what do you charge for your services?"

He waggled his eyebrow, a cheeky light in his eye, then clearly he remembered he was in the dog house with me and coughed instead. I tried desperately not to let the heat building inside me push out and make my cheeks glow.

"Well, it tends to depend on the amount of work I've got to do and the amount of materials. I reckon it'll be about two grand all in. But I won't know till I get going. Might go up a bit if the walls are in bad nick, or come down if they're not too bad."

"All right, sounds reasonable." I nodded. "I'll have to give you a check, though. I can't get out to an ATM in this weather."

"Sure, no problem." Ryan nodded then turned to me. "I know I'm asking a lot, but do you think I could have half up front? It's just—"

"Really, Ryan?" The unease in the pit of my stomach started to bubble up into mistrust. "You stole nigh on twenty grand worth of rare books from me and still try to get money up front for the work I'm asking you to do!"

"I know, I know, I'm sorry." He ran his free hand through his fringe. "I wouldn't have asked but honestly, Katrina, I'm in the shit. I've got this bill to pay and I swear to God I didn't take those books."

"No, you might not have, but I bet Eve did and you two are practically married!" I was incensed and seriously considering telling him to bugger off. I'd wait out the weather and get someone from Wakefield in instead.

"Nowhere near married." He sighed. "And she's gone missing. I've not seen her since I confronted her about your phone call on Friday. She's gone missing. Ring anyone on my phone, they'll tell you I've been ringing round, trying to chase her up ever since. Look." He put down his cup on the kitchen table and pulled his phone from his pocket. He scrolled through a few things then held the screen up for me to see.

Soz Ryan ain't seen her since our last shift together at factory. Ave you tried Karen?

"Oh." I sighed. "Right, well, fine. I don't believe you one bit but I need to get this job done so I can leave this horrid mess behind me. So I'll do you a check for one thousand five hundred pounds. It's more than half of what you said but I'm convinced it's not going to be a simple job. I'll pay whatever the balance is when you finish."

"That'd be great, thanks. But I wish you'd believe I was telling you the truth, too."

"Ryan" — I shook my head — "I'm not stupid. I barely know you. An expensive item only you and I knew about went missing. Until I get evidence otherwise, you've taken them. It's logic. I have to work on that."

He nodded dejectedly and put his phone down on the table then picked up his mug again.

"Come on, the fuse box is in the cellar, just by the stairs. I had to get to it when I first arrived."

I switched on the cellar light for the first time since I'd gotten the building. I'd been down to switch on the fuse when I'd had just a torch to light my way but hadn't bothered going down since.

"Oh, it doesn't seem so cluttered down here," Ryan chirped as we walked down the dust-laden stone stairs.

It was only when we got to the bottom, directly in front of the fuse box, that I realized how wrong his statement had been. I looked right, through a second doorway and into the main body of the cellar then looked at him.

"Well, crap." I sighed. The fuse box and gas stop cock were easily reached at the bottom of the stairs in their own self-contained area but the rest of the cellar through the second doorway was packed with junk. I saw remains of old chairs, broken toys, odd bits of wood and metal, a watering can with a hole and piles and piles of, yes, yet more books.

"God, Mary mustn't have ever thrown anything away." Ryan shook his head. "Well, the good news is the fuse box looks in pretty good nick. It shouldn't be too much of a chore to update it. However, it looks like there's some more shit needs shifting first."

"How observant of you," I snapped. "Thanks for stating the bloody obvious."

"All right, calm down. I was only —"

"I know. Just stop it, would you? I don't really want you here, I don't really want to clean out more crap, but I'm stuck with both." I'd been trying to keep calm but this was too much for me.

"Look" — Ryan turned to face me — "I'm sorry. I can't say anything else but I'm sorry. I made a stupid mistake and I regret it. It'll probably be the end of my relationship and it certainly has been the end of a pleasant working relationship with you. So maybe you could stop rubbing it in my face, all right?"

"Well, maybe you could give me my bloody property back then," I growled, pointing my finger viciously in his direction. Something snapped inside and all the anger and upset I'd managed to just hold back broke the barrier and burst forth.

"I don't have it," he yelled. "I don't have the fucking case. If I had the damn thing you'd have it back, I promise you. God, woman, are you always this paranoid?"

"Paranoid!" I shook with built-up frustration and adrenaline. "Paranoid! I've explained this to you once already, but apparently you're too fucking thick to understand. I found the books, you saw the books, and you and I were the only ones who did. The books were stolen therefore you have to have had something to do with it. Straightforward bloody logic, Ryan."

In my shaking fury I managed to take a few steps toward him so when I finished my spiel I was almost chest to chest with the man.

"I realize that," Ryan ground out between gritted teeth. "But I'm trying to tell you I didn't steal them. Yes, I stupidly told my girlfriend about the books. And yes, she probably took the damn things. For that I'm sorry, but you don't have to keep accusing me of something I haven't done, I wouldn't do, I couldn't do. Fuck, Katrina, I thought we'd become friends."

"Friends don't steal from friends," I snapped.

"I didn't steal from you," he yelled so loudly and with such intensity that I stepped backwards in fright. Sadly something, a pipe, a broom, a ball or something similar got lodged beneath my heel and I stumbled. Ryan shot his hand forward and tried to grab me but I was already stumbling and falling backwards. I tried to straighten myself but I couldn't get my feet flat to the floor. My back hit something relatively soft then something hard hit my head and I collapsed into the middle of the junk. There was a loud and long roar that I couldn't identify, and I felt things moving around me and over me. When the world around me stopped spinning and shaking I was covered with stuff. I could breath, there didn't seem to be anything directly covering my face, but when I managed to open my eyes I could see criss-crossed shadows across the light. I was either hallucinating or something was resting above me.

"Don't move!" Ryan yelled. "I'm coming in for you. Can you hear me?"

"Yes," I shouted—well, I tried to shout but it seemed to come out muffled.

"Okay, thank God for that. Are you hurt?"

"I don't know, I hit my head and my legs are under something."

"I'm coming. I'm going to move things as carefully as I can but if anything slips shout up. I don't want to disturb whatever is above you."

"Okay," I coughed. Things around me creaked but nothing moved. I could hear Ryan moving things but it sounded as though he was far away. He couldn't have been that far away, though, the cellar wasn't that big.

"Katrina?"

"Yes?"

"Just making sure you're awake," Ryan replied.

"I am," I sighed. "Well, I think I am. My head feels fuzzy."

"Hang in there, love. I'll get to you soon. I'm working as fast as I can."

"Thanks." My senses came back to me and I attempted to wiggle my extremities. My fingers moved freely but my toes weren't responding.

"I can't feel my toes," I gasped, tears slipping from my eyes.

"Don't panic, sugar. It's probably just something heavy lying on your feet. I'm getting closer to you and there's some kind of metal thing I can see. Maybe you're under that."

"Okay," I responded. "I can move my fingers."

"Good, that's great. Really positive. I'm going to heave this iron thing, might be a gate or something, out of the way. God knows how Mary got it down here. Anyway, brace yourself — some items might shift around it."

I tensed myself, heard wood squeaking and felt things slide around me. Everything went dark but the frame of whatever was around my head kept my face from being hit by falling debris.

"I can see your feet," Ryan yelled. "Katrina, can you hear me?"

"Yes," I said. "I'm okay."

"Good, good, can you move your toes now?"

I waggled them — it hurt a lot but they moved.

"Yes, it's a bit painful but they're moving."

"Great," he shouted. "Thank God for that. Okay, I should have the stuff cleared off you soon. Just keep lying still, Katrina, okay?"

"Okay," I replied, incredibly relieved to be able to feel my feet again even if they were tingling painfully with pins and needles

More detritus moved and shifted as Ryan worked to clear me.

"I can see your legs now. I've got to be a bit careful here, though. There's a lot of stuff behind you which might slide down as I shift things."

"Take your time," I gasped, suddenly choked up again. "I'll be okay."

Ryan squeezed my knee gently, sending completely inappropriate zings of lust up from where his fingers laid.

"Don't worry, love. I'm here. Won't be long now. It won't, I promise."

He moved his hands and the noise of removal was a lot louder so I knew he was moving things directly above me.

"I'm clearing a few things around the sides, shoring up the big items behind. There's a lot of things that seem to be quite precariously balanced. I want to make them as secure as possible so I can help you move without fear of another avalanche."

"Okay but, Ryan—?"

"What, love?"

"I'm scared."

Chapter Sixteen

Ryan Taylor

I'd imagined pining Katrina down many times but none of them had included an avalanche of hoarded crap. It all happened so fast. I was scared shitless when the stuff stopped moving and it went silent. I couldn't see anything of her, just the sole of one shoe. But thank God she was talking to me. It wasn't a simple extraction. Lots of the piled up junk had fallen but much more was still piled high behind her. I had to be careful not to dislodge anything important and end up crushing her again.

I cleared Katrina's legs and just touched her for comfort—hers and mine if I'm truthful but my damn cock decided to get excited. I wished it would stop dicking about and let me concentrate on the crisis at hand.

My strategy was to move the smaller things first, and find out where the larger items originated from. I cleared up to her waist that way but then it became a little more complicated.

"Okay, Katrina, there's a huge tarpaulin which has fallen down over the top of your top half. Now the bit over you is free but it seems the rest is trapped in the junk behind you. I'm going to try to fold it back slowly and carefully to see what's under it, okay?"

"Yeah," she replied shakily. "Okay. Erm, when the tarp wasn't over me I could see bands of something over my face like a cage. I don't know what it was, but thought I should tell you."

"Thanks, love." I kept my tone light and airy but my insides were rocking and rolling like a small boat on a rough sea. There were some seriously big pieces of shit behind her, a lawnmower being the most disturbing. I could just see the old-fashioned enclosure at the front but if the blades were in place behind that, we didn't want it moving at all.

I rolled the plastic back inch by inch, moving off taps and washers, plugs and plungers, screws, tools and all sorts of debris. I reached the cage-like structure Katrina had mentioned — it seemed to be an old rattan chair.

"Hello, you." I smiled down as I pushed the crinkly cover back to reveal her face. She blinked, pulling distorted faces, then when she accustomed herself to the light she smiled.

"Hiya."

She looked remarkably well intact, just a bit of dust that might have been hiding bruises and cuts.

"Right, well, the good news is, this chair is all that's over you now." I grinned. "The bad news is, it's well and truly embedded in the junk behind you. So I'm not sure what we should do."

"If you can lever up the bit resting across my chest, I could wiggle down and out," Katrina suggested.

"We'll give it a try but I want you to go slowly. There are items beneath you that could set off the avalanche above."

"Good point. I'll be careful. Are you ready?"

I positioned myself to the left of her, my hands dug under the bar of the chair and I tried not to think of the fact that my knuckles were digging into her breasts. *Damn dick, mind of its bloody own.*

"Ready," she replied.

I ignored my sex mad man bits and lifted slowly and with great care. Something creaked, a few small items bounced down from the hill, but the majority of it stayed put.

"Can you move down now? Just carefully, all right?"

"Yeah, I'm trying." She hissed in pain. "Fuck, that hurt."

"Don't damage yourself, love. If it's hurting stay still and I'll work out another way to —"

"No, I'm okay now, I am. It was just, oh, I don't know, but I'm moving. It's not so bad."

"Slowly does it," I replied. "I'm watching the pile and it's stable right now."

"Good because I'm going to have to move a bit more, my hair is trapped in something."

"Right, I've got you."

She squirmed. The groaning sound echoed around us again and things started to move.

"Are you free?"

"Yes!" Katrina exclaimed triumphantly.

"Then move, move, move!" I yelled back — the junk was going to collapse, I could see it tipping forward.

She scrambled down beside my legs — it wasn't an easy position to move from. I watched as the top of the pile teetered farther and farther forward and braced myself for impact.

"I'm out!" she screamed and pulled on my arm. "Come on."

I dropped the chair and moved back toward the entrance, awkwardly skidding and tripping on the crap that littered the way. The tide was too quick for us, so I grabbed Katrina and turned away from the avalanche, holding still and hoping to God that the lawnmower wouldn't barrel into the back of my head. The noise dissipated and the movement stopped.

Katrina collapsed against me and sobbed.

"Oh, you're okay. We're okay, now." I wrapped my arms around her and held her tightly to me. "Don't worry, love, it's going to be fine."

She clung to me, I stroked her back. The light, candy fragrance that was her signature lingered under the musty dustiness of the collapsing cellar. Her hair was soft against my cheek, her body was soft against the rest of me, and I willed my wayward dick to behave itself. The poor woman needed comfort, not poking.

"Sorry," she spouted between the tears. "Sorry, I just went a bit to pieces." She pushed herself back out of my arms.

I tried to step back but found my way impeded.

"Sorry." I smiled awkwardly. "I'd give you more room but I seem to be a little stuck."

"Hang on." She pressed herself against the junk behind her, coincidentally pushing out her breasts very noticeably under my nose. I gulped and looked up. She inched her way to the right, carefully, with a few stumbles.

"You've got a lawnmower in the back of your legs. Can you move into the space I vacated?"

I tensed my leg to move forward.

"But not yet!" she exclaimed. "Let me see if I can hold onto the mower so it stays in place—there's a pile of crap behind it."

She edged around me—there was a small sink hole in the center of the sea of junk around us. I wasn't sure, but we couldn't have been far away from the doorway.

"All right, you got it?"

"Yep," she said from behind me. "Go for it."

Stepping forward wasn't a problem but as I heard the creak of stuff behind me I lunged right.

"Let go!" I yelled and sharply turned.

Katrina was letting go but the avalanche was on the move again. I stumbled forward and put my body between her and the advancing stuff. But it stopped in its tracks within a split second.

"Might have overreacted a bit there." I shrugged, and let her go, my cheeks heating with embarrassment.

"Well, you weren't to know. Seems the stuff's lighter in this corner."

I looked behind me and sure enough there were just a few things piled around us, but the corner seemed fairly clear. A bit farther to the right the pile loomed higher but it was nothing compared to the junk in the middle of the room.

"Oh shit," I cursed when I realized that the doorway was blocked with all the crap that had tumbled around us.

"I was just thinking the same thing." Katrina laughed then winced and grabbed her abdomen.

"Are you all right?" I asked.

"Yeah, yeah, think there's a bit of bruising, that's all."

"Fine, well, let's clear a bit of this floor and sit down and think what to do next."

It didn't take long to kick and push away the couple of inches of debris behind us. I sat on the floor, back to the wall, and Katrina sat next to me, again with a wince.

"I'm sorry I got us in this mess," I sighed.

"No, it was me, I wasn't thinking."

"But if I hadn't—"

"Look," Katrina sighed. "Let's not do the blame game now, eh? Let's work out how the fuck we're going to get out of here."

"Good plan. Do you have a mobile?"

"No." She shook her head. "I left it charging this morning. You?"

I patted my pockets then remembered.

"No, I left it on the table in the kitchen before. Bugger."

"Right, so we're not calling for help, then." Katrina sighed. "We'll have to do it ourselves."

"Someone might come to the house and—"

"Ryan, the village is snowed in. No one comes to the house but you—we're not getting help any time soon."

"Right, right. Hold on. I've been down here before, with Janet when I was little. We had a fort down here one summer when it was too hot to play outside."

"I don't think making a blanket fort will help matters," Katrina snapped.

"No, wait, no. I remember there was a sink down here, in the corner. We filled it and played for hours making boats and seeing if they'd float. It's just in this corner here, where the debris is the shallowest. You can see the corner of the cupboard sticking out.

"And?" Katrina looked puzzled.

I let her off—she clearly wasn't thinking straight after having a half ton of shit fall on her head.

"And we'll have a water source, if it still works, but I'm sure it will. God knows how long it'll take to clear this lot, but if we've got water, it'll make us a bit more comfortable."

"Oh, right, yeah." Katrina nodded. "I'm sorry, I knocked my head. I don't think I'm quite with it yet."

"You're probably a bit concussed like I was. Sit still and rest, I'll go and clear this sink. It's only a little farther up the wall here, I'm sure."

"That's probably a good idea since the world is spinning around me." Katrina smiled weakly.

I didn't like how pale her face looked, but from my own experience I knew rest was probably the best thing for her. It was the best care she could get in the circumstances since I couldn't get her to a hospital.

It was relatively simple to reach the sink. I pushed all the debris outwards from me into the rest of the avalanche.

I found a watering can, but on further inspection it had a huge hole in the bottom so I discarded it. I did find an intact jar, a planter with a chip out of one corner and a copper-colored container that I thought might have been a bin once with a huge dint in the side. All of them would hold water, though, thank goodness. I put them behind me in the middle of my cleared area, for easy retrieval, and continued.

"Katrina." I looked round and her eyes were closed. "Katrina, are you all right?"

"Mmm," she replied. It wasn't exactly the most encouraging answer she could have given but at least it indicated she was still alive. I was trying not to panic but there was a distinct possibility that she had horrific internal injuries that I just wouldn't know about. Any indication that she was still breathing acted to stave off hysteria.

"Yes!" I fist bumped the air when I reached the corner of the cabinet and danced a fairly unmanly quick-step of glee when the silver draining board peeked out from below the pile of discarded plant pots.

"What's happened?"

"I've found the sink," I said, brushing the top clean. "Not got to the taps yet but I'm working on it."

"Cool. I need a drink, Gran. I'm thirsty."

She hit her head good and proper. Brains banged about, poor love. And all because of me. I pushed back the guilt trip—I didn't have time to wallow in that. A little more digging unearthed the taps and a sink filled with broken jars, old paintbrushes and various debris. I found an old tatty bit of cloth and wrapped it round my hand as I cleared out the debris. I tried not to cut myself to shreds and I also didn't want to flood the damn cellar by running the taps onto the junk.

I got the stuff out with just a few little pricks and left it in a pile on the drainer.

"Okay, here goes, Katrina. Let's see if they work."

The taps were manky looking—clearly they'd not seen the light of day for a while. I twisted and at first nothing happened. I tried again and with a crack it gave and water ran forth.

"Water!" I exclaimed, running it over my fingers then cupping some in my palm to drink. It was cold, wet and possibly poisoned from dodgy old pipes but I didn't care about that at the time.

I turned back and picked up the jar. I cleaned it out best I could then filled it to the brim. I took it over to Katrina, leaving the tap running. It had been a struggle to undo it. I had to be careful not to lose the water source completely until I'd filled my containers.

"Katrina." I offered her the jar but she didn't move or respond. "Katrina?"

I squatted beside her, prodded her arm, and she wriggled.

"Hmm?"

"I've got a drink for you, love."

"Oh, ta, Ry. My mouth tastes like a sock drawer."

Katrina had never shortened my name—it sounded weird yet felt familiar and comforting. It reminded me of Janet. She used to call it me in response to my insistence on calling her Janie.

Her eyes flickered open and I offered her the jar. She smiled and took a long swig, the water glugging in big bursting bubbles. She stopped, wiped her lips with the back of her hand then belched in a very unladylike manner.

"That's better."

"Do you want some more?"

"No, not now, I'm tired." Katrina pouted. "But my eyes hurt." She prodded around a bit and loosened what seemed to be contact lenses. She threw them onto the floor one by one and sighed. "That's better."

It was as though the knock on her head had loosened her inhibitions. She was reacting like a child who hadn't been shamed and molded into expected behaviors yet.

"Are you all right? Can you see without those in?" She nodded and yawned again. "Yeah, clear as crystal," Katrina insisted.

"Okay, if you say so."

Her eyes were a much paler blue without the contacts. I didn't realize they changed a person's eye color that much.

"I'm going to clear this junk here, we're not far from the door, and I'll get you out of this mess, okay?"

"I know you will, you always do."

That was cryptic, but clearly the woman was babbling. I wish I could wrap her in a blanket or offer her some kind of home comfort but I had nothing.

"Are you warm enough?" I asked her. I'd not felt the chill because of the constant moving, and, well, I'd had other things to think about. She'd been sitting still.

"I'm okay," she said.

I wasn't convinced.

"Here." I stood up and pulled off my jumper. "Put this on."

"Okay." She smiled fuzzily again, as though she'd had a little too much to drink. "But how do I do that?"

"No worries, I'll help. Sweaters are difficult."

"I know, right? All the different holes and stuff." She nodded sagely with the seriousness of a five-year-old.

I knelt in front of her and pondered. I'd not had any experience with dressing children, so it took a couple of moments for me to work out how the hell to get the damn thing on her.

"I'll pop this over your head. Lean forward for me, love." I wouldn't normally use the pet names with her, but they were comforting. Possibly more for me than for her.

The back of her hair was matted, and when I popped the opening of my jumper over her head she winced. I helped her push her arms into the woolen ones and pulled the middle down over her stomach. My dick observed how delicious her curves were but my brain was still concerned about the bleeding and the back of her head. I didn't have time to admire her beauty—I had to make sure she was safe.

"Katrina, just lean forward for me, love, I think you might have cut your head."

"Okay, Ryan." She dipped her head forward and I ran my fingers gently over her hair. There was definitely a lump and when I pulled my hand away blood clung to my fingers, but at least it was dark and clotted.

"You gave that a good old bump," I said, "but you'll be all right. You can bob your head back up now."

"Don't wanna, makes me go dizzy."

"I know, sweetheart, but you'll hurt your neck bent forward like that. Hang on, I know what we'll do."

I undid the buttons on my shirt. I knew all about working and walking in the cold. I had layers on and I had a lot of work to do once I had gotten Katrina comfy, so being in just my T-shirt sleeves wouldn't bother me.

Katrina giggled.

"What's so funny?"

"You." She chuckled. "Looking after me. It's funny."

"Well, I'm doing my best," I replied with a wry smile. "I'm not very good at this caring lark, though."

"Usually me doing the caring." She sighed. "But my head feels like it might come off if I start caring now."

"I know what you mean." I wadded up my shirt and placed it on the cleared bit of floor next to her.

"Here, sweetheart, lie down."

"Okay, Ry." Katrina leaned the other way but I caught her shoulder before she tumbled the wrong way.

"No, no, the other way, I've made you a pillow."

She let me lead her head in the other direction and snuggled into my shirt when she lay down. It couldn't have been very comfy. I shifted a bit more junk from around her feet, clearing her a little more space, then

moved sideward on my knees to check on her head
end of things.

I stroked a curl out of her face and she smiled. I was
about to move away when she shot her hand out and
stopped me.

"Don't go yet, Ry. Stay until I sleep. Mum won't
mind."

"Okay, love," I soothed. I wondered if she had me
muddled with someone from her childhood. Ryan
was a pretty common name. But then maybe she was
just feeling a bit addled. I knew I'd spouted a lot of
rubbish after my head knock. I'd even slept with Eve
I'd been so bloody loopy.

I slipped sideways, rested on my butt to give my
knees a rest. I was starting to feel my own bumps and
bruises as the adrenaline rushed away. The backs of
my calves killed and random spots over my body felt
bruised and irritated.

Katrina's hand rested on my chest and as her
breathing evened out it slipped down. She started a
little and pulled her arm in close to herself, cuddling
her body. She looked frail and delicate, and I hoped
beyond hope that she'd be okay. When I knew she
was asleep I turned around and faced my nemesis.

We'd joked a few times when we'd been upstairs
about cave-ins but when the junk was mostly books
and papers it hadn't seemed so menacing. Down here
it was very different. The doorway was blocked with
twisted metal, maybe littered with broken glass,
ceramics and God knew what else.

And where was I going to put the caved in crap?
There was only so much space. And one wrong move
could set off another avalanche. Before I moved
anything I filled up the three containers with water. I

switched the tap off and just hoped I'd be able to turn it on again if needed.

I placed the containers of water on the end of the drainer. I'd cleared out the space between Katrina's feet and the sink. I'd dug out a rough rectangle around Katrina and the basin. But there was still a solid wodge of crap between us and the blocked doorway. I didn't have a clue how long it'd take to get out of the cellar but I knew it wouldn't be an easy job. The workman in me had estimated it as at least a half day of hard labor.

I stood in front of the pile and thought. I could try to pile the rubbish back on top of what was already there, but if the base wasn't strong enough, we'd be in the shit again. I'd have to work things into the clear space we'd made in front of the sink. Pile it up to save space and be secure. It wasn't ideal, but we had the containers of water that would keep us going for quite a while and the sink was the one bit of space we had.

So I started by refilling the sink and clearing the small bits of debris on the edges of our area. It felt counter-productive at first but I needed a space to move things to. I needed to make them secure. I didn't know how long it took to clear the ankle-deep slurry to the sink and around it but in the end I had everything piled up in the corner as neatly as I could with junk, about six foot of open floor, a thirst and a rumbling stomach.

I had to take a break, so I sat on the floor near Katrina and drank from the filled jar.

"Oooh, my head," Katrina groaned.

"Hey, sunshine." I turned to look at her—the poor woman was looking decidedly pale.

"Oooh, my head," she repeated.

"Want some water?" I dipped the jar into the bin of water beside me and offered it to her.

"Since there's nothing stronger, water will have to do." She took a gulp and winced. "How long was I asleep?"

"I don't know—no watch—but a while, I think."

"You look knackered," Katrina continued, then sipped the water again.

"Well, I've been working on getting us out of here."

"That I approve of. I'll help. Well, when the world stops spinning."

"No, no, you need to rest, trust me. You try and do too much with that bang on your head, you'll feel a lot worse. I'm going to get back to it in a minute. Just needed a quick drink break."

"We're not going to die down here, are we?" Katrina knitted her eyebrows and leaned back against the wall beside me.

"No." I shook my head. "No way. It's not going to take too much longer to get through the doorway and we've got water."

"I'm starving." She sighed.

"I know, I am too. But you can live without food for days if you've got water."

"Sorry, Ryan, I'm not helping much, am I?" Her shoulders slumped.

"Don't worry, love, I understand. But I promise I'll get us out of here soon."

She nodded, biting down on her bottom lip. I was surprised to feel her hand over mine. Katrina didn't speak. I didn't know what to say so I just sat there, the weight of her hand over mine. I would get us out of the mess, I was determined.

"I best get back to work."

"Okay, but just stay here a minute longer, please?" she pleaded.

"Sure, sure. Are you all right?" I turned to face her.

She was smiling, but it was simply because she was straining her muscles in that direction, there was no warmth behind it.

"I'm fine," she squeaked, pulling her hand from mine, "just fine."

"Oh, Katrina." I sighed. "I'm so sorry — if it wasn't for me we wouldn't be in this stupid mess but I'll get you out of this, promise."

She burst into tears.

How the hell do you deal with a crying woman? I sat frozen in place as I tried to work out what to do next. As I had no chocolate I decided that a reassuring pat on the back would have to do. She turned to me and latched her arms around me, sobbing into my chest. I did all I could do in the situation — I wrapped my arms around her and held her close.

Talk about unexpected. She'd been screaming blue murder at me, had told me in no uncertain terms how much she didn't trust or even like me, and yet she was holding onto me as though I was the only thing preventing her from drowning. Words failed me. I stroked Katrina's back and hoped that the sobbing would stop. The poor woman was shaken, shocked and probably concussed, but I needed to carry on working to get us out of the dire situation we were in.

Katrina felt so good in my arms — soft and giving. She smelled faintly of citrus and fruit drops and in any other place at any other time I'd have been pressing to kiss her, undress her and more. Apparently being trapped wasn't terribly good for my libido, or maybe that was the hard work shifting the crap. I was worn out.

After a few minutes her sobs slowed, and she started to release her grip on me.

"Sorry," she sniveled. "I'll let you go now."

"Are you all right?" She pulled back, but I left my hands cupping her shoulders.

"Not really, but I'll hold it together." She smiled. "I can take on anything when I'm acting — I'm a complete cowardly wreck when I'm simply myself."

"You're quite allowed to be, given the circumstances. I'm going to get us out, though, okay?"

She nodded. "Go on, go, before I grab you and cry all over you again."

"Okay. Just shout if you need me, though."

"Sure. Thanks, Ryan."

"No problem." I heaved myself up and tried not to wince. I ached all over but I had a lot of work in front of me.

Chapter Seventeen

Katrina Quinn

One minute I was trapped under a deluge of stuff, the next I was waking up leaning on a masculine-smelling shirt and wearing an unfamiliar jumper. I honestly had no recollection of anything in between, which was my excuse for keeping hold of Ryan even though I was just having a Janet moment. Ryan had always been my comfort way back when and I didn't want him to move, in case he never came back again. Stupid, I know, but I blamed the head injury.

I realized as I blinked my eyes to rid them of tears that I didn't have my contacts in. A shot of fear injected my stomach with ice and crawled up my veins until I shuddered with it. Ryan was seeing my real eye color for the first time since I'd met him as Katrina. Would it be enough for him to recognize me? He hadn't already, but then the situation had him distracted. I'd just have to grab my spare pair as soon as we got out. I wasn't quite blind without them but the world was a much fuzzier place.

"Is there anything I can do?" I asked when I got sick of winding myself up with worry.

"Hmm, you should be resting," Ryan replied with a frown.

"I know, but I feel useless and trapped just sat here."

He looked around for a few moments, focusing on the floor nearest to me.

"I know — see all the bits scattered around near you? Can you pile them near the wall? I know it sounds pretty silly but the more space I have to fill with the crap blocking the door, the better."

"I can do that." I grinned. It was menial and boring, but least I knew I was contributing to the escape plan.

"Just let me move the containers of water into the area where you were sitting first, though. We don't want to block that in with this lot on the sink."

"No, true." He lifted down the impromptu water jars and I worked on getting to my feet. It wasn't that simple. It would have been quicker to list the parts of me that didn't ache and I was hungry and aware that eventually bodily functions would want to happen. I didn't want to attempt to go to the loo without an actual toilet or in the presence of a bloke.

"Don't get up," he said when he noticed me. "Just work at floor level for now."

"Okay," I agreed. It seemed the wisest course of action.

Ryan was deeply engrossed in moving stuff. It clearly wasn't an easy task — one false move and we could be engulfed in crap again. It didn't take me too long to clear the floor and, as my head seemed to be pretty stable, I walked over to Ryan.

"Can I help?"

I'm glad he didn't have anything in hand because he jumped at my words.

"Oh, I didn't mean to startle you." I laughed.

He chuckled but looked down at his feet, his cheeks pinkened.

"Sorry, I was deep in thought. What are you doing stood here?"

"Erm, talking to you," I replied as if humoring a child.

"You're meant to be sitting and resting, not standing and scaring me."

"I needed to move, to stretch. I won't overdo it, I promise. But if you pass the things you dislodge to me, I'll pile them in the corner and it'll help things move a little quicker."

His stern look didn't fill me with confidence so I continued, "Oh, just for a little while, please let me help, Ryan, please?"

Eventually he gave in. "All right, but I will move anything heavy and you must stop if you start to feel woozy."

"I will, I will!" I would have bounced but I was still feeling delicate.

Ryan shook his head and carried on, pulling gently on a chair and managing to dislodge it without any rumbles or collapses. He passed the rickety frame to me and I confidently moved it over to the corner and placed it carefully on top of the other stuff.

We set up a rhythm and it seemed that things were moving much quicker with both of us involved. It was weird working in such close proximity with him, knowing the argument we'd had meant we were stuck in this stupid situation. The more I worked, the more aware I was of the tension in the air between us. In the end I had to speak up.

"Look, Ryan, I really quite like you."

He didn't look round, so I kept on going. I thought it best to start out with a positive.

"And I just want a straight answer. Once I get it I'll file it away and we'll move on from here with the slate wiped clean." That was the way Gran had always operated and I was willing to give it a go. If it would lift the tension in the air and around my heart.

"Okay," his reply was hesitant. He still didn't look at me.

"Promise me you'll tell me the truth," I demanded.

"I will." He passed me a bent, wire magazine rack. Our gazes met.

"Did you take those books?"

"No, I didn't," Ryan replied without a flinch or a flicker of an eyelid.

"Okay, I believe you." I did. I'd wanted to all along and I let go of doubt and went for it.

"I honestly think Eve took them, Katrina. And I'm so sorry I told her about them."

"Well, you weren't to know. I didn't swear you to secrecy." I didn't want him to feel bad.

He turned back to the pile of junk, and I wondered what was going through his mind.

"When I see Eve again I'm going to make her give them back to you."

"When you see her? Where's she been?" I asked.

"God knows." He passed a dislodged cardboard box to me. "She's not answering her phone."

"Crap, I'm sorry, you told me that already."

Shrugging, he turned back to pull out a large tin and its rattling contents.

"I'm sure she's all right. I'd have heard if she wasn't. And I'm pissed off with her anyway."

"It might not have been her..." I tried not to upset him, well, more upset.

"Come on, Katrina. Who else could it be?" Ryan sighed and turned toward me again. "I've been with Eve for years, since we were both in secondary school even."

I simply nodded. He obviously needed to talk.

"And in all that time we've done everything together." He passed me the tin then kept working—I didn't think anything would distract him from the blockage.

"Some of it wasn't very clever. God, I was incredibly nasty to my childhood best friend because of Eve. I've done stupid and illegal things with Eve."

I stumbled with the tin, shaking it loudly. He snapped round to look at me. I smiled reassuringly.

"But always we've done it together. Talked about everything, made plans together. But recently she's been avoiding me. Probably since she was busy racking up thousands of pounds' worth of debt on my credit card."

"Not good," I interjected.

"No, not good. Really not good. The kind of not good that makes you doubt you ever actually loved the girl in the first place."

The tin slipped from my hands and hit the floor with a loud bang.

"Oh, fuck." I dropped to my knees, which made my head explode with pain. "Sorry about that." I winced.

"No, no problem. Are you okay? Did you go dizzy? Do you need to rest?"

His concern was sweet but I felt bad as the exploding tin was simply me being clumsy, nothing to do with the head injury. I couldn't believe I'd just heard him confess he might never have really loved Eve.

"I'm all right, just clumsy."

We scrabbled to pick up the nuts and bolts that rolled across the floor in all directions. I dropped in a few and clashed hands with him.

"I think we should have a break. Just ten minutes."

I wasn't sure if he needed the break or if he just wanted to stop me working for a while but I nodded my agreement.

"We're closer to the door now, anyway. It's going better than I thought."

"Mm. You've done a great job." He had. We'd be able to get out soon, I was sure.

"Well, needs must." He sighed, took the tin then placed it in the corner of crap.

I'm not sure he was talking about the same thing I was. He had a faraway look in his eye.

"What you going to do about Eve, then?"

We sat propped up against the wall, next to the water containers, looking over what still needed to be done.

"I don't know, Katrina. I mean, I should tell her to sling her hook, but can I? We've been with each other so long now, could I live without her?"

Silence reigned.

"I'm sorry, I shouldn't be rabbiting on about Eve."

"It's fine." I waved my hands and smiled.

"No, I'll shut up now, get on with getting us out. God, it's like the bloody *Great Escape* but without the Nazis."

I laughed. "Yeah and with more junk."

"Good point." He heaved himself to his feet.

"I'll help." I stood, holding down the wooziness.

"Only if you're sure."

"Sooner we're out, the better."

It took me some time to process why I was so affected by Ryan's confession. Why should it bother me? Clearly our time had been over many years ago when I had still been Janet. His confession that he might never have loved Eve just made it all the worse. That would mean that all the crap, the bullying tactics he had used back when we were teens, had actually been him speaking, not Eve.

And you couldn't know about love after one experience with it. I didn't know about love and I'd had a few encounters with it. I knew it wasn't like in the movies. No big dramatic moments of overwhelming emotion—I never knew I was truly in love. Infatuated, yes. Flattered, having a good time, sexually aroused, definitely. But I was fairly sure that true love was a myth. Especially as the one man I'd every truly been convinced I'd loved was Ryan and how could that be? If I let myself love him I was opening up to rejection.

Love was different for every person who felt it and when that bloom of a new relationship shined it was as though you had found the one. Ryan would have felt like that with Eve all those years ago.

I should have reassured him, told him about my theories, but I wasn't sure it was a suitable conversation for an employer to have with her employee.

"I'll pay you for today," I exclaimed, without thinking.

"What?" he gasped.

"I'll pay you for your time today."

"No, you don't have to do that."

"I want to—it's not fair you missing out on a day of work because of me."

"I'm not going to accept your charity," Ryan snapped.

"It's not— I mean it's— I just wanted to help." I sighed.

"God, I'm sorry. I don't want to start an argument. We're both tense and saying things in the heat of the moment. Thank you for your offer, Katrina, but this isn't your fault. If this was a regular job under usual circumstances I'd accept the money but it isn't. So I don't want paying. Tomorrow when I come to shift this crap properly and the days after when I rewire your house, then you can pay me, but not for this."

"Fair enough. I didn't think it through, just blurted it, you know. I forget sometimes that people do things for motivations other than money."

"Is that really how it seems for you?"

We continued moving stuff, crisis over.

"Yeah, mostly. Everyone is motivated by money or power in my world. Even me, I guess."

"No, I can't believe that. "

"It's true. I knew Brian was married, I knew I shouldn't have slept with him, but I did it anyway because I wanted to. It was a power trip—me, Katrina Quinn—I fucked the guy I'd had a teenage crush on."

"Well, that's just chemistry," he said. "Hang on, I'll take this, it's heavy." He lugged an old metal doorstop to the pile of crap. "And it takes two to tango."

"That's what I thought but it's not the way the media painted it."

"Well, they make it into something that will sell them newspapers whether it's the truth or not. And he showed his true colors in the end by dating that young model, didn't he?"

"Hmm, it was a bit late for me by then. The damage was already done." I sighed.

"Oh, it'll be forgotten soon enough. Everyone will be onto something else, someone else."

Ryan edged back past me. The pile was in two distinct parts now, with about a foot of space between the stuff blocking the door and the rubbish piled at the corner of the room. Our pile of nicely packed crap was growing and leaving less space for us to maneuver in.

"And in my opinion he's the one at fault. You're single, he was the married one. It was his responsibility to remember that and not give in to his urges. Even around a sexy woman like you. I can see it'd be a challenge but he made the wedding vows."

I was flustered by his words. Not only was he the first person to say the incident wasn't my fault, but he'd confessed that he found me sexy.

"Thanks," I whispered, shifting the box in my hand to the crap pile. "You're the only person who's said that."

"That you're sexy? Oh I don't believe that. I saw a top ten list of sexy birds in a mag recently and you were top of it."

I laughed. "No, not that bit. I hear that all the time. Which is weird 'cause I never did when I was younger. I'm still not sure people mean it."

"Of course they mean it, you're gorgeous!"

"You're making me blush now." I giggled.

"Well, if that makes you blush I won't tell you about the stash of pictures of you I've got."

"Oh, God, please don't. They Photoshop me to the high heavens in them things, you know. I must be a real disappointment in the flesh."

Ryan turned and looked me up and down. His gaze lingered on every curve from my ankle to my ear.

"I know you're not on top form today, what with being concussed and everything, but, Katrina, you *are* sexier in the flesh."

He held my gaze the whole time he spoke and either he was a master liar or he meant every word.

"You're making me blush again." I broke the eye contact and looked down to the floor, my cheeks blazing with heat, my chest tightened with lust right the way from my heart to the tips of my nipples.

"Am I?" He lifted my chin with a finger. "So I am." He grinned.

"Stop it." I slapped his hand away playfully. "You're being mean now."

"For telling you you're sexy?" He laughed. "That's not mean."

"No, for making me squirm."

"I'm making Katrina Quinn squirm, oh my."

There was a great retort for that comment somewhere in the back of my brain but it wouldn't connect with my lips. I just opened and closed them like a marionette.

"I can make you squirm too!" I finally exclaimed.

"Yeah?" he questioned, one eyebrow cocked.

"Yeah." I reached out and traced a finger along his cheek and jawline.

"You'll have to do better than that." His voice was low and gravelly.

The squirming had started, I was sure, but I wasn't one to back down from a challenge. So I put my Katrina smile on full beam and pressed my smile to his relaxed lips, cupping his cheek with my fingers.

He resisted for all of half a second, before the set line of his lips melted and melded with mine. We set up a rhythm that felt like the tossing of the sea, or maybe that was just the concussion talking. Ryan didn't stop kissing me back, he pulled me to him, holding me round my waist and running his hands up my back. It had started as a silly little game. I was only going to press my lips to his, make him blush and pull back. All I wanted was to be balanced again. In control. I managed control for as long as Ryan resisted my kiss then I rolled into complete and utter surrendering chaos.

I was just pushing my hands up under his T-shirt when Ryan pulled back with a shuddering breath.

"As much as I'd like this to continue — and I really, really would — we need to get out of here. I'd much prefer to fuck you on a bed than against this bumpy wall."

"Sure, yeah." I vibrated my head up and down for a while with nervous energy but then the room started to spin so I stopped.

What else could I say to that? I couldn't really. We got back to work and there was a zing of something waiting to happen between us every time our fingers touched. It was like being in the center of a charged cloud, just waiting for it to reach the point where it had to discharge. I was almost sure that my hair was standing on end, my skin was tingling with the tension so much.

And I was starting to feel the call of nature rather urgently. What a bizarre mix of sensations that was — turned on and full up in a truly unpleasant way.

"I can see light!" Ryan exclaimed. "I don't think much of the crap got through the doorframe 'cause this bedframe's blocking the bottom half."

"That's brilliant!"

"We should be through soon."

We moved quicker then, grabbing and moving, not worrying too much about where we put the stuff we removed. The top was eaten away quickly and we could see the stairs leading to freedom on the other side.

"Do you think I can climb over that last bit?" I asked once there was just the bedframe and some debris left. I'd held on as long as I could and my bladder was going to explode.

"I don't know, you might be able to, but I'd be happier—"

"I'm going to wet myself if I don't get to the loo soon," I moaned.

"Ah, right, okay then. You can't go in a tin in the corner like I did, can you?"

"Erm, no," I replied, screwing up my face in distaste. "So help me past this damn bed."

He craned his neck and looked over the debris and checked the other side.

"Okay, so just be careful on the other side—there's lots of rubbish and it might slip and slide about."

"Yeah, yeah, come on!" I gasped, standing by the edge of the bedframe that was most exposed.

"Okay, okay." He laughed, and let me scramble up him to get my foot on top of the metal frame then ease it over the other side.

"Can you get across?" Ryan gasped. I was leaning quite heavily on him, poor man.

"There's something under my foot, it seems pretty secure… I'm going for it."

I let go of him and grabbed the wall, throwing my balance onto the leg on the outside of the cellar. It hurt like buggery but I didn't care. I wobbled on the crate beneath me but it held so I scooped my other leg over.

"Thank God I do yoga!" I exclaimed. "I'm on the other side. I'll go pay a visit then I'll come back and help you."

"Okay." He chuckled. "Just be careful as you go—don't want you tripping up in your haste."

"I won't." I raced up the cellar steps to sweet, sweet relief. I giggled gleefully as I ran up the stairs, glad to be free from the cellar, but once I had paid a visit—another term Gran would use—I started to think.

All the reasons I shouldn't fuck Ryan queued up in my mind as I made my way downstairs. I'd had a nasty knock to the back of the head and I should have gone directly to the hospital. I had kissed him when I wasn't fully myself. I couldn't let it go any further. I had to wait until I was fully in my right mind again. I wasn't paying too much attention to where I was going until I became aware of a thumping sound and looked at where I was stepping next. Ryan was there. I didn't stop my forward momentum quite quickly enough so we bumped together, his face lodged between my breasts.

"Oops, sorry."

We gasped at the same moment then laughed.

"I moved a few more things, then I thought 'Stuff it' and jumped over the bedframe too."

"We can clear it properly tomorrow," I said.

"We can," he replied, "now we've got something far more urgent to see to."

He lifted his face up toward me, and I dipped down so we met in the middle. So much for waiting for my right mind. Sparks flew, my breath hitched and all I thought of was getting him closer to me.

Ryan ran his hands under my T-shirt, showing his eagerness to get me naked. I pulled my lips from his with a pop.

"Bedroom, now," I growled. My tone even surprised me with its huskiness. I turned then ran up the few stairs left to the landing and heard his steps behind me.

Giggling I headed for the spare room, crazy flashbacks zooming through my mind's eye of him chasing me as a kid. This wasn't the same, though. Then I had been taken with youthful exuberance and joy. This giggling run was inspired by one thing only — lust.

"Hey, slow down, I've been working hard," he said, the sternness of his tone belittled by the huge smile on his face.

"And I'm desperate to get out of these clothes."

I'd already kicked off my shoes at the bedroom door and to illustrate further my need I pulled off the jumper and my T-shirt in one go.

"Okay, you win." He came toward me, covering the space between us in just a few strides. His strong hands on my skin were hot, rough and mucky. I didn't care because I was as equally covered in dirt.

I ran my hands up inside his T-shirt — our mouths met and melded together. Each kiss was as thrilling as the first, scorching the imprint of him on me time and time again. He pulled back to let me discard his T-shirt and we pushed together, flesh to flesh once more. He quickly sought out the clasp at the back of my bra, and after a couple of tries he freed me.

I was barely aware of anything around me — the cold air, the darkness outside the window or the simple single bed behind me. I didn't have time to worry about not living up to his expectation, my real body blemished and marked more than the Photoshopped one the media showed. My belly jiggle, the stretch marks acquired in the battle with my puppy fat and the wobbly flesh of my thighs are part of what make me me. I'd honed my body in recent years and I was much healthier than I once was but I still had curves because they were intrinsically part of my womanliness.

All that mattered was that Ryan was touching me. I held my breath for a moment and he pushed off my jeans and knickers, pausing over the birthmark on my left hip. Did Ryan know about that birthmark when I was little? I wasn't sure. If he did, he didn't jump to conclusions because after circling it with his thumb he pushed my trousers lower, denuding my lower body easily.

I evened the odds, despite the distraction of his lips on my chest, trailing lower to my breasts and nipples. I was fairly competent in the removal of clothing generally but I misfired unhooking his button several times too many before eventually beating it and roughly sliding the jeans down his legs.

He felt good beneath my fingertips — warm and supple like just-proved dough with a hard center I really wanted to get down to. I kissed into the curve of his shoulder, catching the cinnamon musk of him beneath the earthy smell of dust and hard work. Ryan traced a finger down my spine and made me shiver against him. He pulled me closer. He was imprinted against my skin and I wanted him even deeper than that.

Getting two fully grown people onto a single bed was a challenge, I didn't think about the logistics and I don't think Ryan did either, we just fell onto it. I loved being crushed beneath his weight. Even my bruises protesting didn't pull me away from the pleasure that was building at the very center of my being.

"Fuck, am I dreaming?" he gasped as my thighs wrapped around him.

"If you are, please don't wake up," I moaned in reply, stretching my neck up to kiss him. I wanted him inside me, I wasn't thinking of anything but satisfaction.

"Katrina, protection," he pushed the words out between his teeth. "I want you so much."

I hadn't thought to pack condoms when I'd flown over here—sex hadn't been on my agenda—but thankfully my pre-packed makeup bag had some in it. I'd have been a Girl Guide if the uniform hadn't been so disgusting.

"In my makeup bag, on the table. Flowers all over."

"The condom?" He cocked his eyebrow.

"You know what I mean!" I slapped his shoulder

"I couldn't help myself."

His cheeky smile melted my heart and I watched on eagerly as he stretched out to fiddle inside the bag, sending a lipstick flying.

"Got one."

He leaned back on his heels to open the package and I entertained myself by devouring his fit body with my gaze. The floppy hair, the soft curve of his lips, the power of his arms and chest—even the dimple in his stomach was sexy. I wanted to touch him all, everywhere and especially there.

His cock was hard and ready, shiny with pre-cum at the tip, plump and pink. I wanted it filling me, really needed it. His thighs were marred with bruises from our cellar adventures, and seeing them reminded me that I was injured. I felt the throbbing in the back of my head where I lay against the pillow. We'd had a harrowing day—or more than a day. I had no idea what time it was, and we deserved this celebration of freedom.

Ryan was still extricating the condom from the packet and my impatience grew. I lifted my hand from the bed, slid it over my thigh and into the curls of my pubic hair. I pressed down onto my clit, a release of pressure coming out of me with a half gasp of pleasure.

I dipped my fingers into the abundance of natural lubrication at my entrance and dragged it up and over my aching clit, the slickness eliciting another moan from my lips, deeper and more insistent this time. I kept my eyes open, eagerly devouring Ryan's body mentally, watching him sheathe himself ready to fuck me.

"Wait for me," Ryan whispered.

I looked up into his stunning green eyes, which were open and sparkling with desire.

"Come on then." I licked my lips nervously, my fingers busy on my clit.

"Yes, ma'am."

He wasted no more time, pressing his cock to my cunt and pushing into me in one slow, luxurious shunt of his hips.

How do you describe the feeling of getting what you've always wanted? It could have been a disappointment, it could have been too much, but it was just perfect. He filled me just enough to press against all my pleasure zones with ease. I was full, but not painfully so, and I squeezed my pussy muscles around him in appreciation.

Some men could be weird about self-pleasure during sex so I dithered over my clit. *Should I remove my hand now and let him do all the work?* I think Ryan read my mind or sensed my hesitation.

"Finger yourself," he commanded.

So I did.

He leaned over me, resting his hands either side of my head, changing his angle and rubbing his pelvis against my fingers.

"God, that's so hot," he groaned.

I strained up against him, my whole body alive with sensation. My breasts wobbled against his chest after each impact, my nipples agitated so pleasantly by his chest hair. My lips met his in an intense kiss that echoed the joining of our lower bodies. I was taking all the ecstasy and intensifying it for myself, pulling his lips tighter to mine, letting him dominate my tongue with his.

I knew I was close. I stilled the working of my finger for a moment to catch my breath. The bedsprings creaked. Ryan moaned and hissed his pleasure against my mouth — everything else was still and silent. It was as though we were the only two people left in the whole world, our orgasms were the only thing that mattered.

With one hand I held a clump of bedclothes but I longed to feel him, have contact with his body in as many ways as I could, so I dug my fingers into the flesh of his shoulder.

"Yes," he exclaimed, the word tickling against my lips. "Oh, fuck, yes."

His body tightened and I knew he was going to come soon. I looked up into his face — his eyes were tightly shut. His chin was darkened with stubble, but one side seemed even darker. Maybe a bruise was coming up there, too. My heart squeezed as I remembered the way he'd rescued me. He was my Ryan, my hero again. We were so in tune. I rubbed at my clit once more, hand trapped between us with limited maneuverability. The merest stroke was all I needed, though, and, as we both climbed closer to the pinnacle, our lips drifted apart until I could just feel the soft warmth of his exhalations.

My eyes were tightly squeezed shut, I tried to preserve this moment forever because I, Janet Davey, was about to come around Ryan Taylor's cock. A dream come true. I wasn't Katrina anymore, I wasn't even trying to pretend I was. Naked and vulnerable beneath him, I was laid bare.

Rearing against him, tightened around him in a vice of delight, I howled out my orgasm. It was a feral sound of completion, and seconds later it blended with the guttural groans of Ryan's climax.

I saw stars, felt heat—I was the epitome of a twee cliché. I broke apart into a million pieces and floated away from my body, one with the spirit realm. It was that intense. An experience I would never forget, an orgasm like none I'd ever experienced before that seemed to roll on to a new level of intensity with every buck and twitch of him. I thought I'd never stop coming but eventually, as he pulled himself from me and eased his body off me, I did.

I rolled to the edge of the bed so he could cling next to me. Both of us pulling in heaving breaths, trying to find equilibrium. It was the sound of Ryan's mobile ringing that broke us apart.

"Shit, I better get that." He leaped from the bed.

I didn't want to open my eyes or move. I wanted to stay in the world where I was fucking Ryan and everything was fine and good and how it should be. I didn't want to let in the avalanche of doubts and fears that I knew would come if I overheard his phone conversation.

Chapter Eighteen

Ryan Taylor

Naked in Mary Davey's hall was not a position I'd ever found myself in before. But then I had never really expected to fuck Katrina Quinn either or be trapped in a cellar of crap. It was turning out to be a day full of the unexpected. Then Eve rang and things got predictable.

"Where have I been?" I screamed. "You've got some cheek!"

"It's gone ten o'clock at night and you're not home," Eve snapped. "I was worried."

"Oh, really? You went missing days ago and I've heard not a word from you. I've rung all your pals and none of them knew where you were and you're the one who's worried."

"Ryan, stop it, you always make it my fault."

"That's because it bloody well always is!" I bellowed.

"Whatever. Where are you? Are you coming home?"

"I'm at Katrina's. I have to do a rewire. I've been trapped in the damn cellar all day under an avalanche of junk, if you actually want to know."

"I don't care, get home. I've got something to show you."

I hoped to God it was Katrina's books.

"It better be something good, Eve," I groaned.

"It is, it is. Hurry."

"Okay, I'll be there soon."

I didn't want to leave Katrina's, but if Eve had the books I could pick them up, dump Eve and come straight back.

I took my phone back upstairs with me. When I reached the bedroom Katrina had a white dressing gown wrapped around her.

"That was Eve." I looked around for my pants and trousers. "She's got something to show me. I'm hoping it's the books."

"Okay," she replied, her tone icy.

"So I'm going to go and get them from her."

"Please do." Her voice was monotone — something was definitely wrong. "I'm going for a shower."

What could I do? As she walked past me to go out to the landing I grabbed at her arms and pulled her to me. She resisted at first then melted into my body and the passionate kiss I pressed against her lips. The desire I'd felt whilst we'd fucked resurfaced.

"I'll be back later," I gasped. "I promise."

She nodded and stepped back from me.

"I... I... I really need to shower, my hair is all..."

"God, yes. Take care, all right? We're snowed in so I can't get you to hospital but I can get Doctor Wallis up if you need him."

"No, I think I'll be okay once I'm washed and dressed and I've eaten."

"Good." I remembered my naked state. "Now I need to dress and go."

"See you." She hurried down the corridor to the bathroom.

I hoped she wasn't regretting what we'd done. Her kiss told me she desired me but a big shot actor like Katrina probably fucked men when she liked, possibly with little attachment. It didn't feel like that, though.

I gathered up my T-shirt, jumper and pants then slung them on. I had no idea what the weather was like. The house was warm, but it was likely to be freezing once I got outside. I grabbed my coat at the door and determinedly trudged into the cold.

Clearly, the snow had stopped earlier in the day. I could see footprints on paths and when I reached the main road the pavements were covered with compacted snow. I decided to walk in the gully of the road, not wanting to slip on the newly forming ice.

What a day I'd had. It seemed almost unreal in the cold lamplight on an ice-laden night. Blocked in, escaped, and well and truly fucked. I still vibrated with post orgasmic awesomeness. I couldn't believe that Katrina wasn't affected by it, too—we were perfectly in tune with each other. I'd never had sex like that before.

It wasn't just that she was famous, either, because, truth be told, I'd forgotten that she even was. Katrina was just the beautiful, sexy woman I'd been working for—I even liked to think we were friends. It had been an amazing fuck, but deeper than just releasing a physical need. I had joined with that woman at a level that wasn't just about bodily functions. It had been spiritual, and, in a way, slightly disturbing.

As I'd been fiddling with the condom, she'd played with herself. What a turn-on that had been but when

I'd looked deep into her eyes for just a split second I'd thought that it was Janet. I quickly banished that thought from my mind. Maybe it was the location we were in or maybe her eye color was very similar but it shook me to the core. It wasn't a bad feeling at all, just weird and unexpected.

There were similarities, in height and smile and eye color, but that was it. I don't understand what made me think of her at that moment at all. It disturbed me because even after so much time I'd gotten an uncomfortable feeling in the pit of my stomach when I remembered all the nasty things I had done to her. It had jarred with the joy of fucking Katrina.

It had passed quickly enough when I'd finally gotten the condom on and thrust into her, though. I wasn't a poet, but the world had become brighter, the sounds had resonated louder and everything I'd felt had been amplified while we were joined so intimately. Just thinking about it made my dick stir. The sooner I could get the books back from Eve and dump her, the better. I was ready to see if sexual encounter number two could live up to the fireworks of the first.

My legs ached by the time I reached my driveway. I'd noticed the bruises when I'd gotten naked and my muscles had ached a bit when we'd fucked but the ecstasy had staved off the pain. The sub-zero trek across the village reminded me of every bruise and overworked muscle.

I held my breath as I pushed open the door. Steadying myself for what was to come next.

"God, Ryan, you look a mess," Eve exclaimed when I stepped into the living room.

"Yeah, having a cellar full of junk collapse on you and consequently digging your way out of said crap is dirty business. Where've you been?"

"Out," she growled. "I've got something for you." She tapped the greenish suitcase beside her.

"Thank fuck," I sighed, striding over to pick up the case. It was too light. "Where are the books?"

"What books? I don't want to show you books. Open it up!"

"No. Jeez, Eve. Do you ever listen to a word I say? Where are the books? I need to take them back to Katrina."

"Do I look as if I give a shit? Not everything's about you, Ryan. That's why I'm leaving you."

"You did that two days ago without a word of warning."

"You pissed me off with your accusations and I came to realize that I don't love you anymore," she yelled.

"Well, that's good because I'm not sure I *ever* loved you. What the fuck did you do with the books?"

"Oh, would you shut up about those scraggy, bloody things. We sold them on already," Eve growled, pulling at her hair in frustration.

"We? You're not the queen, you know!"

She shook her head at me and huffed. "I mean me and Roy. He's my new supervisor at work. I've been fucking him for weeks and you've not noticed. I nearly brought him in here when you had your concussion. We were going to fuck in our bed, but you mucked that up so I fucked you instead. A pity fuck. Anyway, he stole the books, while you were busy giggling with that Katrina tart."

I rubbed at my temples in disbelief. "You had an accomplice?"

"Whatever. He stole them, we sold them, now we're going to leave this Godforsaken place forever."

"Crap, what am I going to tell Katrina? Eve, don't you ever think of anyone but yourself?"

She shrugged. "I've packed me stuff. Roy's waiting for me in the square. I really wanted to see you open that box – my parting gift to you – but as you're being an absolute bastard about it I'm going to go. Can't keep my true love waiting."

"Oh, no, of course you can't. Well, I hope you're both happy together. I'm thrilled to see the back of you."

"The feeling's mutual."

"Don't worry about the debt you've left me in, I'll sort out some way to pay it," I added sarcastically.

"I'm sure you will."

Eve stood and tottered out of the room, in her impractical red heels. I didn't watch her go. I just hoped she'd make it to the village square without falling and breaking an ankle because I sure as hell wasn't going to run to her rescue.

I slumped down onto the sofa. All the wind had been taken out of my sails. I hadn't known what was going to happen but I'd been fairly confident that I was going to be the one calling the shots and doing the dumping. But no, Eve had even managed to ruin that.

I wasn't quite sure how Katrina would take the news. Sure, we'd talked it out in the cellar and come to an amicable truce. Would she be as easy-going once she heard that a stranger had managed to break into her house without detection? I felt bad – it had to be my fault that the guy had gotten in. It didn't surprise me that Eve had been having an affair. She was incapable of doing anything on her own and as she wasn't doing anything with me... It made sense that she'd gotten someone else to lean on.

At least I could take the case back to Katrina. She was adamant about personal belongings making their way back to relatives. It was sheer curiosity that made me open it. I shouldn't have, simply because Eve wanted me to, but I was scared it might be booby-trapped and I was afraid Katrina could get hurt.

Inside, snuggled in the faded cream interior, was a pile of letters held together with a red elastic band. I flicked through—they were all addressed to Mary with American stamps on the envelopes. The postal dates showed they weren't very old—all from within the past decade and all from the same address in Hollywood.

I opened the first one in the pile and started reading.

Dear Gran,

Well, I'm finally here. I miss you like crazy, but everything is such a whirl, I almost feel like it's all a dream. Thank you so much for understanding, Gran. I had to do this, start over and make that break. I hope to be able to sneak back to Thornleydale to you soon — the food over here in America is definitely different and nothing like your home cooking.

The weather is amazing, though, warm and sunny, and the people are so friendly. I've made so many mates among those on set already. They're really good at helping me get used to how it all works too — I'm such a newbie when it comes to film. It's nothing like acting on stage.

I'll write again soon, I promise.

Lots of love,

Janet

I hadn't realized that Janet was an actor. Mary would never give me details, no matter how much I asked. I read on, desperate to find out more about my friend and what she'd moved on to do. The letters continued in a similar vein, and I was just thinking about taking down the address then going back to Katrina's when I read something that stopped me in my tracks.

Dear Gran,

Working on Snow Mountain *has been amazing. I met Harrison Ford and got his autograph for you. I'll put it in this letter for you. He was wonderfully charming. It was strange working with him and even weirder kissing him, even if just on the cheek. I never imagined I'd get to kiss a Hollywood legend.*

And, Gran, I must confess that I love working opposite David Stretford. He is gorgeous, witty and so charming. I'm loving being his leading lady. I'm hoping to be more by the time the film is over...

Everything else blurred. I struggled to take in what I was reading. Katrina Quinn had been the lead in that film, she'd played opposite David Stretford and all the rumors said that they had been shagging. I knew for certain that Katrina was in that movie. I walked over to my DVD collection and pulled it out. There she was on the cover.

Well, that explained why I had thought of Janie when I'd looked into her eyes. Katrina Quinn was Janet Davey. I was crushed. Why had Janie gone to such lengths to disappear and why hadn't she told me who she was when we'd crossed paths again? I'd been a bastard to her once upon a time but I didn't deserve to be lied to like that. I couldn't believe what I'd discovered. Janie had a secret identity and she hadn't told me.

I'd had plans to shower and freshen up before heading back to Copse Cottage but I didn't. I took that revelation along with the suitcase and letters back out into the cold December night. I'd wanted to hear news of Janet for so long, wanted to see her and put things straight. That desire had soured when I realized that I'd been lied to.

Of course a woman could change. She could dye her hair, remove a tooth, get a tan and take on an accent. But why hadn't she revealed who she was to me? Okay, I'd been a bastard to her—maybe she had thought I couldn't be trusted—but surely she trusted me now, she'd fucked me! Why hadn't she told me who she really was before that?

I'd walked those few miles to Copse Cottage so many times in my life that I barely took notice of where I was going. Even in the snow I was sure-footed. A car zoomed past me, beeped its horn, but I didn't look up. I had no desire to see Eve gloating.

If I'd not opened the case, I wouldn't have known. I could have gone back and enjoyed all Katrina's delights again. Maybe we'd have gotten together properly, a real relationship. Perfection, but built on lies. As much as I knew that Eve had only given me the letters back out of spite, she'd actually done me a favor. I needed to know the truth.

I hammered on the door, and, after a few seconds that stretched on into infinity, Katrina opened it, beaming.

"Oh, thank God you've come back." She sighed. "Come in, come in. It's freezing out there."

She ducked back into the corridor and I followed her.

"I was so scared you'd go back to Eve and never come back here again. I didn't want to think it, but I did. I mean, you told me you've been with her for years, you clearly had a strong relationship once."

"Stop it," I snapped.

She turned to look at me. "Stop what?" Her brow crinkled, and her hands wavered at her side, as though they wanted to travel up to her mouth. Janet had been a nervous nail nibbler back in the day.

"Lying." I lifted the case from the side of my leg and offered it forward to her. "Stop lying to me, Janet. I know your secret now."

"Oh God. " Those hands flew to her face, her eyes widening in fear. "Oh God, no."

"Why didn't you tell me?" I threw the case to the floor between us.

She shook her head, eyes tearing over.

"I've built up a whole new life, Ryan. I'm someone else now. I'm not Janie anymore."

"But you are!" I roared. "You are and you never told me. We were the best of friends, Janie."

"We were," she yelled back. "Then you got in with Eve and you might have forgotten, but I haven't. You made my life hell for seven years."

She had a point but I was still angry.

"But you lied to me. You lied. You fucked me, Janie, under false pretenses."

"Well, can you blame me? For years I was under the impression you hated me. Janet Davey was the lowest of the low in your eyes. But as Katrina I had an opportunity to get what I've wanted since, well, forever. I didn't want to be geeky Janet you hated, I wanted to be foxy Katrina who you really fancied."

I shook my head. "Janet, oh, Janet. I wanted you just as much. Yes, even when I was being a bastard. At the time I didn't realize just how much my words and deeds hurt you. I was that thick. I thought under all of it you knew that you were still my Janie, the only girl in the world I've ever trusted fully. I thought you knew. You acted like you did."

Janet shook her head and stretched a hand out behind her to find the newel post of the stairs. Making contact she let herself collapse back onto the stairs.

"How could I have known, Ryan? You told me you hated me on a regular basis. You pulled every trick in the book with me as the target. You were Eve's completely. I didn't know, Ryan. I didn't. I hurt so much for all that time because I loved you. I really loved you."

Now that was a revelation I hadn't been expecting.

"Then why didn't you tell me who you were? Why did you continue to lie?"

"Ryan Taylor, use your fucking brain for once, would you? I loved you, you hated me. Why would I tell you I was your Janie when you were so dismissive of her but so enamored with Katrina?"

"But we talked about Janie all the time when we were clearing this place out—you must have realized my true feelings for you through that?" I was too hot and flustered in my coat and jumper, but I couldn't take them off. I wasn't staying.

"You were reminiscing. You told me nothing."

I shook my head and heaved a sigh.

"So you read the letters," she continued, nodding toward the case.

"Yeah. Eve did too."

"Shit." The sob bubbled from the back of her throat and racked her body with its intensity. "It'll all come out now. Everyone will know."

She was right. Eve wouldn't keep this tasty nugget to herself, not when the world's media would be clamoring for it. I felt sorry for her for a split second then it just built my fury further.

"So that's what you're so upset about? Your secret identity being uncovered? You're not at all upset about me. About what you've done to me?"

"How can you say that?" she yelled, voice gruff, forced through her tears. "Ryan, don't you know me at all?"

"Well, apparently not. I thought I knew Janet. I thought I knew Katrina, and now it turns out I didn't know either of them. I don't think I know anyone. Not even fucking Eve who I was so sure I'd worked out. She didn't steal the books, her lover did. They've sold them and are off to live happily fucking ever after. She's screwed me over, too. So now not only am I fucking heartbroken, I'm fucking skint, too. My life is officially shit. I'm screwed."

"Money. In all this you're still fixating on the money?" Janet looked up at me.

It was so weird thinking of her as Janet but now I knew I just couldn't see her as Katrina anymore.

"Well, Ms Multi-millionaire, I don't suppose it's anything for you but I'm screwed. Eighteen grand's worth of debt all courtesy of the woman who just dumped me and I've barely got a penny to my name. I'll lose my home, my reputation... I could even go to prison. Yes, that matters to me."

"Fine, fine." She threw her hands in the air and a moment later she sprung up from the stair. She stormed into the living room. I didn't move. I had no idea what she was doing. Was that the end of the conversation? I'd just turned a fraction, ready to leave, when she flew back into the hallway, brandishing a piece of paper.

"Here, take it. Means nothing to me. Take it, go. Don't come back."

She waved the rectangle of cream paper before my face, the air wafting against my hot cheeks, the crackling sound amplified in the silence.

"Go on then," she whispered. "Go."

Chapter Nineteen

Katrina Quinn

When he'd walked out of the door to go back to Eve I'd known things were going to go wrong but I hadn't had a clue as to exactly how wrong.

I'd been so relieved when he'd come back—I had honestly thought he wouldn't—then he'd dropped the bomb. He knew who I really was. I was stunned, heartbroken then intensely angry. Eve and Ryan had made my life hell—that's why I'd changed from Janet to Katrina all those years ago. They'd done it again. Ruined my life. It'd be in the media before I could blink. My real name, my real roots and the fact that I'd been living a lie for so long.

What did he care for me, though? I had confessed my love for him and what was Ryan worried about? Money. Just the money. So I'd written him a check for twenty thousand pounds and handed it to him.

"You're paying me off?"

"If you want to think of it like that, yes. I'm giving you the money you're so desperate for. Call it a severance payment."

"This is what all this boils down to, to you?" He reached out, but didn't touch the check. His fingertips were less than an inch away.

"It's what you want."

Ryan clasped the check, and I let go of it.

I cried. I didn't stop crying, I wasn't sure I ever would. Ryan stood, quietly, check held out as if he'd not made the decision to keep it yet. He was still marred with dust and dirt. The bruise I'd noticed earlier was coming up darker along his jawline.

"We could have been so good." Ryan pushed the check into his pocket, then without a second glance he turned to leave. "Bye, Janie."

I bit down on my top lip to hold in the howl of sheer misery that bubbled within me. I couldn't fall apart. If I did, I might never be able to put myself back together again. Alone.

I watched him walk away from me, stepped forward once, twice, three times. I wanted to stop him, needed to make him understand. I was whole again when we were together. The gap that had existed in my life for so long had finally been filled. I couldn't let him just leave. I needed him to understand.

When he abruptly turned I mis-stepped and we bumped against each other. He gasped—in shock or arousal I wasn't sure—but then his lips were on mine, scorching me with passion. His musk enveloped me, the spice of him inspiring the memories of Ryan inside me, making love to me.

I kissed him back, my wet cheeks pressed against his. I reached around him, wanting to hold him to me and stop him from leaving. But somewhere deep within, I knew that was the last kiss we'd ever share. There was something different in the molding of his lips to mine—regret, longing, separation. We both knew it was the end of something that could have been so very perfect. That our lives, which should have been intertwined, had been plucked apart so far that they had snapped.

Eventually he pulled back. I gripped my fingers in his coat, but he dragged himself away. I was close to begging, to calling him back. I needed to explain why I'd done what I'd done. But I couldn't find my voice. Tears rained down my cheeks and my throat was filled with regret. I opened my mouth to speak but nothing came out.

When the door clicked shut behind him with a gentle sigh, I collapsed to the floor, my body racked with sobs. My whole world had broken apart. I don't know how long I just sat there in the hallway and cried. I told myself over and over that I was being pathetic. I needed to get up. I just couldn't move. My grief weighed so heavy I just couldn't move a limb.

For a brief time I had thought we could make it. When we were together there was nothing but me and him. We blended together so perfectly. I had thought we could be something special together. I hadn't thought it through, though. Would I have confessed who I was or just lived a lie forever? I'd been too caught up in the ecstasy of the moment.

I had known when he'd left that something was going to go wrong but I'd thought we'd overcome it, whatever it was. I had been ready for Eve to come here shouting the odds, I'd been pumped up and ready for battle, but everything falling apart hadn't even crossed my mind.

How stupid of me to have thought that Eve would have just gotten rid of the case and its contents. I had honestly thought that they would have been dumped somewhere after the books had been removed. I'd not even worried about them at that point. I'd mourned the letters passing but hadn't contemplated their misuse.

However, the revelation that Katrina Quinn had lied about her childhood to the world didn't bother me anymore. I wasn't thinking about my career, my life back in the US, I just had Ryan on my mind. Eventually, when I was so cold that my teeth were chattering and I couldn't feel my toes, I dragged myself into the living room and collapsed onto the sofa. I wrapped the old, crocheted throw around my shoulders and stared into the fireplace.

* * * *

Copse Cottage, 1994

"Oh, you shouldn't let it get to you," Gran said, patting my hair. "He's a bloody idiot, always has been."

I snuggled back into the throw and sighed.

"Really, Janet. You need to move on and forget him, he's not worth the heartache."

"But, Gran, Ryan's my best friend." I coughed and spluttered. I'd had a soaking at Ryan's hands in the stream at the back of the village. It wouldn't have been a problem if it hadn't been late November. Since my dunking I'd had an awful cold.

"He was, love. Boys change once the hormones kick in." Gran placed a hand on my forehead, measured my temperature and shook her head.

"But we said we'd always be friends. It's always been Ryan and me."

"I know, love, I know. I'm not saying it's right, it's just the way it is, and if you want to avoid heartbreak you need to distance yourself from him now, accept he's moved on."

"But I don't want to." I coughed again and pulled the throw tighter around me.

"I know, sweetheart. That's because you're so kind-hearted and loyal. I'm going to go and make you a hot honey and lemon, ease that poor cough, okay?"

I nodded, and Gran straightened with a wince then gracefully walked toward the door. She'd never had dancing lessons but her deportment and balance had always been superb. The chill breeze from the hall carried the scent of damp fallen leaves and the memory of being dumped in the cold water by him.

He'd stood laughing with Eve and a gang of other older kids beside him. No one had offered to help me. They'd jeered as I'd hauled myself out of the thankfully shallow stream and dragged myself and my sodden bag and books home, their laughs and jeers ringing in my ears.

I heard a noise, a tapping, but I put it down to more ringing in my ears. Then the rapid knocking happened again, louder and more insistent. I carefully sat up and looked at the window. Ryan stood on the other side.

I almost collapsed back onto the sofa and took Gran's advice, but he smiled and beckoned me over. I heaved myself up. My whole body ached and I was racked with another coughing fit, which I tried hard to stifle. If Gran saw Ryan at the window she'd have a fit.

I opened the right pane.

"Hey, Janie." He itched the back of his head nervously.

"What do you want?" I exclaimed.

"To see if you were all right, you've not been in school since—"

"You pushed me into the stream to entertain your new friends?" I snapped.

He at least had the decency to look sheepish, his pale cheeks highlighted with autumn sunset pink.

"Sorry," he mumbled.

"So you should be." I sighed, coughed a little more and grabbed for the windowsill as I felt the world tip around me.

"Feel better soon, Janie." Ryan reached into the window and clasped the top of my arm for a moment. There was so much in that touch, a sorrow in his eyes. He was trying to tell me something, I knew it, but he didn't say another word.

"I will. You be careful, okay? Don't do anything else stupid."

"I don't think I can manage that." He shrugged and pulled his arm back through the window. "You know what I'm like."

He ran off across the garden, before disappearing into the gap between the bushes, unfastened blazer flaring out behind him. I shut the window and scurried back to the sofa. The ensuing coughing fit covered the real reason I had tears in my eyes.

* * * *

I must have drifted off to sleep because when I woke I could have sworn I was my twelve-year-old self, my body cold and aching all over. A knock on the window made me jump—was it Ryan? Had he come back? When I lifted myself, untangled the blanket and peeped over the back of the sofa, I realized it wasn't. It was a man with a camera. I ducked down again quickly. I didn't think he'd gotten a shot of me. I thanked God that I hadn't taken down the dusty net curtains when we'd been clearing. I wrapped the blanket completely around me and rushed out into the hallway where the door vibrated with knocking, and a clamor of voices started up from the other side. The letterbox was open.

I raced upstairs, ignoring the clamor and my aching bones, and shut myself in my room. I sat on the edge of my bed and groaned. Outside the sun was rising, lighting the snow-dusted garden prettily. I couldn't appreciate it, though.

"There goes my privacy." I sighed and shook my head.

I picked up my phone—there were several missed calls and irate messages from my agent, from the director of my upcoming movie, and one that made me smile.

Call me, sugar, if you need backup. Matt x

I didn't check to see what time it was, I just hit the key to ring him back.

"Matt?" I gasped.

"Mm, Katrina?" He yawned. "Need the white horse treatment?"

"More than ever, Matt." I sighed, tears rolling down my cheeks.

"Okay, well it's stupid o'clock here, but I'll be on the next plane."

"Thank you," I sobbed.

"Hey, it's what you pay me for. Chin up, boss. It'll all be yesterday's news soon enough."

"I guess." I sniffed. "You know the address, don't you?"

"Yep, I'll be there as soon as I can."

"Sorry," I sniveled.

"Oh, hush, who needs sleep anyway? I'll see you soon. Get yourself packed and ready. Don't answer the phone or the door unless you know it's me. You know the score. Hold tight, I'll be there soon."

Thank God for Matt. At least there was someone in the big, cruel world whom I could rely on. There were no calls or messages from Ryan—not that I expected any but their absence made my heart throb again. I sighed deeply. I'd have time to mourn and berate myself once I was back in the comfort of my own home. I had to pull myself together and pack.

First stop was the bathroom for a hot shower. My body was speckled with bruises—dried blood still came free when I washed my hair, too. I fought back the memories, the horror of being buried beneath all that junk, the ecstasy of being with Ryan—I pushed it all down. I pretended it was a movie I'd worked on. Just a script, completely unreal, and moved to the very back of my mind.

A couple of painkillers and a change of clothes later I felt more able to deal with the situation I was in. I went around the house and closed all the curtains. I'd learnt how to do it without showing my face at the window. The paps might have gotten a few photos of my arm but they would have gotten little else. With the curtains closed I could move around the house more freely. The last thing on my mind was eating but as I'd not had a bite of anything since the previous morning I nibbled on a banana. I concentrated on packing my things, with only the odd glance to my phone. Matt was true to his word and texted me an hour and a half after I'd woken him with details of his flight and plans for the journey up to me. He'd be in Thornleydale by eight p.m.

I was going to be good, I wasn't going to ring Ryan. Definitely not, what a bad idea. But I had my phone in my hand, and somehow I managed to dial him. He didn't answer so I left a message.

"Ryan, Gran's is overrun with paparazzi. I'm leaving later today for America. I just wanted to let you know."

I nearly pressed to end the call but something stopped me.

"And I just want to tell you I'm sorry. I fucked up big style, but, Ryan, I'll always be your Janie and you'll always be the only boy for me."

I ended the call and let the tears flow. I couldn't beat them back, couldn't pretend that it was all make-believe any longer. A part of me hoped that Ryan would try to make contact that day. Maybe he'd turn up at the cottage, beat off the hordes at my door and sweep me off my feet and into his arms. I had always been a romantic.

It didn't happen.

I got a message from Matt at seven. I was sat in my bedroom, packing the last of the precious memories we'd found as we'd cleared the house. I glanced at my mobile and saw Matt's name.

On the way. The driver reckons we're about 30 mins away. I'll use the knock when I arrive so you know it's me. Be ready.

I'd struggled with myself over what to take back with me. So many of the photos and memories I'd found were intrinsically tied to Ryan as well as to this house and my gran. When I lifted out the box, hand-crafted by Ryan and filled with my precious things, my heart tore in two. I couldn't breathe, couldn't see, I was broken.

But I couldn't leave it. In the end I packed it all up to take with me. I could deal with the memories and unpack the emotional baggage once I was safely back home.

I carried my two cases downstairs, the modern wheeler I'd brought with me in my left hand and the sea-green retro case in the other. It was still packed with the letters and memorabilia I wanted to keep. I'd instruct Grant to sell the property as it was once I was back Stateside. I wouldn't be coming back. It wasn't my home anymore, not without Gran.

I saw her then, like a projection of an old film, stood in the doorway, orange, floral pinny around her waist, beaming at the little children who were racing. The little girl grabbed her round the waist. The lad ran past straight into the kitchen.

"I've not baked that pie yet, Ryan Taylor, so don't try to eat it."

She beamed down at the little girl who giggled back.

"Oh, you're just the most beautiful thing in my world, Janet Davey."

"And you're my bestest thing, Gran. Always."

My eyes misted with tears and the memory faded. And although every wall echoed with similar, precious memories, that wasn't the only place they existed. They'd forever be within my heart.

The knock came but I knew it was Matt long before that. His booming voice cut through the clamoring press. I'd know that tone anywhere, even if I couldn't hear his words. I opened the door, keeping it between me and what was on the other side just as Matt had taught me. He stepped in and we both pushed the barrier shut again.

"Dear God, I thought the Yank paps were crazy. Whoooweee."

"Welcome to Britain." I smiled.

Matt opened his arms wide and I threw myself into his embrace.

"Girl, I shouldn't let you out of my sight, should I?"

I shook my head against his shoulder, too overcome with emotion to speak.

"Don't worry now, I've got you. The driver's waiting for us in his bad ass cab. So we've got to go. All right?"

I drew in another lungful of his comforting scent, clean soap and pine then pulled myself away.

"Yep." I sniffed. "Yep, just let me put my hat and sunnies on."

Matt grabbed the largest bag. "You'll have to carry that green one, I'll use the other one as a barrier. No fine china in there, right?"

"No fine china." I nodded.

"Okay, then, darling, let's go."

Chapter Twenty

Ryan Taylor

The really shit thing about living in an out of the way village was that the pub shut at eleven. So what did I decide to do? To walk the ten miles to Wakefield and find a pub that was open. It made perfect sense to me at the time. I trudged along the main road and kept my mind firmly fixed on the drink I would have at the end of the line.

I very firmly pushed down any thoughts of Janie because when they pushed to the surface I got a very unmanly urge to sob. I wasn't sure who I was more annoyed at, her or me. Yes, she had held the information back from me, she'd pretended to be someone else but I hadn't caught on to it. How?

I knew her inside and out, which was why I had managed in successfully teasing the hell out of her in secondary. I knew all her buttons and how to press them. I'd often pissed her off by knowing what she was going to say before she even said it.

How had I not recognized her? It was a fruitless line of inquiry so I stopped thinking about it. Janet was out of my life forever, even if my stomach sank like a brick to think it. I noticed how cold my hands were after a few miles of walking. I dug them into my coat pockets and found the crumpled up check with my fingertips.

Twenty grand in my pocket. That had never happened before and was pretty scary. My irrational desire to rip it up and throw it to the four winds was even scarier. How could I accept it? It was a payoff, a settlement. It was guilt money. That check had bitterness written all over it. How could I take that money? She had given it to me in anger, an insult to add to my injuries.

If I cashed it I'd prove to her that I was just in it for the money. If I didn't I couldn't pay my debt and God knows what would happen to me then. Talk about being stuck between a rock and a hard place. There were a few days until I needed to pay the first installment of three grand to the credit card company — I didn't have it and was about to blow a chunk of it on getting pissed.

It hurt me that she thought it all boiled down to money. It didn't. What mattered was that the one person in all the world I'd thought was good and honest and incapable of lying to me had turned out to be a fraud, a fantasy. Did the Janie I remembered ever actually exist or had I twisted everything in my memories to make her perfect?

The solid foundation my world was established on was shaken. I'd built Janet up to be my perfect woman. Honest, pretty, funny. But what if that was all imagined? We'd gotten on as kids, but then didn't most children? We'd been together all the time because the town was so small — there hadn't been many others of our age around. Was that the only reason we'd hung out together?

Clearly I didn't mean as much to her as she did to me. But then the bundle of wooden guilt in my gullet flipped and churned. Maybe I had but when I'd been busy proving my love to Eve I'd broken apart that bond with Janet. Maybe I had been so nasty to her that I'd driven her away for good.

The flashing of a car's lights through the hazy, lazy smattering of snow that was half-heartedly spinning to the ground took me back in time to the prom.

* * * *

College Prom, 1998

Eve hadn't wanted to go, didn't understand why I did, but in the end she'd humored me.

"We'll go in, fuck it all up somehow then scarper when it gets leery."

I'd nodded, not really listening. I had one reason to go to that party and I couldn't tell it to Eve, she'd kill me. It was set up in the function room of the hotel up the road from the college. There was little to no decoration, just a few balloons at either end of the trestle table full of food. There were a few flashing lights dotted around the place, and a glitter ball that was more ball than glitter. The place was packed, we'd turned up over an hour late. Posh frocks and stiff suits seemed like the informal uniform to replace the blazers and striped ties of school days.

Eve disappeared off and I dug in, trying to find the person I wanted. I knew she'd be there but where? Of course, searching for one person in a body of students wasn't easy — I got sidetracked by greetings, pints and girlish giggles several times. It would have been rude to just walk past and ignore them. It was the last time we would all be together. I'd probably never see the majority of them ever again. And I never said no to a pint.

So the party was winding down by the time I found her on a table in the back. She wore a red dress that glittered with sparkle. Her hair was down, swept up on one side with a clip, and a fresh rose sat nestling next to her face.

"Janie, would you like to dance?"

Instant mistrust flashed in her eyes.

"For old times' sake." I smiled. "I promise not to step on your toes."

A smile spread from cheek to cheek and to her pretty blue eyes. She took my proffered hand, and I pulled her onto the dance floor with me. Under the uneven sparkle of the old glitter ball I wrapped my arms around her. She slipped hers around my waist and we leaned on each other, swaying to the beat.

"I came here tonight just to speak to you," I said, my mouth beside her hair.

She stiffened—even then I think she was worried that I was going to pull a joke on her.

"I had to tell you something before you left for university. It's important."

We swayed more. I didn't register what song was playing, just her body next to mine. She'd grown up. I remembered little Janie whom I'd played with, taunted and teased, and gotten into many awful scrapes with. She'd grown into such a beautiful woman.

"I've made a mistake—" I was going to say so much more but I screamed in pain as my hair was pulled hard at the scalp. Of course, it was Eve.

"Come on, you. We're going."

"I was just—"

Her withering stare stopped me in my tracks. I looked back over my shoulder.

"Sorry," I shouted toward Janet. "Really sorry."

* * * *

I'd wanted to say a lot more than that. How I had hated hurting her and hadn't realized how much damage I'd been doing until it was too late. That my stupid boy hormones had ruined the one true friendship I'd ever had and that she really was the best girl in the world.

I'd wanted my Janie back. Even then, I'd actually wanted her, not Eve. But Janet had gone off to university and I'd barely seen her after that. The one time I had, she'd been hand in hand with a lad. If she'd been alone I might have said hello, but I had been intimidated by her being with her boyfriend.

When I reached the city I walked into the first place that was open. It was a dive. I didn't care. I ordered a double Scotch then another and as they blurred into each other I forgot the world around me and disappeared into my world of despair.

"I've called you a cab," the loud, large barman told me. "I'm cutting you off."

I had no idea what time it was, where I was or even who I was. I don't think I was very co-operative but they got me into the cab eventually.

"Where you going, mate?"

"God knows," I spouted. "To the fucking dogs, I think."

"Oh, dear, terrible for you, mate. But what address am I taking you to?"

"Thornleydale," I said on the third time of trying.

"Right, don't throw up or I'll have to charge you double."

I nodded off in the back of the cab, only came round when he switched off the engine.

"That's forty-eight pounds seventy," the driver said, and I scrabbled through the last of my cash.

"I've got forty, a bit of change and, erm, a furry mint."

"Give us the forty and change, you can keep the mint. You didn't throw up after all."

I paid the driver then got out of the cab. My head pounded, my stomach rolled and my ears were buzzing. The noise increased the closer I got to the path of my house.

It was bad enough dragging myself home after a heavy drinking session but doing that and dodging a garden full of journalists was not something I'd wish on my worst enemies.

"Mr Taylor, did you know about Katrina's secret identity?"

One guy shoved a mic under my nose. I shook my head and continued to walk forward.

"Are you and Ms Quinn in a relationship?" asked a blonde with a squeaky voice.

I kept walking forward, determined to get to my front door.

"What do you think about her lying to the world like that?"

"Is she going back to America?"

"Is her career over?"

The questions flew in one ear and out the other. I was drunk but wasn't going to say anything in front of them. It was bad enough that the whole village would know what had happened without me airing my dirty laundry for the world's press to poke fun at.

Eventually I reached the door and, after a few attempts, fitted the key in the latch. I slammed it shut but the clamor of questions from the other side still broke through. I went straight into the living room, switched on the TV and turned the volume right up. It hurt my ears but I couldn't hear the journos anymore. I wound my way upstairs, sprawled in bed, ignored the noise and slept.

* * * *

To say I felt like shit when I woke up was an understatement. I'd suffered with a few hangovers in my time but none as nasty as this. My whole body ached, even the backs of my eyeballs and the hairs inside my ears. Noise was intolerable and light even more so. I stumbled to the bathroom. After some painkillers and a long hot shower, the red-hot pokers in my brain stilled a little.

It hurt all over again when I remembered why I'd gotten so drunk in the first place. I peeked out of the bedroom window and the sea of paparazzi was still there. I shut the curtains, blinking at the brightness, and fell back into bed. I had nothing to do. Eve was gone, there was no work to do, and the one woman I'd ever loved had turned out to be the celebrity I'd lusted over and now they'd both fucked off out of my life. It was like a script from a soap opera.

There was something I needed to decide. What to do with the damn check. Now where had I put my coat? It was halfway up the stairs, of course. I sat down, my shoulder against the spindles, to check the pockets. I got the check and pulled my phone out of the same pocket. I had a message. It was from her.

Of course I wasn't going to listen to it—that would have been really stupid of me—it was just that my finger slipped and I clicked to listen. It was purely incidental, though.

"Ryan, Gran's is overrun with paparazzi. I'm leaving later today for America. I just wanted to let you know. And I just want to tell you I'm sorry. I fucked up big style but, Ryan, I'll always be your Janie and you'll always be the only boy for me."

The phone dropped from my fingers. Hearing her voice, strained and full of emotion, hit me full in the stomach. Then there was a moment of realization. She was my Janie. Did the rest of the crap truly matter? I'd missed out on years and years of being with her because I'd made the wrong decision. Could I do the same again and lose her forever?

I ran down the stairs, shoved on my shoes then hustled out of the door. I forced my way through the crowds outside and headed off toward Copse Cottage without glancing back. It was only when I was halfway there that I realized how dark it was. I tapped my pockets for my phone then realized it was still somewhere on my stairs. I had no clue what time it was but when I reached Copse Cottage it was deserted.

I knocked on the door just in case but didn't hold out much hope.

"You looking for Katrina?" a gruff voice with a London accent croaked behind me.

"Yeah." I turned round.

"She left about an hour or so ago." The voice was attached to a short, wide fellow sat on one of those foldaway fishing stools.

"Oh." I sighed.

"Her and an 'eavy-set man pushed their way through and zoomed off. My mates are following 'em. I drew the short straw. You're not someone interesting, are you?"

"No." I shook my head. "I'm not."

"Bugger."

I walked off again. Mind buzzing. Who was the heavy-set man? Where was Janie going? Walking back home, it struck me that the media would be following her. They'd let me know where Janie was going.

"We're not a library, you know," Dilly from behind the counter shouted over to me.

"I know, I know, I just need to see if any of 'em have the story in them I want to see then I'll buy one."

It wasn't just a case of finding one with the story, it was finding one with the most detail.

"Oh, I'll save you the bother. She's gone back to America. Flew out last night. You're looking for stuff about Katrina Quinn, right? I knew she looked familiar when she came in that time. Who'd have thought our Janet would become a star."

"She's always been a star to me."

Finally I had a purpose, something to do. I hoped to God that it was the right thing.

Chapter Twenty-One

Katrina Quinn

The journey home passed in a blur. I slept for a lot of it then Matt made me go to see a doctor when I got back on US turf. I went just to shut him up. There was nothing the doctor could do for me and apparently the bump to my noggin had done me no permanent ill effect.

Eventually I had to talk to my agent.

"I wish you'd told me, Katrina, then I'd have been prepared, but don't worry, it'll all pass. All I need you to do is give a big, high-profile exclusive interview to one of the rags, and bang! This whole episode will be underlined and forgotten."

"Are you sure?" I asked, nibbling my bottom lip.

"Sure I'm sure! It's a fairy tale story — the star who made up her past to protect her real loved ones. You'll be lauded for it, mark my words."

And he was right. We picked a magazine almost at random and sold them my exclusive rags to riches story. I even teared up a bit, genuinely, too, when I started to talk about Gran's death. I refused to say anything about Ryan, though the woman interviewing me tried time and again to dig up that dirt.

The media outside my window lessened day by day until there were none left. Filming started on *Flames and Dragons* and I worked really hard. Thank God I played a hard-hearted, butt-kicking kind of woman because I was in no state for romance. I kept waiting for a phone call or even a message from Ryan, but it never came. Then about a week after I'd left Yorkshire I noticed twenty grand leave my bank account. He'd cashed the check.

I was gutted then disappointed by my reaction. I'd given the man a huge amount of money, why wouldn't he take it? Maybe he was just all about the money. What if he'd lied about Eve and the guy who'd stolen the books? What if it was all one big conspiracy all along?

I tried not to think about it. Ryan was out of my life for good. I'd lived for years without him around — surely it wouldn't be too hard to go back to that casual dismissal of him? I tried to pretend that was exactly what I wanted but the inscribed wooden box beside my bed told a different story.

* * * *

It had been two weeks and three days since I'd left the UK — I'd counted every one of them. It had been a long day on set. I'd spent ages hanging in the air and had flipped over more times than a human should have to and I'd said all of three lines. Action and adventure films were great on the big screen but sometimes the filming was less than stimulating.

It was raining, which fitted my mood perfectly. Matt was jabbering on about the wedding. I was pretending to listen. The world outside the limo was gray, the streets deserted. The rain would disappear as quickly as it had come. It wasn't proper rain, the determined type we got in Yorkshire. If it started raining in Thornleydale it wouldn't let up for days.

I was feeling nostalgic over rain, a sure indication that I was in a bad way.

"Jeez, I thought the paps had all gone home."

"Hmm, they had." I sighed.

"Well, there's a guy at the gate now."

I looked out of the limo window, and there was a figure there. Tall, wide-shouldered, with dirty blond hair plastered down to his face.

"Stop!" I yelled. "Stop the car!"

"Whoa, whoa, why do you want to stop? He might be a psycho," Matt exclaimed.

"I know him, I know who he is. Stop the car now."

"You heard the boss lady." Matt shrugged.

The driver pulled the car to a stop, and I opened the door.

"Get in, Ryan," I yelled.

He ducked out of the rain, pulling a small rucksack in behind him.

"Hey." He pulled the door shut. "Erm, surprise."

"Ryan?" Matt exclaimed. "*That* Ryan?"

I nodded, afraid to speak.

"And who are you?" Ryan snapped.

"I'm Matt, good to meet you." Matt held out his hand. Ryan didn't take it.

"Well, that didn't take you long," he growled. "Maybe I should just jump back out of this car and leave you and your new fancy man alone."

"Fancy man?" I squeaked with shock then I couldn't help but laugh. "Matt?"

"Oh, sweetie, I fancy you more than I fancy her." He winked.

"What, is he taking the piss?" If Ryan had fur his bristles would have stood on end.

"Down, tiger." I shook my head. "Matt's gay. He's marrying his boyfriend next month and they're both wearing pink on the big day."

"Oh." Ryan looked sheepish. "Right, then."

"I'm Katrina's bodyguard, PA and all round dogsbody."

"Well, someone's got to do it." Ryan smiled and held out his hand. "Nice to meet you, mate."

Matt clasped it and the peaked testosterone in the confined space edged away. We moved smoothly down the drive and reached the front of the house. I stepped out of the vehicle and tried to calm my heart rate. I couldn't get my head around what was happening.

"Well, boss, I'll leave you to it. I'll be in the lodge if you need me." Matt walked off whistling and left me and Ryan on the doorstep of the mansion.

"Nice place you've got." Ryan coughed. "A bit bigger than Copse Cottage."

"A little." I smiled. "Come in out of the rain."

He followed me inside, wiping his feet on the large mat in the sparkling hallway. It amazed me how the cleaner kept it looking so pristinely white. She was a miracle.

I led Ryan into the living room and carefully sat down on one end of the huge red leather sofa. I knitted my fingers together in my lap and tried to stop shaking.

"Okay, so this is the bit I've been rehearsing over and over in my head since I left Yorkshire." Ryan sighed. "Every time I've said it or thought it, it's come out different, so bear with me."

I nodded, folded my fingers together in my lap and leaned over them, then stretched back. I couldn't get comfortable—I didn't know how to sit, what to do. I wanted to get up and pull him close. I longed to kiss him until I couldn't breathe. It was irrational but that's all I desired.

"That voice message you left me on my phone, well, it made me remember something really important. We were the best of mates, inseparable. We were Ry and Janie. We went together, were rarely apart. Then I did something to ruin that. I'm not proud, I'm gutted actually. I've been disappointed ever since. You know that day at Prom? I was trying to tell you how much I missed you. How you were the best friend a boy could ever have. Wanted to wish you well, tell you to go find a good man to marry."

I remembered that night and had always thought it was the greatest humiliation. He'd asked me to dance—I'd thought he was going to tell me all the things I longed to hear—then Eve had dragged him away from me.

"Sorry," he'd mouthed. I was certain he'd meant that that's how I'd looked— Sorry. Sad and alone.

"I wanted to find you, wanted to tell you all this, but it never happened. I had Eve, my parents died and things just got complicated. Before I knew it I was nearly twice as old as when we danced at the Prom and at least twice as sad.

"At your Gran's funeral I kept looking for you, just couldn't believe you weren't there. I was heartbroken to see Mary go, she was the last connection to you that

I had. When the funeral ended and there was no sign of you, I felt like that was it, I'd never see you again. It hurt. I didn't understand why at first and I felt really guilty about it. Even though my girlfriend was an abusive alcoholic."

He ran his hand through his damp hair, the resulting furrows staying put because of the rain.

"I swear I didn't ramble this much in my practice runs." He shrugged.

I should have said something, anything, but I was struck dumb. The sheer weight of wishing to hear something good, some promise for the future, crushed my ability to speak.

"Anyway, my point. My point is that we should be together. Even when you were Katrina and I didn't know you were Janie I should have done because there's just one person who could make me feel the way you do and that's you. My Janie." His voice stuttered, he coughed, shifted from foot to foot. "I've been incomplete for all these years, Janie, and then we were together and—"

He didn't finish what he was going to say because I sprang up from my seat and threw myself at him. He wrapped his arms around me and I knew I was back where I belonged. Our lips met and I melted into him. All the words I wanted to say swirled around my mouth and I kissed them into his without spilling one.

"I'm so sorry, Janie." He sobbed into my hair, as I kissed down his stubbled cheek, inhaling his musk with a fresh hint of Hollywood rain. "I'm so sorry."

"I'm sorry." I sniffed. "I should have told you but—" The words stuck in the back of my throat.

He kissed along that curve and freed them.

"But I was so scared that you'd reject me. I couldn't take that again, Ryan. I couldn't face knowing I'd have to live the rest of my life without you in it."

"No, never. We're meant to be, you and me, remember?"

I nodded. We'd always said we'd be together forever no matter what.

"I can't believe you're here." I cupped his face in my hands. "How are you here?"

"Love and determination," he replied with a grin that melted my heart.

Then words became superfluous, all we needed was to touch and kiss. I celebrated our reunion by kissing him all over, peeling off his wet clothes as I traveled over his familiar terrain. I disrobed him, and he plucked at my clothing and kissed and stroked any flesh that he could reach. When we were naked we rolled onto my sofa. Large and encompassing, it was more comfortable than the single bed at Thornleydale and even a little bit wider.

I had him beneath me, my thighs between his, his cock pressing against my stomach as I lay in his arms, kissing him, drinking him in. I was in no rush and would be happy if it lasted forever. Each brush of his fingers set off sparkle trails of excitement across my flesh. I wanted to revel in his proximity, drink him in, savor every nibble, every taste.

He growled as I kissed down to his cock, my lips lying tantalizingly close to his shaft, the warm air of my breath caressing him. I touched them to the bottom of his erection, and he whimpered with joy and frustration. I peppered his dick with tight-lipped kisses until he was writhing and moaning. Next I slipped my mouth around his darkened tip. He tasted of salt and caramel. I ran my mouth down over him as far as I could manage.

"Janie, Janie," he crooned. "I'll come if you keep that up. Let me fuck you, now, please, I need to fuck you."

I needed that too so I let him go with a pop, and reached over to the coffee table at the end of the sofa. Secreted in the drawer was a condom. I've always been a frustrated Girl Guide. I turned round and carefully pulled the wrapper open. It was a delicious role reversal as he caressed his dick and I removed the sheath. I waited for him to realize I was waiting for him and when he moved his big, work-worn hand away I rolled the thin protection down over his cock.

Poised above him, my gaze locked with his, I took in the moment. The heat of his legs against the soft coolness of my inner thighs, the rise and fall of his chest, the pout of his lips, the brightness in his eyes. His deep musk mixed with mine in a heavy and seductive cocktail, and I heard and felt the hitch of his breath when I lowered myself closer to him. He groaned as I slid onto him. My eyes closed with the weight of ecstasy and I reveled in the girth of him, the length of him, filling and satisfying me so completely.

I couldn't open my eyes, the weight of arousal was too heavy. I listened to his breathing, his moans, and felt the vibrations of his thighs as he thrust up to meet me. I felt everything so intensely I thought I might vibrate out of my skin with pleasure.

We were together and that was the most important thing in the whole world. We were meant to be together. My heart swelled with joy and I moved before that bubble burst. He gripped my hips, his thumbs pressing into the concave either side of my stomach. I leaned a hand on his chest, stars popping behind my eyes, their fiery trails seeming to scorch down my body to the juncture of my body and his.

I moved slowly at first and upped the tempo as I needed more and more friction from him to head closer to the climax that lodged somewhere between his body and my clit. Ryan slipped his hand around to sit his thumb between my pussy lips. He pressed down making me jolt and purr at the sensation. He wanted my orgasm, I wanted his. We both labored toward our goal, panting and groaning, a symphony of lust.

As I squeezed tight around him he throbbed inside me and we shook and shuddered out our pleasure. The rolling tide of ecstasy left me limp and lethargic but fully blissed out. I pulled away from Ryan long enough for him to do the essential tidying up then I flopped on top of him again, my back to the sofa cushions, my front pushed against him.

We lay in silence for a while. I was content. Ryan was there with me. I wanted to just accept it, not question, to move on, but I needed to know, I wanted clarification.

"Ryan?" I whispered.

"Hmm?" He rubbed his hand up and down my arm.

"Don't leave me, okay?"

"I'm not planning to." He pulled me close. "I love you, Janet Davey Katrina Quinn. I'm not going anywhere without you."

"Good." I kissed his chin. "Because I love you, too. I want to show you something."

I got up and pulled him behind me.

"Where are we going?" He laughed.

"To my bedroom."

"Oh, lead on," he purred.

I giggled and pulled him toward the stairs. I let go and jogged up. He followed after me – I could feel the heat of his gaze on my arse. I suppose I should have felt self-conscious being completely naked but I didn't. Ryan put me completely at my ease.

I ran through the soft pelt of my carpet floor and sat down at the head of my bed. Seconds later Ryan joined me.

"Nice," he crooned. "Well worth looking at. This is a great room. What a view."

Sheltered by the side of a hill and many trees, the vista through the wall-long window was breathtaking.

"I know, but it's not what I want to show you. Look, do you recognize this?"

I placed the wooden box he'd carved for me all those years ago into his hands.

"Oh, wow," he exclaimed. "Janie, I didn't know you still had this." He ran his fingers lovingly over the grain, tracing the letters of my name like he'd traced my curves moments before.

"Look what's inside."

He flicked open the catch and pulled out the mustard thread, the disfigured lucky penny and all the other special items that snuggled in there.

"Janie" – his eyes were wide, sparkling with unshed tears – "I'm so sorry."

"Shush." I pushed a finger to his lips and shut the box with my other hand. "No regrets now, okay? We're together and it's all that matters."

"Oh, Janie, you're still the best girl in the world." He smiled.

"And you're not bad for a boy."

About the Author

Victoria Blisse is a mother, wife, Christian, Manchester United fan and award winning erotica author. She is also the editor of several Bigger Briefs collections, and the co-editor of the fabulous Smut Alfresco and Smut in the City and Smut by the Sea Anthologies.

She is equally at home behind a laptop or a cooker (She is TEB's resident 'Naked Chef') and she loves to create stories, poems, cakes and biscuits that make people happy. She was born near Manchester, England and her northern English quirkiness shows through in all of her stories.

Passion, love and laughter fill her works, just as they fill her busy life.

Victoria Blisse loves to hear from readers. You can find her contact information, website details and author profile page at http://www.totallybound.com.

Totally Bound Publishing

www.ingramcontent.com/pod-product-compliance
Lightning Source LLC
Chambersburg PA
CBHW020602260626
47157CB00003B/835